To Rise, I Must Fall.

His eyes pierce me, but fear rests there too. I can make him burn. I can make him fall.

It's time I take the fight into my own hands. I'm surrounded by lies. With no one left to trust, the only one I can turn to is myself. Beelzebub is up to no good. The Seven Princes are gathering demons outside Hell. But why?

I will discover the secrets and weed out the lies. I will learn to harness my powers and bring angels and demons to their knees.

I'm ready now. Let Raphael come. I want to face the Archangel who took everything from me.

BOOKS BY L. M. PERALTA

the seven princes of hell

THE ARCADIAN STEEL SEQUENCE
BOOK THREE

L. M. PERALTA

either the product of the author's imagination or are used fictitiously. Any resemblance to actual persons, living or dead, events, or locales is entirely coincidental.

Summary: Lia, the girl who can make angels fall, faces Raphael, the Archangel who killed her parents. But before she battles Raphael, she must learn more about her powers.

ISBN: 978-1-946470-02-7

acknowledgements

I want to thank the following three people, in particular and in no special order, for dedicating their time and talents to this novel.

My husband, Joey Gagliano, who tirelessly poured over my manuscript and showed up every day to make me smile. My father and original editor, Lorne Peralta, who has read all my books from beginning to end and back again. My friend, Gwen St. Pierre, who helped me perfect this series.

And also,

My mother, Juanita Peralta, without whom I would not be the person I am today. My grandmother and spokesperson, Marie Peralta. My grandmother, Gloria Latour, whose charm and sass inspired at least one of the characters in this novel. My grandfather, Louis Latour, who was there for me in the Spring when my world was shaken up and I needed someone.

My brother, Jacob, who has enjoyed this series more than I would have guessed. My sisters, Taren and Demi, who took me out of my little world and into theirs.

And to all the readers, thank you for taking the time to read my novel.

prologue

LUCIFER lifted the curtain and gazed out the window above the clouds. Light emitted from the tear in the sky, a tear the angels made. Angels in Hell. Her kingdom. Raphael had no right. The angels would return, but this time Lucifer and her army would have a weapon that not even Michael could resist.

Lucifer had a prisoner, a prisoner Michael had searched out for centuries. She had kept him for a long time in the bowels of Hell.

She found him scribbling notes in a cave, hiding because he could not Veil himself. Poor creature. Such an abomination.

She smiled. Michael would be pacing Heaven's pearly gates right now, wondering what she wanted with the one-winged angel, the one he so despised.

She let the curtain fall. Darkness encased the room, but a lamp pushed the darkness away, making the shadows fade in its glow.

She intended to win this war, and if it costs Heaven a few angels, that was no skin off her back.

Michael issued the decree, banishing her to Hell, a place that didn't yet exist. He was all too happy to carry out the *order*. All the angels loved Lucifer. She had been beautiful and strong, the strongest light in Heaven.

But she made Hell work. Pride would never let her be defeated. Her tongue was as silver as her armor when she fell, and she used it to embolden the angels who fell beside her.

She separated her soul into seven distinct personalities: Pride, Gluttony, Greed, Lust, Sloth, Envy, and Wrath. *The Seven Princes of Hell.*

She brought fire and ice to the hellish Circles. Sheol was a barren wasteland until she molded it from the darkness. She knew ways of tormenting human souls and manipulating desires.

She dared Michael to come. She would be ready.

Lucifer's heels clicked along the floor as she paced the room. The blackened bones, which had once displayed beautiful, white feathers, were tucked against her back. She stopped and observed the man sitting in the chair before her.

His back was turned. Stacks of books rose in front of him. A single white feathered wing graced one side of his back. On the other side was a stump.

The walls were covered in drawings of the Staff, the only weapon that could kill angels. Scribbled notes surrounded the drawings. Gibberish.

Lucifer approached the table.

The angel's back muscles tensed as her voice tickled his ear. "Is it finished?"

His hand gripped protectively around the Staff. Etched into the weapon was a story from long ago—when angels mated with humans. "What will you do with it?" he asked.

"I will use it for its purpose."

"To kill him?"

"Perhaps."

"He'll hunt me down, you know," the one-winged angel said. "Especially after he hears I helped you." His voice trembled like a dried leaf, threatened by the wind to lose its place on the tree.

Lucifer placed her hands on his shoulders and pressed them down into a more relaxed position. "If he wants you, my skilled friend, he'll have to go through me."

"You don't mean that. You will cast me out when I am no use to you." The one-winged angel lowered his head.

Why did he sound so frightened? She hadn't meant to scare him. Maybe it was the way her voice sometimes overlapped itself with a deeper one.

That was the consequence of splitting yourself into seven. Fragments were left inside her like tiny pieces of glass that the broom missed.

"Why would I lie to you?" Lucifer tried to keep the deeper voice back.

"Because you lie to everyone. I don't think you mean to anymore. You just do."

Lucifer raked her long fingernails along his shoulders. "That bastard tossed me out of my own home. You can guarantee I want that Staff deep in his heart. He's the greatest liar of us all."

part one

luminous

One

HE demon lunged at me.

I wrenched a cushion from the sofa. The blade sank into the fabric and the fluffy bowels.

Caiduc cowered behind a folding screen.

The Jinn was good for nothing in a fight. He was afraid. Something I didn't understand since his true form was impervious, right? So, why was he frightened of everything that moved?

I tossed the pillow aside and reached for my dagger. The room looked ransacked.

Fragments of glass from the vase I threw at the demon littered floor. The television screen was cracked when I was thrown against it. Tufts of pillow guts snowed down.

Who had broken the lamp?

This was *not* where I asked Caiduc to bring me.

The demon grinned at me with his pointed, yellow teeth. He had blotches of flaky, burnt skin. The rest of him looked human.

He rushed me.

Damn it.

He had a kitchen knife. I had a dagger of Arcadian Steel.

Our blades met. His cracked in two.

The blade clattered to the floor. The handle was still in the demon's grasp. His face fell.

I rammed my dagger into his shoulder. Dark blood oozed over my hand. The blood was hot and thicker than a human's.

It covered my hand like gummy tar. *Gross.*

"Witch." He ground his teeth.

"Cockroach." I twisted the dagger.

Pain rode up my side. The demon brought his fist into me again. I winced.

I yanked my dagger out of his shoulder, ready to give him a mortal wound, but he punched me again. I doubled over.

This was *not* going well.

I looked up.

A clawed hand swiped across my cheek. The side of my face burned. Drops of red blood spattered the floor.

Shit!

How would I explain this one to Nash and Adriel?

The demon dove at me again.

I wouldn't have to do any explaining if I was dead. No, I still might. Nash would march into the Circles and pull me out just to tell me how stupid I was.

I threw myself to the floor, and the demon narrowly missed me. Holding my side, I sank my dagger into his foot. Blood sprayed my face.

The demon howled.

Wasn't expecting that one, huh, buddy?

I rolled onto my back and stood, trying to straighten myself despite the pain in my side. Was his hand made of brick?

I could see more of him now. His eyes were solid red. His head was covered in burnt skin that couldn't keep the blood in.

What had he been doing in this house? Did he *live* here?

But now was no time for a demon census report.

The demon picked up a golden Buddha and swung it at me. I stepped back, and the back of my leg hit the coffee table. I fell onto the glass surface.

Before I knew what was happening, the demon was on top of me. The Buddha clenched in his hand.

My dagger had fallen under the glass table, out of my reach.

The demon raised the Buddha like he was playing Whac-A-Mole.

Shit! Shit! Shit!

A crack ran through the glass table. My mind burned. I slammed my fist onto the surface.

The glass shattered.

I hit the floor. It felt like I had pebbles under my back. The demon fell with me, but I barely noticed his weight.

My hand gripped the dagger. He swung the Buddha toward my head, but I was faster. I plunged my blade into his neck.

"Go back to Hell!" I screamed.

His mouth morphed into a circle. The Buddha fell from his hand.

I withdrew my dagger. Blood spurted from his wound. He was falling on top of me, but he disappeared to dust before the descent.

I laid on the floor, my arms stretched out. A burst of laughter erupted from my lungs. It hurt my side to laugh.

I hoped all my ribs were intact. I sat up, which wasn't easy to do.

Caiduc stood before me, scratching his wrist.

"Well, you weren't any help," I said.

"You told me not to," he said.

"I told you not to transport me. Didn't mean I couldn't use your help. Are you feeling okay?"

"Yes." Caiduc's eyes darted.

My lips pursed into a frown.

Caiduc touched the string of wooden beads dangling from his ear.

"Let's go," I said. "I have no idea where you've brought us."

I tried to stand, but pain flared up my side. "Some help."

Caiduc approached me with his hands held to his chest. He gingerly offered one to me.

I took his branchy hand in mine and used his weight as leverage to hoist myself up. I brushed the crumbles of glass from my back.

"You fought well," Caiduc said. "You are getting better."

Did he want me to get better? Was that why he hadn't stepped in with his mysterious Jinni magic? Or was it because he didn't want me to see what he could do? Maybe that would be against Jinni code or something.

"At least I didn't get myself stabbed this time." When that demon stabbed me back in Sheol, I would have died if someone hadn't come and healed me.

I stepped over the cushions, the pillows, and the broken glass. Tearing open the front door, I walked out into the street. Rain misted the cobblestone road.

I missed the rain.

The white face of the tower peeked from the trees blanketing the hill. *Fengdu Ghost City.*

"Huh, this is the right place. You were close, Caiduc."

I followed the road. Despite the misty rain, people explored the city. Tour guides spoke over loud speakers. Tourists carried umbrellas and backpacks.

Trying to make myself inconspicuous, I joined a group of tourists as I moved through the city. We climbed the steps lined with devil sculptures. Splotches of green stained the statues.

After we went over the bridge, I separated myself from the crowd. The green hills overlapped each other in the distance. Water met the rocky base of the island.

Past the river was a tiered tower with red columns and eaves that curled up at their points.

This place was beautiful.

Without Adriel to guide me, I became lost in the twists and turns of the streets. Night fell before I found a familiar street and followed it. Caiduc trailed behind me.

"Why did you attack that demon?" Caiduc asked.

"Because he's a demon."

"But your friends are demons."

"That's different," I said. "My friends don't possess people. They don't make people do bad things."

"They did though. They all had contracts with Lucifer. That's why they are demons."

"Look, I don't want to talk to you about morality."

"Is that because it confuses you?" he asked.

"No, it's because I'm not Tom. I don't like talking for the sake of it."

The small shop sat among the clusters of buildings at the base of the green hill. Its timber beams were straight and narrow. The corners of the roof curved up to the sky. The sign above the door read: *Miss Jiao's Tea House.*

"This is it," I said.

Mist curled through the dark streets. The cobblestone walkway was damp from the rain. Clouds covered the moon and stars, and streetlamps let off a cold, blue glow.

Caiduc stood beside me with his hands clasped. "Do I have to go in?" His fingers trembled.

"Not if you don't want to."

"I won't then." Caiduc disappeared.

Demons were one thing, but I wondered what would make a Jinn so afraid of a small woman like Jiao. She was no taller than four eleven, and her slim frame was far from imposing.

I opened the door to the tea house. The bell chimed above the door. "Hello?"

Low tables surrounded by sitting mats were evenly spaced on the tiled floor. Wooden columns trimmed in gold held up the recessed ceiling. Lanterns with red tassels hung from every fourth ceiling tile.

A cherry blossom grew in the center of the room. It wasn't there the first time I visited. The tree was in full bloom. Pink flowers littered the floor around it.

I walked up to the tree and cradled a delicate, pink flower.

"Don't touch that!"

I jumped.

An old woman stepped from behind the folding wall. She carried a tea kettle. She wore a black robe with a thick, red band around her waist. She looked frail. Her brown skin was thin and wrinkled. Her hair was as white as snow and wispy like the feathers of a bird.

"I'm sorry. I'm looking for Jiao."

She glanced up at me. "You're the girl who came with Adriel."

"That's right." *How did she know that?* She wasn't here when I came with Adriel. Maybe she watched us from that folding screen in the back.

"What happened to you?"

I touched my cheek. The blood had dried. "It's nothing. Is Jiao here?"

The old woman smirked. She set the tea kettle down on one of the low tables. "Sit," she said.

I looked around before approaching the table. Maybe this was Jiao's grandmother or maybe her great-grandmother. I sat at the table with her as she poured the tea.

"Thank you." I reached for the cup.

She slapped my hand away. "Do you want to be a babe in arms again?"

I raised my eyebrows. "I'm sorry I thought . . ."

"You assumed," the old woman said. She lifted the tea cup and took a long sip from it.

My eyes widened.

The wrinkles on her face disappeared like someone pulled her skin tight. Her gray hair darkened to a rich, glossy black. Her eyes brightened, and her frail body grew less bony. Her back straightened. Her lips became plumper.

"Jiao?" I asked.

"You think I would let some old woman take over my tea house?"

"But you're . . ."

"If you call me old, I just might force some of this tea down your throat. You'll be a third trimester fetus on the floor before you can blink." The bite in her tone told me not to ask any questions. It also told me something stressed her out more than my sudden appearance.

"I need your help," I said.

Jiao raised an eyebrow before narrowing her eyes. "Adriel has you thinking I do favors?"

"I need to find my father. Well, both my fathers actually . . ."

Jiao raised an eyebrow.

". . . and my mom, my adoptive mom."

"And I'm assuming your *other* father adopted you."

I nodded. "Can you find them for me?"

"Well, that's an awful lot of people that went missing on you."

"My mom and dad died."

Jiao shook her head. "Can't find dead people," she said. "Unless you want to find out where they're buried."

"You can't find out where they . . . went?"

"Hell no," Jiao said. "What kind of teas do you think I'm brewing? You don't mess with the afterlife. *I* don't mess with the afterlife." She folded her arms. I didn't know if she was trying to convince me or herself.

"But my dad, my bio-dad I mean, he's not dead. He's alive somewhere. I just don't know where he is."

"I can't find people without something they have touched."

"But I don't have anything. I never knew him."

"Well, you're out of luck," Jiao said. "It's not like Google. You're going to need more than a name. Speaking of, have you tried Google yet?"

I doubted an internet search would be of much help. All I *had* was a name. It wouldn't be as easy as Jiao was making it out to be. Besides, after what my bio-mom said about him wanting to get away from her, maybe he changed his name.

"You should probably start there before you start messing with magic," Jiao said.

Magic. Witchcraft. What if Adrianna was right?

"I need to ask you something."

Jiao sipped her tea, and the circles under her eyes diminished. She had lost fifty, maybe sixty years, in a matter of minutes. She looked like the twenty-something college girl I thought she was when I'd first met her.

"I have this power," I said. "I can move people with my mind."

"What do you mean?"

"I can toss them against walls, throw them backward. When I was sixteen, I threw myself from a burning car. I don't know how I'm doing it. I think I might be a witch."

Jiao paused and put her cup down. "Witches need incantations and herbs. What you are doing isn't witchcraft."

"Then what is it?"

Jiao shook her head. "Witchcraft is something that is taught. Did anyone ever teach you?"

"No."

"Did you ever drink demon blood?"

"No." I drank angel blood. Should I tell her that?

"Then, what you are doing is something else entirely. Give me your hands."

"What are you going to do?"

"I'm going to bite your fingers off." Jaio chomped her teeth. My skin jumped.

She rolled her eyes. "I'm just going to take a look."

I placed my hands across the table. Jiao clasped them in hers and closed her eyes. She had a bored look, like she was leafing through a magazine in the waiting room of a doctor's office. But something changed. A pained expression flashed across her face. She released my hands.

"What? What did you see?"

"What are you?" she hissed. "You stole an angel's grace?"

I shook my head. "I don't know what you're talking about."

"Get out!" she screamed. "Get out now!"

I stood, and she pushed me out the door.

Ŧwo

RAIN fell outside Miss Jiao's Tea House. It felt good on my skin even though I had been tossed out into it. The answers I needed weren't here. I would never find my father, and if my powers didn't come from witchcraft, where did they come from?

You drank angel blood. That had to be the origin of my powers. But something seemed so wrong about it. That's why I hesitated to tell Jiao. And now that she knew, she was afraid of me, angry at me or both.

I had done worse things than drink angel blood. I made angels fall, angels that weren't working for Raphael.

Mom and Dad. Where were they? Had they gone to Heaven? How could I know for sure? Wherever they were, that's where I wanted to be, even if it meant an eternity in Sheol. I would make it work.

I couldn't imagine them being assigned to any of the Circles. They were good people.

I shook my head. I changed my contract. I didn't have a choice on where I would be going.

Caiduc looked up at me. "Where to?"

"Huh?"

"Where do you want to go?"

Home. "Bring me back to Sheol," I said. "I should have never come here."

Caiduc's branchy fingers touched my arm.

The flash was blinding. Water crashed around me.

I blinked until my vision came back into focus. I was in my room at Nash's place with its cold, unwelcoming, hospital-white walls and the chill that wouldn't leave the air.

Glancing around the room, I discovered Caiduc gone. Maybe he could sense I needed a moment alone with my thoughts. But no matter what I needed, I didn't want to be alone.

So many questions were left unanswered. How could I know I was doing the right thing if I didn't know enough?

I pulled a sweater on. I reached for the door.

Wait.

That nasty cut on my cheek.

I couldn't walk downstairs like this. Nash would see the cut, and I wouldn't hear the end of it.

Maybe I could cover it up.

I leaned over the sink and peered into the bathroom mirror. I pressed down on my cheek. Dried blood flaked from the cut. The skin pulled apart.

Too deep to cover up.

Damn it!

I wet a towel and dabbed the cut. It looked better without the dried blood, but it still looked nasty.

I sighed and dropped the towel to the ground.

I'm going to have to be honest with Nash. At least one of us wouldn't be lying.

Wait. What was that?

The area around the cut seemed to shimmer. I peered closer. The skin sealed up like Playdough pressed together.

My mouth hung open as I touched the skin where the cut had been. The skin was smooth. What in the world? Had *I* done that?

My side no longer hurt either. Somehow, I had healed that too. No one helped me as I bled in that alley. I had helped myself.

Whoa. It would be great if I knew how to control it.

I rinsed my face and wandered down the hall to the stairs. As I reached the bottom of the stairs, the front door opened, and Nash walked in.

I kept my head down and tried to pass him, but he grabbed my arm.

"Lia . . ." My name left his lips in a breath.

I clenched my teeth. How dare he? I worried about a kiss while he had done much more with the Queen of Hell.

I tried to shrug him off, but he maintained his grip.

"I can't let you go," he whispered.

Liar. He let me go the moment he slipped into Lucifer's arms.

Why should I be surprised? They were one in the same, both fallen angels. I was human, temporary, and damned to the Circles. I shook my head. That might be the way it worked when you're immortal, but it wasn't the way it worked with me.

His words echoed in my head: *I can't let you go.*

"You have to, eventually," I said. "Bob made it very clear to me. Lucifer needs to fill my bio-mom's place when she leaves. So, once I've defeated Raphael, my mom will be released to Heaven. Then, it's off to the Seventh Circle of Hell for me." A man signed a contract to take Lydia's place, but that was a bandaid. After what he had done to that girl in the basement, he was destined for Hell. He had his place to fill, and I had mine.

"I won't let that happen," Nash said. His voice was like gravel. He sounded sincere, but I couldn't trust him.

"How are you going to stop the Devil?" I spat. I pulled my arm away from him and walked out the door.

I felt his gaze on my back, but I didn't turn to look at him. I didn't know where I was going, but I couldn't bear to be in the same room with Nash for another second.

Chandra was right. Nash moved fast. But something told me that he was seeing Lucifer long before we broke up. That kiss they shared was passionate, but it was also too comfortable, too familiar. Their bodies molded together like the missing pieces of a puzzle.

I walked a couple blocks before I unclenched my fists, and the tension left my shoulders.

"Lia?"

I turned around.

"I saw you leave," Adriel said.

"When?" I asked.

"I was on the stairs."

"You saw me and Nash." My lip quivered.

Adriel put his arms around me. He didn't judge. He didn't press. He held me as I cried against him.

I was warm and safe in his arms. I never wanted to leave.

CHANDRA and I crossed staffs.

She pushed me back. I swayed and caught myself before I stumbled to the ground. She lunged forward, her staff above me.

I held my staff in two hands and blocked her blow. She tried hitting me with the end of the staff, but I managed to block that one too.

Chandra ground her teeth.

She rocked back. I imitated her, and our weapons met in the middle.

Chandra jabbed her staff at me. I pivoted to defend, knocking her weapon off course. She approached me, twirling her staff as I retreated. She swung at me. I blocked.

Chandra forced my staff to the ground with hers. Her staff swung up. *She's trying to take my head off!* I ducked, and her staff whooshed above me.

She buffeted my legs.

I winced, but maintained my balance. I blocked a second blow to my face.

Chandra twisted her staff. It was behind my legs, but before I could defend, the ground rushed up to meet me.

Chandra smirked.

I thought I was getting better, but I'd never be able to beat Chandra.

She went to the weapons table and grabbed her water bottle. I stood, rubbing my back. Good thing we trained on the grass.

Adriel fought with Nash farther down the field. Nash gave Adriel a room in his house although Adriel didn't have any belongings to keep there, and like Nash, he never slept. They were getting along, but they were far from friends.

They were brothers. Both Seraphim. Now both fallen angels.

"Hello, sweetheart."

I spun.

Bob stood with his hands in his pockets. He wore his customary black suit, black shirt, and red tie. His height was impressive. It wasn't practical to be so tall.

"What do you want?" I asked.

"My key." Bob held out his hand.

"I don't have it," I said.

He narrowed his eyes.

"After I took it from you, I lost it. Might have left it in the elevator. Don't know."

Bob smiled.

What did it take to wipe that grin off his face? Did I have to hit him again? I did have a staff in my hands.

"That's too bad. You're going to get me into a lot of trouble."

I don't care. Bob was the Redeemer, and he was trying to get Nash killed, but why?

Maybe he didn't like how Lucifer favored Nash. Although I couldn't imagine Bob and Lucifer together.

"What are you doing here?" Nash stepped up beside me. He folded his arms.

"I'm always a welcomed guest here." Bob grinned. "Why don't you invite me for dinner? My trunk is full of food."

"I don't cook meat."

"And I don't eat meat." Bob winked. "Well, not tonight anyway. I'll be a vegetarian just for you, just for tonight."

The last thing I wanted was to have dinner with Bob. It would be like a mouse dining with a cat. The mouse could never be sure when the cat might ignore the food and take a bite of mousy flesh instead.

After seeing Bob alone with a table full of food, I kept having dreams about him gorging himself sick. All that food had to go somewhere. If it wasn't ending up on Bob's lanky frame, it must be ending up on the floor.

"I can't host tonight," Nash said. "We're hunting."

This was the first I was hearing of it. Why didn't he tell me?

"Well, some other time." Bob turned on his heels and left the training field.

"What did he want?" Nash asked.

"I stole his key," I said.

Nash raised an eyebrow.

"His elevator key." I moved my staff from one hand to the other.

"Where is it?"

What was that on his face? Nerves, anxiety, why?

"I lost it," I said. I didn't feel so bad about lying to him. He was lying to me.

"You shouldn't be taking things from one of the Princes of Hell," Nash said.

I cocked my head. "Why aren't you a Prince of Hell? Lucifer seems to like you enough."

Nash looked to the side. "You don't understand what the Princes of Hell are."

"Lucifer's seven personalities. She split herself up into pieces. Bob is one of those pieces."

"I'm not one of Lucifer's personalities," Nash said. "We're not that close."

"But you are close." I tossed him the staff. "I have to get ready. I didn't know we were demon hunting tonight. Or were you lying about that?"

I turned and marched toward the house. When I got to my bedroom, I tied my hair in a tight bun and grabbed my sword and dagger. I stopped at the window in the hallway outside my room.

Tom and Kiran trained on the field. They met blades. Tom stopped and dropped his sword. He said something to Kiran. Tom's brow furrowed, and he frowned. Kiran stepped forward and pressed a finger to his lips.

What are they up to? Whatever it was, Kiran wanted to keep it quiet. *They're hiding something. Why not?* Everyone else has something to hide.

MY head hit the brick wall, and my world spun. I tried to pick myself up, but in my dizziness, I stumbled. Water dripped from the ceiling of the dark basement.

Drip. Drip.

I opened my eyes. It felt like I was underwater. My vision blurred. Sounds dulled. *The world is a fiddle, and its music screams.*

I held my head between my hands, trying to stop the world from spinning and blurring like paints mixing on a palette.

The Surgat stood under the swinging light bulb as it blinked on and off. The demon held a massive sword shaped like a giant old-style key, its edges ridged and ending in a sharp, straight horizontal tip. The blade met Nash's with a clang.

Adrianna knelt in one corner of the room as she put pressure on a wound on Kiran's leg. Adriel approached and reached out his hand to touch the wound, but pulled back. *He can't heal anymore.*

But I can? Can I heal others? I wasn't sure how I healed myself.

Adriel looked toward me. He was coming to see if I was okay. *No, you have to help Nash.*

Chandra came up behind the demon while he and Nash fought. The silver keys around the Surgat's neck clinked together. He ducked to avoid Chandra's brass knuckles meeting his skull.

Chandra attempted to hit the demon again, but one long arm swung back and grabbed her wrist. The Surgat twisted. *Crack!*

Chandra screamed. Her hand hung limp, folding down against her arm. *Clink!* The brass knuckles slipped from her fingers.

Nash ground his teeth. His sword was caught on one of the ridges in the Surgat's blade. The Surgat swung his sword, and Nash's blade clattered to the ground.

The Surgat's long, thin leg kicked Nash in the chest, sending him backward onto the concrete floor. He turned his gray, skinny body to Chandra. His black eyes leaked smoke.

Gripping Chandra around the neck, he lifted her from the floor. He turned her and bent her body forward.

Adriel gripped his sword and rushed the demon, but he was too late.

The demon took his large key blade, plunged it into Chandra's back, and turned it.

Chandra's mouth leaked blood and spit. She lifted her head. Her head was so close to her spine that her neck sloped like a snake's. Her eyes were solid black.

The Surgat released her.

Chandra's skin hardened to a thick, black shell. Her hands became pinchers. She grew a long, black tail with a stinger. Her hair turned red and grew in tufts down her back. She gazed at me.

Oh shit!

Chandra's pinchers snapped at me.

I pinned myself to the wall and narrowly avoided being sliced in half.

"Chandra, it's me!" Like that would help. Chandra *did* want to kill me, but what did that demon do to her.

Nash's sword met the Surgat's blade. "He controls her now."

Adriel's longsword blocked Chandra's pincher from attacking me again. The blade glanced off the shell, but Chandra couldn't move it anymore.

She turned on Adriel, her stinger whipping around behind her. The stinger lunged forward. Adriel dodged it, and Chandra buried the stinger into the floor.

She pulled the stinger out, causing concrete pebbles and dust to pop into the air. Adriel blocked another pincher as Chandra reached for him.

Clang!

Nash's blade met the Surgat's sword.

The sword. That's what set Chandra against us. I needed to get that key blade to turn her back.

What could I do?

I ran to the demon and leapt onto his back. I grabbed the necklace. It had a hundred keys strung around it, making it heavy. I yanked it, cutting into the demon's neck.

The Surgat tried to reach behind himself to grab me, but I held tight. Chandra pinned Adriel to the ground.

He buffeted her in the head with his sword, but the shell acted like armor. Perhaps it could only be penetrated by pure Arcadian Steel and not the lesser alloy of the blade Adriel wielded.

But we weren't trying to kill Chandra.

With his sword and my distraction, Nash forced the key blade from the demon's grasp. He slashed the Surgat's chest. The demon howled.

I leapt from his back and grabbed the blade. It was so heavy I had to drag it to where Chandra had Adriel pinned.

With every ounce of strength I possessed, I lifted the blade and sank it into Chandra's back. I turned the key.

Chandra's body went limp like a doll's. *Did I kill her?*

The shell turned back to smooth skin. The tail disappeared.

Adriel rolled from under her.

Chandra fell to her knees. "What happened?" She grabbed her broken wrist.

"You lost control of yourself and your Veil," Adrianna said. "You tried to kill Adriel and Lia."

Keys rattled.

I turned.

Nash and Adriel ran the Surgat through with their swords, Nash from the front, Adriel from behind.

The demon turned to smoke, and his necklace of keys dropped to the floor.

Nash knelt and inspected the keys, taking one and turning it in his hands. "These keys can open any lock in the world."

"There are more than a hundred locks in the world," I said.

"They work like skeleton keys," Nash said. "Large groups of locks can be opened with one key. You just have to know which one."

I shrugged. "Maybe we can gift one to Bob since I lost his."

Nash gave me a look that said he wasn't in the mood for my jokes. When *was* he in the mood for jokes? I wished he would stop looking at me like a snake that had crawled into his boot.

He lifted the string of keys from the ground. "Let's get out of here." He opened the portal.

Adrianna helped Kiran to his feet and walked with him through the opening. Chandra followed, scooping up her brass knuckles.

"What are you going to use those keys for?" I asked.

"I don't know," Nash said. "But they might come in handy."

"They are dangerous," Adriel said. "They open doors you should not enter."

I doubted Nash would heed his warning.

MUSIC blared through my earbuds. I folded my arms against the railing of the balcony as I gazed upon the training field.

My head and neck still ached from the battle with the Surgat. I wished I knew how to control my special healing ability or any of my abilities for that matter. How many more did I possess and didn't know about?

The one that made angels fall was easy to understand. I touch them, and poof—flames. It was the getting to them that was the hard part, but at least that ability never failed.

But who could I turn to to teach me about my powers? I was force-fed angel blood. Was there anyone else like me?

Adriel leaned his arms against the railing.

I pulled the wires of my earbuds, and they popped out of my ears.

"You have a key that you're not supposed to have," Adriel said.

"Yeah," I said. "But I'm not returning it. Bob's the Redeemer, and he's trying to have Nash killed. I'm going to find out why."

"You're not going to talk to Nash about it."

I looked at my hands. "I don't want to talk to Nash at all." I sighed. "Last time we discussed it . . ."

He kissed me. Then he tried to take it back, but you can't take back a kiss any more than you can take back the feelings it awakens.

". . . he didn't seem to take it very seriously. I didn't know it was Bob, but I knew someone was after him."

"He wants to stop him *and you*," Adriel said.

"But why? That's what I keep wondering. Bob has as much of an interest as Lucifer in stopping Raphael or Michael or any angel. Why does Bob want Nash dead if he's the head of the team that kills angels?"

Adriel shook his head.

"I'm going to find out," I said. "No one is going to keep any more secrets from me."

Three

OONLIGHT flooded through the open window. A steady, summer breeze rolled in. My mouth was dry so I got out of bed to get a glass of water.

Something crinkled under my bare feet. Stooping, I picked it up. It was a picture drawn by a young child.

A flat two-dimensional house was drawn in the background. In the foreground were three stick figures with the traditional round circles for heads. Two of the figures had triangles drawn midway up their torsos to depict dresses. The two taller figures were a mother and a father, and the little girl in the center was me.

I smiled at the childish attempt, so like the drawings I used to draw in school when I was little. My finger traced the drawing of my father. Where was he, and why didn't he try to find me?

I placed the drawing on the desk beside the door and wandered down the hallway. The walls were bare, and the tiled floor was cold against my feet.

I stopped outside the door to my mother's bedroom. Her back was to me. She placed something inside the drawer at her bedside.

"What's that mommy?" The words tumbled out of my mouth expectantly like I was in a living memory where all the lines were pre-written.

My mom paused with the object still in her hand and the drawer still open. She turned to me.

She held a book. She approached and knelt to look at me. "This?" she asked. "This was your father's. It's called *A Tale of Two Cities.*"

I touched the book gingerly as if it was something sacred.

"It's the only thing he left us. So, it's special," she said. "You must never take it out without asking."

"Can you read it to me?" I asked.

"For a little while." She put the book on the dresser and helped me onto the bed. She curled up beside me and opened the book to the first page: *It was the best of times, it was the worst of times, it was the age of wisdom, it was the age of foolishness, it was the epoch of belief, it was the epoch of incredulity, it was the season of Light, it was the season of Darkness. . ."*

I sat up abruptly. Sweat painted my brow. That was it. Something my father had touched.

"Caiduc?" I whispered into the darkness.

Caiduc's dark form appeared on the edge of my bed. If I had seen him in the night, I might have jumped out of my skin. But I was used to him now. Even if his nightly visits were creepy.

He turned his head to me.

"Can you take me somewhere?" I asked.

Caiduc nodded. "Where do you want to go?"

"I know where I can find something of my father's to bring back to Jiao. I need to go back to my childhood home. Can you bring me?"

Caiduc nodded.

Jinn powers were confusing. How could he know where my childhood home was? To know that, he must be omniscient.

Getting up from bed, I grabbed my dagger and belt and wrapped it around my waist. I wore my pajamas: a t-shirt and a pair of shorts. I didn't bother getting dressed.

I pulled on my boots and tied back my hair. "I'm ready."

Caiduc gripped my arm, and *splash!*

I gasped in the air.

Caiduc and I stood in the bare living room where my mother used to read. It had never been hers, but she and I had occupied it. The house smelled musty. No one lived there for years.

I wondered if it was a happy home like Mom and Dad's was. I still remembered the wooden, creaky stairs, the worn bannister, the old floorboards, and Dad's studio that was connected to the house. I frowned. Did they let it go to shambles like this?

I guess I own it now. Although I wasn't sure how all that was going to work out since I was a runaway, and all my paperwork was with family services.

I'd figure all that out later. The house wasn't what mattered to me. The memories did, and I carried those with me.

I bumped into what I thought might be a couch and a coffee table, but I found the hallway.

"What are you looking for?" Caiduc asked. "Maybe I could help."

"It's a book." I felt my way along the wall. "Hopefully it's still in my mother's bedside drawer where she left it."

I stopped abruptly. My bio-mom's room was bare except for a large silver cage and silver blood that had dried upon the floor.

Silver shoeprints blanketed the ground. The police who found me all those years ago couldn't see the blood that pooled there.

A memory flashed before my eyes of me crying in the corner of the room. My face was stained with the blood of the angel that my mother had killed. A stranger approached me in a police uniform, holding out his hands like I was a wild animal.

Not there. Not there. Not there.

"It's not in here," I said. "She moved all the furniture."

I glanced at the door to the adjoining room, a small study that we had rarely ever used. I opened the door.

My mother's bed and mattress were piled inside along with her room's other furnishings, clothes, and long mirror. I climbed over the bed to the small bedside drawer and opened it.

The old paperback book nestled inside. I pulled it from the drawer and met Caiduc in the hallway.

"Is that what you were looking for?" he asked.

"It is," I said. "Hopefully, it's good enough for Jiao to help me find my father."

I looked down at the book. *A Tale of Two Cities*. The memory played in my head again like a movie, like I wasn't really there.

"What will you say to him when you find him?" Caiduc asked.

I hesitated, not because I didn't know what I planned to say but because it was difficult for me to say it. I'd better get used to it if I had to say it to my dad soon. "Why didn't you try to find me?"

I turned the paperback book over in my hands. To me, that old book was more valuable than any of the books in Nash's library. I read over the first chapter three times.

Every time I heard my mother's voice reading it back to me. It felt strange to remember her. I was two people with two families: Lia Hebert, daughter of Micah and Alexandria Hebert, and Rachel Palermo, daughter of Robert and Lydia Palermo.

Rachel. I didn't *feel* like a Rachel. *My name is Lia.*

I opened my bedside drawer and placed the book inside.

On my way to the training field, I stopped outside the library. Adriel sat on the couch with a book in his hands.

"What are you reading?" I sat beside him.

He looked up, eyes wide. "Ah, nothing." He closed the book.

I read the title. "*Jikininki: The Corpse-Eating Specters.* I didn't know you were interested in demons. I've seen a Jikininki. I could tell you about it, if you want."

"I . . ." He put the book on the table beside the couch. "That's okay," he said. "I was just . . . browsing."

"I found a book today," I said. "*A Tale of Two Cities.* I started reading it. It was a favorite of my dad's. My real dad, not the one who adopted me. He was a painter. Didn't read much. But he was brilliant. Just the most beautiful paintings."

"I've seen your father's paintings."

"You have?"

Adriel nodded. "They are *moving.*"

"Thank you." An ache rose in my throat. Tears wet my eyes. I tried to blink them away. "I'm so afraid that they're not up there. They deserve to be, but . . ."

Adriel took my hands. "They're in Heaven."

"How do you know?"

"Because of you. Only good people could have made you what you are."

"But good people end up here," I said.

Adriel shook his head.

"But they do, and spend an eternity suffering. How is that fair?"

"People who have done wrong have sin in their hearts. They are capable of a countless number of wrongs. So, though the punishment is eternal, it is appropriate."

"But can't you change your mind?" I asked. "People change all the time. Sometimes they don't know what they're doing is wrong. Given time, like say an eternity in Hell, they might *find God*."

I clamped my mouth shut. I was starting to sound like Tom.

"Brava!"

Speak of the Devil.

Tom sat in the chair across from us. "Whoa, Lia. I didn't think you had it in you." He looked at Adriel. "She's right. If God's so merciful, where is his mercy when someone down here repents? I've never seen someone ripped out of the Circles with a one-way ticket to Arcadia."

Adriel frowned. "Hell is not infinity. It is an unchangeable present."

Tom narrowed his eyes. "Did you just throw Sisyphus at me? Tell me, Seraph, what *is* the difference between infinity and an unchanging present?"

Adriel glared at him.

Tom's voice raised in pitch. "Because once I have your answer, I'll truck over to the Circles to tell old Sisyphus, 'It's okay. You're not rolling a boulder up a hill forever. You're rolling a boulder up a hill today. It just so happens that every day is today.'"

Happy Groundhog Day! I thought.

Adriel stood. "I will not stay here while you make a mockery of God's justice." He left the room.

"Why do you do that?" I asked.

"Because it's so much fun," Tom said. "Finally, someone who can hold his own in a debate. Too bad he gets so heated. I was just getting to the good stuff."

"It's not good for him. Every time you mention it, he has to think about Heaven." *A place to which he can't return. Because of me.*

"I guess I could argue with you instead," Tom said. "You showed some brilliance just now. Too bad we're on the same side of the debate." He winked.

"Hope I'm not interrupting." Bob stepped into the library. "So many books." He looked around the room. "I've always been impressed by Nash's collection."

"Ah, look at that." Tom picked up the book Adriel had been reading. "I found the book I want." He flashed a tight-lipped smile and ducked out of the room.

"The boss wants to see you, sweetheart," Bob said.

What did Lucifer want with me now? "Fine," I said.

I walked with Bob to his car and sat in the passenger seat. Bob folded in after me, turning the ignition.

Redeemer. I'm on to you.

"Is this about the key?" I asked.

He turned to me and grinned. "No."

I settled back in my seat with my arms folded and braced myself for the ride.

Bob drove like someone was going to drown his cat if he didn't make it to his destination in under ten minutes. The cat drowned. We made it in thirteen.

"What is this about?" I asked as we got into the elevator.

"I can't tell you that, sweetheart." Bob pushed a button, and the doors closed.

I folded my arms.

Bob pulled a key out of his pocket and turned it in the keyhole in the elevator panel. *So, he got a new one.*

The elevator jolted as it took us up.

"Why does everything have to be a secret around here?" I asked.

"You'll find out soon." Bob put his hands in his pockets.

"I don't like surprises." It wasn't surprises I didn't like but bad news. Every time I saw Bob, it was bad news. I wanted to brace myself for it, like you would as you neared the peak before the rollercoaster drops you, but I needed an inkling of what I was preparing myself for.

"This shouldn't come as a surprise."

Maybe Lucifer didn't like that we hadn't gone out to burn down angels in over a year. But she wouldn't be calling me in for that. She would have spoken with Nash.

Or maybe this was about Adriel. I had made him fall, but I did that to save him from the Pit. Shortly after that, I asked that he be released from the Angel District. Did Lucifer think I might be playing both sides?

Perhaps Bob *did* tell her about the key, and I would be lectured on how I couldn't go around beating up on Lucifer's right-hand demon.

Show me your true face, Beelzebub. It'll make it easier to kick you in the teeth.

The elevator chimed, and the doors opened. I followed Bob down the hall. A clone secretary passed us with a silver platter of food.

The scent of roasted asparagus wafted down the hall. I peered over my shoulder as she placed the platter down inside one of the rooms. She closed the door and locked it with a key from her skirt pocket.

You don't deliver food to empty rooms. Lucifer was keeping someone locked up. My mother?

Bob opened the door to Lucifer's office. "After you, sweetheart."

I walked past him into the room. Lucifer lounged on the sofa across from the two black, leather chairs. But she wasn't the only one in the room.

Nash stood at the window, sipping from a mug.

Of course, he's here already.

He didn't look at me when I walked in.

Lucifer stood from the sofa and sat behind her mahogany desk. "Sit." She gestured to the chair across from the desk.

I frowned, but sat.

Nash hadn't moved. What was so damn interesting at the window?

Lucifer's fingers twined together. Bob was behind me. I felt like I was trapped between a snake and a scorpion.

Lucifer smiled. Her lips were a different shade of red every day. Today they reminded me of a traffic light.

If Nash was here, why did she need me? Nash could deliver her message. Then I wouldn't have to sit across from her like a zebra trying to stare down a tiger.

"Why am I here?"

Nash shot me a look. I wasn't surprised the first look of the day was a jab.

Lucifer continued to smile like she was made of stone and I was made of glass. I could shout and complain all I want, but in the end, she could shatter me.

But I wasn't going to let her frighten me.

"I've spoken with Nash," Lucifer said. "But I wanted to make sure you heard this from me."

Was her trust in Nash breaking?

"There's an angel out in the desert. I've asked Nash to find him. Now, that I have you, I have the leverage I need to bring him down here."

I folded my arms. "What do you want with this angel?"

Lucifer's glare pinned me. Good thing she separated herself from Wrath or she might have reached over the table and scratched my eyes out. "His name is Azazel. And he is very important to me. Thousands of years ago, Michael ordered Raphael to bind and blindfold him and leave him in the desert to suffer."

"Didn't really answer my question."

Nash stabbed me with his eyes.

"I don't have to answer your questions. I want Azazel taken with his Grace intact. That's why you are not to touch him. You will be there as a threat but not a weapon. Do you understand?"

"Yeah. It'll bring me joy to set a guy free that Michael and Raphael hate for some reason. Thank you for the opportunity. Is that it? Or are you going to tell me, you need twenty more angels from me?"

Lucifer's lips curled into a smile. She's thinking of all the ways she will have me tortured once I'm down here permanently. "That's it," she said.

four

ASH sighed. As he gripped the wheel, his knuckles turned white.

"What are *you* sighing about?"

He looked at me like I asked him if Earth was round. "Lucifer is the Queen of Hell."

I narrowed my eyes at him. "Don't talk to me like I'm stupid."

Nash shook his head. "Well, you didn't seem to know that back there. Are you trying to get me thrown into the Pit?"

I folded my arms. "Lucifer won't throw *you* into the Pit."

"Lucifer uses people," Nash said. "I'm a tool to her. Like you."

Does Lucifer passionately kiss her tools?

"Are you afraid she'll replace you with Azazel? Who is he anyway?"

"He was one of the Watchers, a group of fallen angels who mated with human women. He spearheaded the whole thing. That's why God ordered Raphael to tie him up in a desert. He didn't want the other angels to be corrupted."

"I thought Lucifer said Michael asked Raphael to do that."

"God speaks through Michael."

"Well, isn't that convenient for Michael? But why does Lucifer think Azazel isn't fallen?"

"Because he would only be fallen if he thought what he had done was wrong."

"But God didn't want him to do it, so . . ."

"Just because God didn't endorse it, doesn't make it wrong."

"Wait. Isn't God the moral compass on everything?"

Nash shook his head. "This is too much for you."

"Stop doing that, and tell me the truth."

"Azazel thought by mixing angels and humans that he could make humans better. But instead he made more imperfect beings. Michael had them hunted down."

"Except one," I said.

Nash nodded. "Metatron. He ran. But when Michael finds him, he'll kill him."

"No one knows where he is?"

Nash looked out the window. "No."

"So, Azazel, what use is he to Lucifer?"

"She's angry with Michael. Eternity is a long time to reflect on sins of the past. Sometimes you repent, other times you decide what you'd done wasn't quite a sin after all."

"But you can't go back," I said. "Hell is forever."

"It's messed up." Nash turned the key in the ignition.

I knocked on the door. Jiao's tea shop was closed, but even if it was broad daylight I doubted Jiao would appreciate me walking right on in. She yelled at the top of her lungs for me to leave last time.

Still, I wasn't sure if she was in the tea room. Both times I had gone to see her, she was in the back.

I knocked harder this time.

A curse and the shuffle of feet came from behind the door. I braced myself for a hard push back into the street. The lock clicked, and the door opened.

Jiao stood in a robe, her hand clasping it to her small body. Standing this close to her, I realized how short she was. I'm no giant, but Jiao was easily a head shorter than me.

"You again," she spat. "I told you to get lost."

"Yeah, you suspected me of stealing an angel's Grace," I said. "I didn't steal anything. Something was forced on me. I—"

"I'm going to stop you right there and pretend that I didn't hear that," Jiao said.

"Why?" I asked.

"Never mind. Just leave now."

She was scared. She would deny it, but that look in her eyes screamed everything. My mother had done something terrible, probably irreversible, and it frightened the hell out of Jiao.

"Please," I said. "I still need your help, and I'll keep knocking at your door all night to get it."

Jiao's eyes darted left and right.

"If I help you," she hissed, "you'll leave me alone for good?"

I nodded.

"Come in before I change my mind." Jiao opened the door wider.

I stepped inside.

"You want to find your father?" she asked.

"Yeah, that's why I'm here."

"And you remember what that would require?"

"I have it here." I pulled the book for the inside of my coat. "It was my dad's."

"Come with me." Jiao led me past the partition to the back of the tea shop.

The hallway was lit with paper lanterns. She turned the corner into a room with shelves full of jars lining the wall. The jars contained powders and pastes of various colors.

"Sit," Jiao said.

I took a seat on one of the cushions next to a low table. On the table was a large, silver dish. I clenched my father's book to my chest.

Jiao grabbed a pot, a jar, and scroll from the shelf and sat down across from me. "Give it to me." She gestured toward the book.

My hand shook as I passed the book to her. I wanted it back as soon as it left my hands. It was the only thing I had left of my bio-dad.

I reached up and gripped the cross and locket that hung around my neck. I could always find comfort there.

Jiao placed my dad's book in the silver tray and took out a long, wooden stick. She blew on the end of the stick, and a tiny flame sparked.

She lit the corner of the book and set it ablaze.

My heart dropped into my stomach. "No!" I reached out.

Jiao put a hand up to stop me. "Do you want to find your father or not?"

I set my jaw, but I settled back. I clenched my fists as the book's pages came under assault by the flames. The fire burned it unnaturally quick and completely. What was once the only thing of my father's I owned turned to dust.

Jiao scooped up the remnants of the book in her hands and poured it into the small pot. The dust dissolved into the hot water. Jiao opened the jar, reached in with two fingers, and scooped out a small amount of powder.

She sprinkled the powder into the pot. She unrolled the scroll. It was a map. She crumpled it in both hands until it was nothing more than a tight ball.

She placed the crumpled paper deep into the pot and covered it with the lid.

"Now, we wait," she said.

"How long?" I asked.

"Tell me about Sheol," Jiao said. It came out like a demand.

I hesitated. "Why do you think I would know anything about that?" I asked.

"You're walking around with a Jinn," Jiao said. "They make appearances on Earth but very rarely. They like to hang out in Sheol."

"How did you know about that?"

"The Jinn?"

I nodded. Caiduc stayed far away from the tea house. Something frightened him.

"Let's just say I have a long history with Jinni. I can smell them. Now, tell me about Hell."

"Hell is . . . different than you'd expect." I wondered if telling Jiao would be against some code and would get me into trouble or something. But then again, what did I care? I already had a place in the Seventh Circle.

"Different how?"

"Can I ask why you want to know?"

"You can ask, but I won't answer," she said.

"What do you want to know about it?"

"Well, everything you know."

"I spend most of my time in the Outer Region. It's a place for demons who complete their contracts. It's . . . okay, I guess. Better than the Seventh Circle. That's all fire, boiling blood, and harpies. And then, there's the Pit."

"The Pit?" The word was a whisper on her tongue.

"Yeah, the name says it all. It's big and endless. If I had to guess, I'd say it's probably bigger than this whole city."

Jiao glanced down. "It's ready." She lifted the lid of the pot and gently pulled the map out with a pair of silver tongs. She placed the map on the table.

I marveled at it. The brew that it had bathed in was dark, so dark that it should have turned the page amber, but the map was mostly clean and white except for one spot.

"He's in Hattiesburg, Mississippi."

Hattiesburg. The only spot on the map that had been darkened by the tea. *He was so close. Maybe two or three hours away all my life.* If I hadn't landed in Hell, I could have thumbed a ride to Hattiesburg.

I had never been to Hattiesburg, but I imagined it would be very difficult to find him without a more precise location.

"Hattiesburg is a big place. Any way you could be more specific?" I asked. *A street address maybe?*

Jiao narrowed her eyes. "You know his name?" she asked.

I nodded. "Robert Palermo."

"Then, I'm sure the rest could be done on the Internet. Don't rely on magic to hand you everything on a silver platter."

Her words were biting.

"Thank you." I got up from my seat. At least, I wouldn't have to search the entire United States and knock on the door of each Robert Palermo in the White Pages.

"Remember our deal." Jiao looked up at me. "You don't bother me again."

"Agreed," I said.

I met Caiduc across the street from the tea shop. He scratched his wrists.

"Did the witch find him?" Caiduc asked.

"He's in Hattiesburg," I said. "I don't know his exact address, but at least we only have one city to search rather than the whole world. I need to get to a public library. One in Hattiesburg if you can manage."

*   *   *

CLEAR water splashed upon my face, but I came out dry on the other side. I stood between two towering shelves. Gray carpet trailed under my feet, and the musty smell of old books filled my nose.

How funny. The sterile smell of Nash's house could overcome the antique scent of books. But this place was consumed by it, although I'm sure the books were far less ancient.

Was this a university library? Without meaning to, I remembered Carson. I remembered feeling normal.

And then a demon showed up in his apartment, and I had to tell him at the risk of sounding crazy. I did sound crazy and scared him away.

What had that demon done to him?

I couldn't think about it. Nothing to do now. I imagined the demon, sinking its claws into Carson's shoulder, whispering for him to do terrible things, things that would land him a spot in Hell.

Things that made middle-aged men lock up girls in basements and drain their blood.

I shook my head.

Not there. Not there. Not there.

"Can I help you?"

I jumped.

A woman wearing glasses and a cardigan narrowed her eyes at me. *The librarian?*

"Umm. No. I was looking for the computers."

She eyed me up and down. "You can't sleep here, you know."

I furrowed my brow. "Of course not. I just need to Google something."

What made her think I planned on sleeping here? I wasn't homeless.

I glanced down at what I was wearing. My shirt was a bit wrinkled. But I showered this morning so I'm sure I smelled fine.

Whatever.

I walked to the computer terminals in the center of the library and logged in under guest. I searched Robert Palermo. The first link that came up was a university site. I clicked on it.

There he was. My father's picture came up on the screen along with a short bio. He was a Professor of Literature at the University of Southern Mississippi. He graduated from Loyola University. Recommended reading: *A Tale of Two Cities*.

The page had no home address, but at least I knew for sure that he was in the city. I clicked back to the search results and scanned the page. A White Pages listing popped up so I clicked the link.

Two Robert Palermos lived in Hattiesburg. One of them had to be him. I jotted the addresses down on a piece of paper and shoved it into my pocket.

Behind the library, I showed Caiduc the first address. "I have two," I said. "Can you take me to this one?"

Caiduc nodded. His earring swung. His rough hand gripped my arm.

I got dizzy from all the in-a-flash traveling, but at least Jinni transportation wasn't as nauseating as portal travel. I held onto Caiduc's shoulder for a second.

"Are you alright?"

"I'm feeling a little sick that's all." I left Caiduc and walked up to the house.

I knocked on the door, and a blond man answered. I remembered my father's face and this wasn't him.

"Sorry," I said. "I must have gotten the wrong house."

The man gave me a tight-lipped smile and shut the door on me.

One down, one to go.

Clenching Caiduc's hand behind the fence, he transported us to the second address. I climbed out of the bushes and brushed the leaves off my clothes.

White picket fences and manicured lawns accented each house along the clear, evening covered street. Trees grew on the median, and all the houses were at least two stories.

I spotted the address. The house was three stories with white flowers in the yard and bushes lining the red brick foundation. Stairs led up to a covered porch. The house must have had twenty windows.

I walked up the driveway. On one side of the house was a massive bay window. Inside a family was having dinner.

A mother, father, and two girls. They were laughing. At the head of the table was a man I recognized—my father. His dark hair was streaked with gray. He helped his youngest daughter cut up her food before leaning back to enjoy his meal.

I swallowed. I could taste the salt of my tears in the back of my throat. He had forgotten me. If I came back into his life now, I would ruin his perfect family. They were his future. I wasn't even a memory.

"You're crying," Caiduc said.

I wiped the tears from my cheeks. "I don't know what I expected," I said.

"Do you want to go in?" he asked.

But I wasn't crying because I felt abandoned by him. I might have wanted a future with him, but he didn't raise me. He wasn't my dad.

I expected him to fill that role for me, but that wouldn't erase the pain.

Mom and Dad were gone. Raphael took them from me. Only one place existed where I could fight him.

I shook my head. "I want to go back where I belong."

 five

I opened my eyes. Caiduc clasped my hands. We knelt together in my room. His dark eyes were sad. Mine were crying. Caiduc placed his branchy fingers against my cheek.

Nothing was said, but nothing was more comforting than the silence that drifted between us. I let the stillness of the room wrap around me, and I wasn't vulnerable anymore.

Safe. For now.

But not for long. Lucifer, Nash, Raphael, Michael, Bob. All of them were up to something. As much as I wanted to take advantage of Caiduc's abilities to mend my abandonment wounds, I needed him for something much more serious.

My first target would be Lucifer. I had to find out what she was up to. People with reputations for lying don't usually tell the truth. I also wanted to get a hold of my contract. Maybe it contained some loophole that could get me out of the whole thing.

The second part should be easy. I was sure Bob would happily get me a copy of my contract. It was signed in *my* blood after all. I was entitled to it.

I hoped I didn't have to oust him as the Redeemer to get what I wanted. Not yet.

But spying on Lucifer, that's where I would need Caiduc's help.

The Jinn seemed pretty content with helping me though I had no idea why. That had been on my list of concerns for some time, but Nash had assured me that finding the answer to that question would be harder than solving a Rubik's Cube.

Maybe Jinn just get bored. Maybe I was Caiduc's entertainment.

It was nice to see that, although he might be terrifying to look at, Caiduc had a heart. Jinn seemed a lot closer to humans than angels or demons.

A car engine turned over.

Caiduc smiled with his eyes before disappearing before mine. The coldness of the room felt heavy.

I walked to the window and peered outside. Nash pulled away from the house. I imagined he was going to see Lucifer so that he could paw her all over her desk.

I marched into the bathroom and rinsed my face with cold water. Strands of my hair were wet from falling into the sink. I rubbed my face with a towel.

I hated myself for thinking about him. He was doing what Chandra said he would. *He doesn't like you,* I thought. *Move on.* He certainly had.

Wrapping myself in the covers, I lay in bed, hoping that sleep would veil me in darkness. I drifted as I listened to the music on my MP3 player.

One moment I was in my room at Nash's house, and then my world shattered like pieces of glass on a broken mirror. I was downstairs in the living room.

Adriel sat on the couch, drinking a cup of coffee. I didn't like how he reminded me of Nash. They were so different, but they looked so much alike now. I wondered why I hadn't seen it before.

He continued to sip his coffee without looking my way.

"Adriel?" I said.

I expected him to turn toward me, but his eyes remained on the white wall. What was he thinking about?

"Adriel? I shouted.

He looked around. His eyes froze on me but saw through me. He turned back to his coffee.

As I approached him, my eyes blinked open. I was in bed. The covers were tight around me.

What in the Hell was that? Maybe it was one of those psychic dream conversations like the one with my mother and the other with the Seven Archangels of Heaven.

But Adriel couldn't hear me. Why was that?

The air outside the covers was cold on my face. My stomach grumbled. The warm sanctuary of the covers beckoned me to stay, but my stomach growled like a hungry animal.

My feet met the cold, marble floor, and I padded across the room to the door and into the hallway. I hesitated at the top of the stairs. Light came from the living room.

Nash? But didn't he leave? How long ago was that?

I tiptoed down the stairs and peered into the living room. Adriel nursed a cup of coffee. Just like in the dream. Or psychic vision.

I needed to learn how to control that. And my other powers too.

"Adriel?"

He turned and looked my way.

"Hi," he said. "Hope I didn't scare you. Nash asked me to watch over you while he was away."

"Did he now?" I failed to keep the ire out of my voice.

"Are you okay?" Adriel asked. "It's the middle of the night. You normally sleep through it. Lately that has changed."

How did he know I slept through the night? Oh, that's right. He's been watching me for years.

"I'm fine," I said. "I just skipped dinner, and now I'm so hungry I could eat an entire buffet."

Adriel frowned and cocked an eyebrow. Did he have to take everything so literally?

I blushed. "Well, maybe only half a buffet. Depends on the size of the restaurant."

"I'll help you make something," Adriel said. "I don't know my way around the kitchen, but I'll do whatever I can."

I laughed.

"What's so funny?"

"I just imagined you in an apron cutting vegetables."

"Why's that so funny?"

"You're a warrior, and you're cutting up veggies."

"Nash is a warrior."

"True. I guess I've just never imagined him in the same way."

"Well, anything so I could take a break from this coffee. The stuff's disgusting." He put the mug down on the table.

"You're telling me."

We made spaghetti. I took out onions, mushrooms, green peppers, garlic, tomatoes, and pasta. That sounded right.

"Can you cut up the rest of the vegetables while I sauté the onions?"

"Sure, can you demonstrate?"

He really didn't know his way around a kitchen if I had to show him how to cut mushrooms, but I gladly demonstrated how to cut each vegetable. I was no Emeril Lagasse, but I had helped Mom in the kitchen a few times.

Working together, we had the kitchen smelling pretty good. I had drained and rinsed the pasta. We hung out on the couch while the sauce finished cooking.

Adriel didn't lounge on the couch like Nash did. Instead, he perched on the edge of it with his feet firmly planted on the floor. If he sat back, he'd crush his featherless wings. They hung on either side of him.

"I saw my father," I said, "my bio-dad I mean."

"When?" he asked.

"Yesterday."

"But how?"

"I don't want to tell you that."

Adriel narrowed his eyes. "Lia. . ."

"But I want to tell you this: I went to meet him. I know it might not change anything. I mean, I'm eighteen now. I missed so much time with him, and I wouldn't take it back because I loved my Mom and Dad. I'm so glad they were the ones who raised me. But he's my dad too."

"He must have been happy to see you after all this time."

I shook my head. "I chickened out."

"Why didn't you meet him?"

"I couldn't do that to him. He left me for a reason. I'm pretty sure he wouldn't want me turning up at his doorstep."

"What if that's exactly what he wants?"

My eyes held Adriel's.

The timer on the stove went off.

"Sauce is ready. I'd better go make sure it doesn't burn."

I took a serving bowl from the cabinet and loaded in the pasta, smothering it with sauce. As I reached for the bowl, Adriel said, "Let me get that."

He lifted the bowl from the counter and headed for the dining room.

"Wait," I said.

Adriel turned.

I didn't like the idea of that big dining room table causing a gulf between me and Adriel. "Let's eat on the sofa. Nash will never know."

Adriel walked to the living room while I grabbed the plates and forks. I put some of the pasta on my plate and rubbed my hands together. "Here goes." I put a forkful in my mouth. "Umm."

I nodded my head as I chewed. I had taken four or five mouthfuls by the time I noticed Adriel hadn't served himself any.

"Try it," I said. "It's good."

He forked some of the pasta onto his plate. "Sorry," he said. "I'm not used to eating."

"Angels never eat?" I asked between bites.

"No," he said. "I've never felt hunger like I do now. It's strange." Dubiously he loaded the spaghetti onto his fork. More than half of it slid off his fork before it made it to his mouth.

I stifled a giggle.

Adriel looked over at me.

"Sorry," I said.

He smiled. "It's okay. I watched humans eat before. It's harder than it looks."

"Not once you get the hang of it," I said.

"Thank you," Adriel said.

I grinned. "Everyone gets the hang of it eventually."

"No." His eyes held mine. "After Sydriel went missing, I was in a very bad place. She and I were close. My heart was dark and cold when I thought something must have happened to her."

He looked down for a moment before meeting my eyes again. "It wasn't the best time in my life. I wondered if I would ever return to Heaven."

He took my hand in his. "But watching you, being your guardian angel, it changed me. I wanted to protect what Sydriel vowed to protect."

I looked down at our joined hands. "You're not my guardian angel anymore," I said. "I don't want you jumping in front of Raphael to protect me."

"You don't understand, Lia." His thumb stroked the palm of my hand, and I felt my pulse quicken. "It doesn't matter if I no longer have my wings. I made a vow, and I must keep it."

KIRAN swung his sword. He widened his stance, his knees bent. He glanced at me as I approached, but continued practicing.

I copied his stance and followed his movements. Even without a sword, my actions were clumsy.

"Drop your shoulders," Kiran said. "You're too stiff."

I sighed. "No amount of instruction can help me beat Chandra."

"You're not trying to beat Chandra."

"Yes, I am."

Kiran shook his head. "Because you know that beating Chandra will mean you will spar against me next. You don't want to spar against me." He didn't say it with smugness in his voice the way Tom might have said it. It was a fact.

"I'll fight you. I'm just not ready. It would be like a snail racing a cheetah."

"You have no reason to lie to me," Kiran said, "and yet you do."

"I'm not lying to you."

"Then you are lying to yourself."

I stopped mid-stance and folded my arms.

"You're afraid that if you beat me, you'll be ready. That you'll have to face the angel that murdered your parents."

I narrowed my eyes. "I want to kill Raphael. You could put him in front of me today, and I would set him on fire."

"But you are still afraid of death."

"Everyone's afraid of death." I stopped. "Well, everyone who is alive is afraid of death."

"You are afraid of something."

Was I? Raphael was ready for me. He was hunting me.

I looked down. "Failure."

"You cannot be afraid of failure," Kiran said, "or you will be frozen forever."

"I don't freeze. I don't hesitate. I act. Despite my fears."

Then why haven't you asked Caiduc to take you to Raphael?

"I'm not the one who's lying," I said.

I grabbed the copy of *A Tale of Two Cities* from Nash's shelf. The book didn't hold the same value to me as my dad's copy, but at least I would get to read it.

Curling up in a chair, I read as I sipped my hot chocolate. Christmas was tomorrow, and I would be celebrating in Sheol. Of course, they didn't celebrate Christmas in Hell.

This would be the third Christmas I missed with my family: Uncle Jonah. I couldn't even send him a Christmas card.

I looked up from my book.

Tom stood at one of the shelves with a book open in his hands.

"Oh, hey. I didn't see you there," I said.

He was unmoving.

"Tom?"

I stood. "Hey." I approached him. "What did I do to deserve the silent treatment?" I reached out to touch his arm.

He disappeared.

What the . . . ?

"You should have a book in your hand if you're going to be in here." Tom walked into the library with a book under his arm.

"Where did you go?" I asked.

"I just got here," Tom said.

"No, you were standing right there." I indicated the spot where Tom stood only moments ago.

Tom cocked his head. "Are you feeling okay?"

I put my hand to my head. "Yeah, I just . . . need to sit down."

"Maybe you should."

Was I doing the dream psychic thing or was that something else? I'd seen Tom standing in Nash's library a thousand times. Could it have been a memory? A memory playing out in real time?

I walked back to the couch and slumped down.

"Where were you this morning?" Tom asked.

"I was training with Kiran."

Tom stiffened. "You train with him a lot without Nash's supervision?"

"No, just this morning. I'm not going to make a habit of it though. Kiran thinks I'm holding back."

"Are you?"

I folded my arms. "Any luck with Lucifer's latest project?"

"You mean finding Azazel? I have a stack of books taller than me upstairs. Tons of references to Dudael, but no indication of where Dudael is. I'm not going to go running around the desert in a headcloth in search of a place that might not exist. In fact, . . ."

I needed to learn how to control my powers. I wasn't a witch. Witches drank demon blood. So, I was the opposite of one, whatever that was called.

Jiao seemed to know something she didn't want to talk about. Maybe she could help me. But she didn't want me anywhere near her.

"You're not listening to me," Tom said.

"Yes, I am," I said. "You were talking about hiking in the desert in a headcloth. I think that's a good idea."

Maybe if I got her something she wanted. What had Adriel given to her last time? Tea! But I'm sure she wouldn't be interested in Chamomile.

She was very interested in Hell.

"Tom, are there any special teas in Sheol?"

He raised an eyebrow. "Nash has some Da Hong Pao. It's the most expensive tea in the world."

"That's not what I'm talking about."

"Tea leaves grow on trees in the Third Circle. They're useless to demons."

"Why? What does the tea do?"

"It makes the drinker immortal, ageless."

"So, it's Eterna-Tea."

"Very clever." He smirked. "It's called Void Mortem."

Useless to demons, but very useful to anyone with a finite lifespan.

six

grabbed Caiduc's arm. "I need you to take me to the Third Circle."

"That is unwise.' Caiduc's voice trembled.

"I don't care. I need to get something from there."

Caiduc shook his head. "Very unwise."

"If you don't bring me, I'll have to go myself, and I'll have to pass through two additional Circles to do that." I plastered resolve on my face, but I cringed inside.

Limbo wouldn't be too bad. Tom said it was like the DMV. Okay, so maybe it would be bad. But what I was really worried about was having to pass through the Second Circle. If the Third wasn't bad enough, the Second was a tearing whirlwind that I'm sure I'd get myself caught up in.

Caiduc scratched his wrists. "I don't like it."

"You don't like anything. Stop thinking about it, and just do it!" I grabbed his hand and placed it on my arm.

Caiduc frowned as best as he could with his protruding deer-face.

My world flashed white.

I pressed my nose into my sleeve. The smell was unbearable. "What is that?"

The sky was a spin of clouds. Cold rain wet my coat. Thick mud encased my boots.

"It is human waste," Caiduc said.

"What? That's disgusting."

"This is where you wanted to go." Caiduc scratched his wrist.

Brown hills rose in the distance, and deep trenches of mud trailed through the area around us. I dry heaved against my coat sleeve. The icy rain had matted my hair to my face.

"I'm looking for tea leaves. Void Mortem. They grow on a tree."

Caiduc looked around. He shook. "Maybe we should go on top the hill." He pointed to a large hill several feet away. "Then we will be able to see."

I slapped Caiduc on the back. "Ha! I knew you were more than just a supernatural taxi service. Come on. Let's go."

My feet hit the ground in loud, wet plops. Splotches of mud dotted my jeans.

A low, deep growl echoed in the distance.

My heart stilled, and I stopped in my tracks.

Shit!

I spun around but didn't see from where the sound had come. I knew what it was. *Cerberus, the three-headed dog, guardian of the Third Circle.*

Something grabbed my boot. Sticking out of the mud was a hand. It gripped my ankle.

The mire birthed a head. "Help me, please!" The man was bald and dirty.

I didn't want to stick my hand in that sludge, but I couldn't let him suffer in the muck. I reached out to him.

"Don't!" Caiduc pulled my shoulder. "You can't save him."

"I can at least get him out of whatever this vile stuff is."

The man took my hand, and his fingers climbed up my arm. I pulled back. He slipped. I pulled. But he managed to climb out of the mud.

His body was covered in it, and that was a good thing because I don't think he wore any clothes underneath.

The roar sounded again.

Caiduc and I raced for the hill. The man followed us. He probably thought we could protect him. Fat chance. We'd be lucky if we could protect ourselves.

At least Caiduc could pull me out if things got mortally dangerous, but this man was stuck here to suffer for wrongs he might have committed decades ago.

My legs burned as I ran up the hill. Caiduc was right. Beyond the hill, plateaus rose from the ground. Upon one plateau, people gathered around a tree.

Below the plateau, people drowned in the mud ravines. They struggled to keep their heads above the muck by pushing down on the people swimming next to them.

That's when I spotted him. *Cerberus.*

It had three heads with a long worm-like neck and patches of black fur over a wrinkly gray body. The beast was ten times bigger than any dog I'd ever seen. Its ears looked like they belonged on a bat. The tail was rat-like. Its teeth were needle-sharp and sank into red, bleeding gums.

Cerberus snapped at the people as they struggled in the mud. Caiduc cowered behind me, pressing his branchy fingers into my arm.

"It doesn't see us," I whispered.

But as if magnetized to us, Cerberus turned its head. Its eyes stabbed me.

Holy shit!

It turned and rushed towards the hill.

"Run!" I screamed.

We ran-slid down the hill. I cursed myself every time I slid in the mud, digging my hands in the thick sludge to get back up.

I couldn't look behind me. *Run!*

Mud coated my arms and hands. Filth was packed so tightly beneath my fingernails, I thought they might pop off. My breath came in short gasps.

Someone grabbed my arm. *Caiduc, now is not the time!* The hands yanked my jacket aside. Teeth sank into my shoulder.

I screamed and spun with my sword in hand. The man covered in mud had a bloody mouth. He reached for me.

I slashed his stomach. He stumbled towards me. I hit him on the center of the forehead with the hilt of my sword and kicked him back into the mire.

Caiduc pulled my arm. "I can take you back," he pleaded.

I looked toward the plateau where the tree grew.

"Look out!"

Cerberus lunged at me with one of its long-necked heads. I gripped my sword. He roared.

The breath knocked me on my back in the mud. It squished under me. All I saw was teeth.

Flash!

The teeth sank into the mud beside me. The heat of Cerberus's breath misted over me. Its mouth filled with mud before it realized that my body wasn't within its jowls.

The second head snapped toward me.

Flash!

The second mouth clotted with mud.

I looked up at Caiduc. His branchy hands were around my arms.

Flash!

The third head descended into the muck. Cerberus turned its heads, coughing up the mud from its lungs.

I stumbled up and ran. Climbing up to one plateau, I raced across it and leapt to the next. Without stopping to think, I kept running, leaping from plateau to plateau until I reached the tree.

People reached for the branches, pulling leaves from the tree, and munching on them. The tree's bark was white. It was bare except for a handful of sage green leaves.

The few leaves that still graced the tree grew on the top branches. The people tried to climb the tree, but their wet, muddy hands were too slick to get a good handhold.

If the leaves were supposed to make a person live forever, why weren't they helping these people?

I wiped my hands on my jeans and grabbed the highest branch I could reach. Climbing to the top, I snatched a fistful of leaves.

The ground shook. I fell from the tree and landed with my back against the rocky ground. Cerberus's large, clawed feet crumbled the edge of the plateau.

I stuffed the leaves into my pocket. "Caiduc!"

Cerberus scrambled onto the plateau. I stood, bracing myself to meet him. Teeth snapped.

I leapt toward it. My blade sank into one black eye. Cerberus howled. Its back legs slipped off the plateau.

Cerberus fell from the plateau. My blade was deep in its eye socket. I gripped the hilt of my sword and tried to remove it from the beast.

We were falling.

I recovered my blade, but it was too late. I slid down Cerberus's neck, trying to hold onto the wrinkly skin when I felt a branchy hand on my arm.

I knelt on the floor of my bedroom and gasped for air. My sword clattered at my side. I reached into my pocket and pulled out a handful of muddied leaves.

*   *   *

ADRIEL hugged me as he flew, but the wind was not harsh in our ears. The air was warm. I felt an overwhelming sense of comfort like I was wrapped in the billowy softness of the coziest bed imaginable. The feathers of his white wings were everywhere, cocooning me in a cave of warmth and security.

My eyes fluttered open. Blackened bones caged my body like prison cell bars. Warmth suffused my back. Adriel slept beside me, his body nestled against mine. The heat of his hand burned into my arm.

My heartbeat was like a hammer in my chest. Adriel's body tensed as if he had awoken surprised to find us like that. His wing arched back, releasing me from its cage.

"I'm sorry," he said.

"No, it's okay." I sat up on the couch.

I didn't like the feeling of awkwardness I felt. I shouldn't feel that way with Adriel. He had protected me for years.

"Orange juice?" I asked.

"Sure," Adriel said.

As I walked to the kitchen, I glanced out the window in the foyer. Nash's car sat in the driveway. Had he returned home and saw Adriel and I spooning in the living room? I didn't care. He was doing much worse with Lucifer.

I grabbed two glasses from the cabinets.

"Good morning."

"Oh, shit!" My hands shook as I brought the second glass down on the counter. I turned. Nash leaned against the counter with a cup of coffee in his hand. "I didn't see you there."

"Slept on the couch last night?" he asked.

"Uh-huh." I grabbed the orange juice from the refrigerator without looking at him. "Where were you last night?"

"Business," Nash said.

"What business? Do you have a desk job in Hell or something?"

Nash took a sip of his coffee. "Do you want me to leave?"

"This is *your* house, isn't it?" I poured the orange juice and took the two glasses into my hands. "I can't ask you to leave your own house." I walked out of the kitchen.

I set the glasses on the coffee table in front of the empty bowls Adriel and I left from the night before. I enjoyed our meals more than I had enjoyed the dinners with Nash. I was glad we made a tradition out of those nightly feasts.

They're dates. No, they're meals between friends. Yeah, right.

Adriel sat upright on the couch. I settled next to him with my arms folded.

"What's wrong?" he asked.

"Nash is home."

"You're still angry with Nash." It wasn't a question.

"He's lying to me," I said.

"What *is* he lying about?"

"He's being sneaky. Always leaving the house. Not telling me where he's going." I didn't want to tell Adriel that I discovered him with Lucifer. I didn't want him to know how much that bothered me.

"You should confront him about it," Adriel said. "Whatever it is, it could affect us all. If you don't, I'll have to."

I didn't want Adriel and Nash fighting again. There wasn't a whole lot of brotherly love between the two of them.

"I'll talk to him," I said. *Not that I really want to.* It was easier to avoid Nash. He wasn't in the house much anyway.

THAT night, Nash left the house again. The car pulled out of the driveway as I leaned against the side of my bed and strummed my guitar. Mud crusted under my fingernails. The dirt was so deep under the nail beds, I wasn't sure if I could ever wash it out.

Caiduc sat not far from me, watching me with intense eyes as I studied my nails.

"I wish you would stop staring," I said.

Caiduc looked away. A shamed expression washed over his face. "I can't help it. Your glow is so brilliant."

"What glow are you talking about?"

Caiduc shook his head, and his eyes fastened back on me. "I don't know what it is, but it's so bright."

My hand left my guitar, and I snapped my fingers in his face. "Well, snap out of it because it's creepy."

"Is it . . . *creepy?*" He said the word slowly like he was testing it in his mouth.

"Yes," I said. "It very much is. Now would you stop?"

Caiduc nodded. "I'll go now."

My heart hurt to hear him say that. "No, wait." I wasn't angry at *him*. I was angry at Nash, and I was taking it out on Caiduc who had helped me without asking for anything in return. "I'm sorry. I have a lot on my mind."

"What is on your mind?"

"Lucifer," I said. "I know she's hiding something from me. I can feel it. She's a liar. The question isn't why would she lie to me. It's why wouldn't she?"

I leaned my guitar against the side of the bed.

"I want to know what she's hiding." I was upset I wouldn't be spending another night on the couch with Adriel. "Can you bring me to Lucifer's skyscraper?"

Caiduc nodded his head slowly. "If that is where you want to go." He reached out his hand.

"Wait!" I said. "There's something I need to get first."

Lucifer was keeping my mother in that room. Why else would she need a clone secretary to deliver food there? But I couldn't get in without a key.

I still had Bob's key, but I doubted it opened every lock in Lucifer's skyscraper. *Not sure if she trusts Bob that much.* Of course, Bob was one of her *personalities.* So, *he* was *her*, is her. That must be confusing.

Shutting the door to my bedroom, I stepped into the hall. Nash's room was across the stairs. I slid the door open and peered inside.

The bed sat on a glass platform with two bedside tables. The bed sheets were black. One pillow was encased in white, the other in black. *A mishap at the laundry mat?*

Against one wall was a loveseat with a black frame and white cushions. Blackout blinds covered the two windows on either side of the bed. Above the bed was a large abstract painting with lines of white that looked like a spider.

The bedroom looked untouched. The bed was made. The floors were clear. It looked thoroughly unlived in.

Nash is a real neat freak. What was I expecting?

I checked one of the beside drawers. Empty. I looked through the opposite one. Same result. I looked under each pillow and searched his closet.

How many black t-shirts did one guy need?

I even hunted through the bathroom. I put my hands on my hips. *Maybe he hadn't hidden them here.*

My eyes swept over the room. A large copy of *Don Quixote* rested on one of the bedside tables. Nash would never leave that there. He'd stick it in his drawer or bring it down to the library.

I lifted the cover of the book. A chain of keys nestled inside the hollowed-out pages. *Damn. Was I really going to bring a hundred keys with me to Lucifer's skyscraper?*

Together, the keys must have weighed twenty pounds. But I'd have to take them all. I didn't know which one would fit.

I carried the keys to my room and grabbed my backpack, stuffing the heavy, metal keys inside. I turned to Caiduc. "Now, I'm ready."

The world was split in two. That happened when I didn't blink. If I blinked right before Caiduc transported me, it was more like waking up in a room I had fallen asleep in after someone splashed water in my face.

It was disorienting but not so much as if I didn't blink. It was like being in two places at once. They overlapped each other like double vision, and my legs became wobbly like I had been spinning around in a circle for five minutes.

I placed my hand on the nearest wall and was bent double until the room stopped vibrating between two realities.

I stood in a hallway in Lucifer's skyscraper, outside her office. I peered through the crack in the door. Lucifer stood at her desk, and Nash was only a foot away from her.

Shit!

I pressed my back against the wall and hoped they hadn't seen me.

"You have some explaining to do, Nash," Lucifer said. "Lia told me that Andromeda wasn't one of Raphael's followers. Andromeda said so herself before she became my Chancellor."

"I don't want to talk about Lia right now," Nash said. "Let's get this over with." He trailed kisses along her neck and bit her ear.

Lucifer didn't flinch. "What are you up to? Where were you last night?"

Wait! He wasn't with Lucifer the night before?

Nash locked eyes with her. "I'm doing what you commanded. Now, please, let me finish what I'm doing right now. I'm your loyal servant. Andromeda has only been here for seven months. Fallen angels can lie. You should know that better than anyone."

"Andromeda is my Chancellor now. She demonized her soul for me."

"And when did she tell you her lies? When she was still a fallen angel, right? Ask her now, I'm sure her story has changed."

She pulled him closer as he kissed the spot under her chin and continued to feather kisses up her jaw until his lips pressed urgently against hers.

Lucifer broke the kiss. "I could lie when I was an angel."

"Only you," Nash said, lifting her into his arms. He carried her out of view.

I wondered if Lucifer knew that Nash used Jinni to find Raphael's followers. I glanced down the hall. Caiduc was nowhere to be found.

Damn it!

I didn't want to be caught here. Before I pounded Nash with every insult and sinful name in the book, I wanted to find out what he was keeping from me. His lies could be tangled up with Lucifer's.

I wandered down the hall. "Caiduc?" I hissed.

Why had he left me here? He knew this was a dangerous place. I might need him any minute to whisk me away back to Nash's. This was not the time to play the Jinni vanishing trick.

"Caiduc?"

As I wandered down the hall, my eyes darted left and right.

A clone secretary turned the corner.

I clenched my teeth and slipped into one of the rooms. The heels tapped louder before fading in the distance. I peered out the door.

The hallway was empty.

Where was that room?

I stared down the hallway. Third door from that end of the hall. I tiptoed until I reached the door.

Before I set my backpack on the floor in front of me, I looked up and down the hall. Clear. I unzipped my bag and grabbed the chain of keys.

Down the hall Lucifer and Nash were making out like the apocalypse was near. *Don't think about it!*

I tried the first key. It wouldn't fit in the lock. I inspected the lock. I inspected the keys. They were all antique. None of them looked as if they could fit in a modern lock.

I ground my teeth and started madly trying each key. One of them fit! It was impossible. The shape of the key didn't match the lock. Were my eyes playing tricks on me?

I turned the key, and the lock clicked!

My mother was on the other side. But how could I get her out of here without Caiduc? I shook my head. *One thing at a time, Lia.*

I pushed the door open and peered inside.

Whoever Lucifer had locked up here, it was not my mother.

Someone was perched on a stool, scribbling on a piece of paper at a small desk. His back was to me. From one shoulder blade hung a feathered, white wing. Beside it was a pink nub.

Lucifer was harboring an angel? That missing wing. Was she the one who maimed him?

My eyes barely had time to focus on the details of the room when the tapping of heels echoed down the hallway. My heart dropped. As I turned my head to see who approached, barky fingers gripped my arm, and light flashed as my feet left the ground.

Seven

I lay on my back as my feet dangled over the edge. Bright light blinded me. I blinked against the glare. The light came from the tear in the sky where Michael burst out of Sheol

I leaned up on my elbows. Before me was the vast, bottomless Pit.

A vise grip squeezed my heart.

I scrambled away from the Pit. I glanced around. Why had Caiduc taken me here?

"Caiduc?" I called, but no one stood for miles across the barren plain surrounding the Pit.

Why did he leave me here?

I stood and dusted the dirt from my shirt and jeans. My hair was matted to my brow. I tried my best to push it away from my face, but loose strands kept invading my vision.

I felt dizzy and sick. Doubling over, I retched. I stayed bent over, breathing heavily as my head spun. Maybe I should consider taking a break from Jinni travel for a while. It looked like a break was being forced on me right now.

To hell with it.

I guess I was walking back.

I couldn't get the image of the one-winged angel out of my head. I cringed whenever I thought of how Nash had mutilated himself that way, but he had sawed off the useless boney wings of a fallen angel. This angel wasn't fallen. Someone had sawed off the downy feathered wing on his right side. Someone had made him deformed.

What did Lucifer want with that angel? He was working on something, but the room was dark, and I hadn't seen what that something was.

I left the dirt path leading to the Pit and walked upon the concrete streets of the Outer Region. I wandered down the street for a few minutes, realizing I headed in the opposite direction of Nash's place. I needed to turn around, but I didn't want to. I didn't want to confront Nash about Lucifer. But Adriel threatened to do it if I didn't.

That's when I saw him.

Nash. He dressed in jeans and a black jacket with the hood up, but I saw his face when he turned to glance behind him. He hadn't noticed me.

How had Nash gotten here so fast? It was only a few minutes ago that I saw him with Lucifer. I thought back to Caiduc. Had something happened when he transported me? Was it possible that I was between places for a while? What *was* between places?

I slowed my pace, not wanting to alert him but not wanting to lose him either. This was my chance. I had to follow him.

He turned the corner down an alley. Where was he going dressed like a Greaser?

I stalked him into the alleyway. He turned another sharp corner, and I threw myself against the wall as he stopped. It looked like a dead end, but he knocked on the wall.

A door appeared where he knocked. *What in the hell?* Nash opened it and stepped inside. After the door closed, it disappeared into the wall.

I stood in awe. I approached the wall and knocked as Nash had. Nothing happened. My shoulders slumped. My lips formed a hard, determined line. I looked along the wall. A brick was out of place. It was discolored: a gray among browns. I rapped on the brick until my knuckles drummed against the transformed, wooden surface.

I grabbed the solid, brass handle and pulled the door open. Warm, humid air hit me. A mix of alcohol and musk stung my nose. The electric buzz of a guitar mingled with an ominous drum beat. They played Rock but not any song I had heard before, and I didn't see a band. The room was dark with spotlights over the bar, tables, dartboards, and a pool table. The door closed behind me but didn't disappear on the other side.

I spotted Nash as he walked over to a table in the back of the room. The light above the table gave off an isolated glow, only lighting the table surface and leaving the area around it veiled in darkness. I slinked along in that darkness, avoiding the light so Nash wouldn't notice me.

A demon sat at the table Nash approached. His skin was yellow and lumpy like he had a bad case of boils. His teeth were filed to fine points.

Nash stood across from him on the other end of the table. They talked, but I couldn't make out what they said over the music. Nash put something down on the table. It glinted in the light.

Was that Arcadian Steel?

I edged closer, but the tables were tightly packed. I bumped into somebody. I heard a growl behind me. The demon pulled me down to his mouth. "Do you want to lose a finger?" he asked. His breath was putrid like sour milk mixed with something alcoholic. His hand was tight around my arm. I was sure he would leave bruises.

He had dirty fingernails and a fat, bloated body. I heard the chair creek under his weight as he pulled me down to the table, into the glow of the light above.

He would have twisted my arm off. I withdrew my Arcadian Steel dagger. With one quick motion, I sliced the fingers of the hand that gripped me. In my panic, I had overestimated the amount of pressure I needed to apply.

The demon's severed fingers popped onto the table. The demon howled above the loud music. A long cut ran along my arm from the shoulder to the elbow. It stung like hell, and I hoped none of that monster's blood mingled with mine. I grabbed my arm before the demon reached for me, wanting revenge.

I pulled the door open and ambled out into the alley. Blood dripped from my arm. I looked down at the cut. It was worse than I thought in the dim light of the bar. It was still superficial but deeper than I assumed.

I had to get out of the alleyway. That demon was probably tearing after me. Holding my arm, hoping to stop the bleeding, I ran down the alleyway until I made it out to the street. I decided the best course of action was to turn as many corners as I could to lose any potential trackers.

Once I felt I was a good distance away, I slumped down on a bus stop bench. Bright red droplets absorbed into the worn wood, changing its color to a deep mahogany. My head swam as I watched the blood paint the bench. The coppery smell reached my nose but didn't serve to sober me.

I could heal myself, couldn't I? But how? How could I do anything while my head was spinning?

I had to get back to Nash's place. I couldn't bleed out on a bus stop bench in Hell. I gripped my arm more tightly despite the pain and got up slowly.

My legs swayed beneath me. It was like I was standing on two stacks of Jenga pieces. I held onto the back of the bench to steady myself.

I had dripped a trail of blood all the way to Nash's house. I ambled up the steps to the door. When I released my arm to turn the handle, a fresh gush of blood escaped from the cut. My hand bloodied the handle. I collapsed to my knees. I dragged myself into the foyer and slumped to the ground.

"Lia!"

Adriel knelt beside me. My vision blurred as I tried to hold onto consciousness, but I couldn't hold on for long.

"LI?"

My vision came back into focus.

Mom stood at the kitchen counter with a carton of orange juice in her hand. "There you are, honey. What's wrong?"

"Mom?" My voice was weak.

"You feeling okay?" she asked.

Dad walked into the kitchen. Dried paint covered his t-shirt. His shoulder-length hair was tied back. His golden cross with silver thorns dangled from his neck.

"Hey, kiddo." He hugged me and kissed the top of my head.

"Lia isn't feeling well," Mom said.

"Oh, that's too bad." He frowned. "Guess it's good it's Sunday. Spend the whole day in bed. No homework." Dad nudged my shoulder.

Mom's lips formed a line. "Yes, homework," she said.

"Yeah," I said, absently. "I have a history paper."

"Okay then," Mom said. "Drink your orange juice."

"I had the weirdest dream," I said. "I thought I went to Hell."

"Oh, yeah." Dad cut into his pancakes. "What did you see?"

"I don't like that." Mom sat, cradling a mug in her hand.

"It was just a dream, Alex," Dad said. "Shows she's creative like her dad."

Mom looked worried.

"I'm okay, Mom," I said. "It *was* a dream."

Sim rubbed against my legs.

"It was just a dream," I whispered.

The world is a saxophone, and its music comforts.

I stood from the chair, reaching down to pick up Sim. My head spun, and I blacked out.

I blinked and cold, white walls surrounded me. The bed was comfortable, but this wasn't my room.

My room was covered in posters and had dirty clothes tossed upon the floor. A small desk in the corner rose above a wastebasket with the crinkled remnants of my failed attempts at writing an essay on American Colonialism.

It was also filled with the warm smell of pancakes that drifted in from the kitchen as Mom made breakfast, and if you touched the floor, you felt the dull vibrations of the music from Dad's studio downstairs.

Adriel's eyes met mine as I searched the room for some sense of familiarity. But everything was so fuzzy. Where was I?

"Lia, can you hear me?" His gentle voice echoed in my ears.

"I have to go downstairs," I said. "Mom only makes pancakes on Sundays. I don't want mine to get cold."

"You've lost a lot of blood," Adriel said. "Tom came in with a bunch of medical books. We patched you up. You're going to be okay. You just need to rest."

I shook my head. I was back home. Mom and Dad were alive. Warm tears wet my cheeks.

Take me back. Take me back. Take me back.

"No!" I shoved him and ground my teeth. "I want to go back."

"Back where?" he asked.

"Home." The word felt so heavy, my voice could barely carry it.

"I'm sorry, Lia." Adriel bowed his head.

"If you're my guardian angel, where were you before they died? Why couldn't you save them?"

Adriel's eyes were on the floor. "It's my duty to protect you."

"But you didn't protect me. You let that monster murder my parents." I slumped back into bed and turned my face away from him.

"What happened to you?" he asked. "Who cut your arm?"

"I did," I said, "on accident."

"How do you cut yourself like that on accident?"

"I was practicing with my dagger."

"Really?"

No, not really. The angle wasn't right. This was possibly the worst lie I'd ever told, and I was telling it to Adriel. I didn't want to lie to him, so I told him something I knew he would see right through.

But I can't tell him. He'll confront Nash and give him the opportunity to tell more lies and cover his tracks.

"I didn't mean what I said." I didn't turn around. "What happened to my parents isn't your fault."

Adriel squeezed my shoulder, and the door slid closed. He was gone. The room felt empty.

FOR the next couple days, I stayed in bed. I rested on and off. Adriel came up to talk with me.

I ate with him, laughed with him.

Nash didn't come to see me. He was probably too busy with Lucifer.

Lucifer imprisoned an angel. I wanted to figure out who he was and why he was in Sheol. But I didn't know who I could enlist to help me. I didn't know who I could trust. I thought I could trust Caiduc, but now he had disappeared. I hadn't seen him for three days. That wasn't like him.

A chill ran down my spine. What if something happened to him? Maybe whoever was walking down the hall saw us before Caiduc could whisk me away. What if he was in trouble, and I had no idea how to help him?

Dark thoughts flooded my mind with a fresh cropping of guilt. He had helped me find my birth mom and dad. Now, when I owed him the most, I didn't know where he was or if he needed me.

I looked around the room. *The keys!*

"My backpack!" I said. "Where is it?"

"What backpack?" Adriel asked.

"The one I had on me when I passed out."

"Oh, it's in the closet."

I tried to get up from bed, but Adriel stopped me, pressing my shoulders back down.

"You need to rest," he said.

I needed to get the keys back to Nash's room before he found out. What if he already found out?

"It's been three days," I said. "I'm fine."

"You're not fine." Nash stood in the doorway. "You're staying here from now on. Don't think I don't know about your little walks. You could have gotten yourself killed. I don't want you leaving this house."

I glared at him. "I don't care what you want."

"You don't have to care," Nash said. "You just have to listen." The tone of his voice did not change. He wasn't angry nor was he any other emotion that I could identify. He said it like he was lecturing a class from a textbook. His dull, matter-of-fact way of speaking, enraged me more. I wasn't a child, and I wouldn't be spoken to like one.

But the look in Adriel's eyes told me not to fight it. It wasn't a fight I would win.

"Fine," I said. "Put me on house arrest."

eight

FOR the rest of the week, the tension in the house hung like the bloated belly of a whale. Nash and I hadn't spoken about our fight or his lies. I couldn't leave the house. Nash took to watching me like a hawk, and, for some reason, Adriel had stopped coming to see me.

Of course, I blamed Nash. He probably kicked him out of the house again. It wouldn't surprise me if Nash blamed Adriel for my recent adventure plus injury. I got a little stir crazy, not only because I was bound to the house, but I also refused to leave my room. I didn't want to run into Nash, and I was on a bit of a hunger strike.

But it was more than being confined to my room that put me on edge. Nash was lying to me and seeing Lucifer behind my back. Nash insisted on checking on me throughout the day though I made it clear to him I didn't want him anywhere near me.

There was nothing I could do about Lucifer's contract. I was bound here forever, but that didn't mean that eternity had to be spent with Nash. Unfortunately, no matter how much I told myself that, it didn't make it any easier to swallow. More than once, he looked upon me with that sadness in his eyes, and I almost fell for it.

More than a few times, I thought *to hell with it*. I should ask him what was between him and Lucifer and have it done with. It was only a mix of curiosity and the possibility of something darker. It wasn't because I still cared about him. I didn't want the confrontation between us. I was resigned to never finding out. I fought a losing battle anyway. It wasn't like Raphael or Michael was stupid enough to let me near them. How was I going to beat them otherwise?

I wasn't going to get near them at all if Nash didn't let me out of this house.

"I have to go," Nash said. "I don't want to leave you like this, but there's something I have to do." At least he could sense what was in the air though we had yet to talk about it. "Believe me, I'd rather tear my eyes out. My leaving will prompt you to once again sneak out of the house and put yourself in danger."

I sat up in bed. "I didn't *sneak* out of the house the first time. I didn't know I was a prisoner."

His face darkened. "You're not a prisoner."

I wasn't going to back down. "I don't know how you define *prisoner*," I said. "But keeping me locked up in this house while I go bored out of my mind fits my definition perfectly."

Hopelessness settled in his eyes. "Your safety might not mean much to you, but it means a lot to me."

"Because Lucifer will toss you into the Pit if anything happens to me?"

"Because I care about you."

My heartbeat hammered in my chest. *Don't fall for it.* "If you have to go, just go. I'll be fine on my own." I wasn't going anywhere, but it would be nice to get out of my room for a while without having to worry about the intense mix of emotions I felt being cooped up with Nash.

He frowned. "I shouldn't leave you."

"Don't worry about me," I said with venom. "I've got a lot of reading to catch up on anyway."

"I hope that you do it here," Nash said.

"Well, as you're ordering me around now, I guess—"

"I'm only doing it for your own good. Have you forgotten that Archangels are after you? That any demon within five miles will want to highjack your body if they find out you are human? I've had to make some tough decisions, and I know all this can't be pleasant for you either." He walked over to the bed, took my arms, and pulled me to my feet. "But none of it has made me change the way I feel about you. Even if you feel differently about me."

He searched my eyes. His dark eyes showed a mixture of pain and finality like he was about to or already had done something that would make me hate him. Leaning down, his lips pressed against mine, taking my breath and the next line of cursing that I had saved up for him.

I was so angry at him, but I found myself kissing back. Still, my rage didn't fly out the window. It was mixed and molded into the passion of the kiss. I was giving it all my wrath and fire.

He broke away.

"What was that for?" I asked.

"In case you needed proof."

I set my teeth. I wanted to spit the knowledge of his affair with Lucifer in his face. But I stopped myself. I wanted him out of the house more than I wanted to confront him. I wanted to find out more before he knew I was on to him. He would be more careful once I ousted him for his affair with Lucifer, and something told me he had things greater to hide.

He looked down at me one last time before walking out the door.

I watched from the window as his car pulled out the driveway, and he sped down the street. What was I going to do? I was trapped in Sheol. All the angels knew where I was, and I was surrounded by liars.

Half an hour crept by as I rested on a chair in Nash's library. *A Tale of Two Cities* was open on my lap, but I wasn't reading it. After I had glazed over a few sentences and lost track of what was going on, I gave up entirely. I shut the book and could have sworn I heard a knock at the front door as I did. I listened. There it was again.

Frowning, I got up from the chair and walked to the front door. Was it Bob inviting me to another one of Lucifer's trials? Or maybe it was Tom wanting to use the library?

I opened the door. Adrianna stood on the steps. Her long blonde hair came down over her shoulders. She wore jeans and a t-shirt. She looked more like a teenager on her way to the mall than a demon warrior.

"Hey, how are you doing?" She stepped into the foyer.

"About as well as anyone held captive in a cold, museum-like mansion."

"Yeah. I heard about that," Adrianna said. "Nash is being overprotective, that's all."

"Overprotective? He's bossing me around."

"So, I guess you wouldn't have any objection to hanging out with me for the day? At my house?"

"Not at all." I hadn't planned on leaving the house. But I'd love the opportunity to get under Nash's skin a little and show him he was not going to keep me shut away.

"Great," Adrianna said. "My car's out front."

"Okay," I said, "let me throw something on. I've been in PJs since my accident."

"No problem," Adrianna said.

I rushed up the stairs. I pulled on a pair of jeans and boots. I tossed a jacket over my t-shirt. I wasn't going to stay in this house another minute.

It was a short drive to Adrianna's house. She drove fast but not as fast as Nash or Bob. She took the turns at a decent speed.

I had been to Adrianna's house once with Nash to pick up Kiran. But I had never been inside. We saw Waylon the blacksmith that day. It was the day I got my sword. That day seemed so long ago, back when I trusted Nash, back when I thought he could help me find and kill my parents' murderer.

I followed Adrianna into the foyer. It could have been a room in itself. Adrianna led me into the living room.

On the coffee table, she had set out a tray of sandwiches. I hoped she was better at making sandwiches than she was at baking.

She *asked* me to come, but I doubted she would have taken "no" for an answer. A couch sat in the center of the room. On the wall behind the couch was a large painting, depicting a man and woman.

The man leaned against a rock. His dark hair was curly. The woman's arms clasped around his neck. Her blonde hair was intricately braided with ribbons and beads. She wore a long, flowing red dress. They kissed each other as the tide washed in. I peered intently at their faces.

"We had that one done in Vienna," Adrianna said. "You don't think it's too over the top, do you?"

"I think it's . . . romantic."

"Kiran thought so too." Adrianna beamed, but her eyes looked sad.

"Where is Kiran?"

Adrianna frowned. "He's been leaving the house a lot lately. I think he's bored . . . with me."

"With you?"

Adrianna laughed and shook her head. "I'm being silly. Never mind." Her eyes darted around the room, and she smoothed her hands over her lap twice.

I pressed my lips together, arming myself with an icepick to break the silence. "How did you meet?" I asked.

"Kiran was a soldier," she said. "I helped him defeat the enemy by giving him an Arcadian Steel sword. The same one he carries to this day."

"You're *older* than Kiran?" Kiran looked to be around thirty. Adrianna looked to be at least ten years his junior.

"I know. I don't look a day over twenty-two." She tossed back her hair.

"Lucifer sent you to Earth to help him?" I asked.

"Hell no, Lucifer sent me to collect souls. I'm a Succubus or *was* a Succubus. I'm retired."

"What does that mean exactly?"

"I seduced men into selling their souls. But I liked Kiran, and he wanted to win the war for his people. So, he traded his soul for a sword that would win the battle."

"Did he win the battle?" I asked.

"Yes, but they lost the war. Kiran died fighting."

"He didn't resent you after that?"

Adrianna walked around the couch. She gazed at the painting. "No. He blamed himself for not negotiating for more. When I found him, he was praying to Baal, the bull god of war. I told him Baal was down here and that he was a demon. He said he should have asked for Baal to strike the enemy with a thunderbolt and send a drought to dry up their crops."

"You knew the sword wouldn't be enough to help him win," I said.

Adrianna shrugged. "They were out-numbered five for every one. One Arcadian weapon wasn't going to turn the tide."

Adrianna had lied to Kiran, and he forgave her.

"You must be starving." Adrianna moved from behind the couch. "Nash said you're not coming down for meals. Please, help yourself." She gestured to the food on the table.

I raised an eyebrow. "When did you talk to Nash?"

"Well, I've still been coming to training, silly." She sat on the couch and patted the seat beside her.

I sat.

"Now, I know it's not as good as anything Nash might make, but I hope your palate hasn't become too refined." She passed me a plate. "Dig in."

The sandwiches were cut into triangles. I grabbed a sandwich from the tray and bit into it. The meat tasted like ham. As far as sandwiches go, it was pretty good, and I was hungry. After the first, I grabbed another. Adrianna had poured some juice for me as I ate. I drank it. It was sweet and tangy. Another flavor was layered in, but I couldn't quite distinguish what it was.

"You like it?" Adrianna asked.

I finished chewing before answering her. "They're good. But I thought you didn't eat meat."

"No, that's just Nash. The only time I don't eat meat is when I go to his house for dinner. Nash doesn't like the idea of eating the flesh of another being. He said it's a strange practice humans do. Well, I was once human."

I frowned. Adrianna had been kind to me, but I never asked her about her past. "What was it like for you before?"

Adrianna considered. "I don't remember much. It was a long time ago when we had to forage for food. I lived in a warm cave with my family, my tribe." She smiled.

"Did you like being human?"

"It was a little rough." Adrianna poured me another glass of juice. "Getting enough to eat was always the main concern. That's how I got here. I fought with my brother over some food

I had foraged. I never planned on bringing it back home to the others. There was so little of it, I was going to keep it for myself. But he came along and tried to take it from me. He hit me on the head with a rock. I don't think he was trying to kill me, only to knock me out long enough to take the food back to the family. His daughter was dying. She was starving. But I wouldn't let go. I hit him with a tree branch. It was thick and solid, and I bashed him in the head with it over and over until his head was nothing but a bloody pulp."

I cringed. I couldn't imagine sweet Adrianna bashing her own brother's brains in. But she seemed saddened by the memory.

Her mood became somber. "I deserved much worse than this," Adrianna said. "But this place isn't meant to punish the wicked. The truly wicked, like me, we're offered contracts commissioning us to do more wicked things to good people. We send even more people down here. People who don't deserve it. Sheol, it's just as evil as what I did."

I never considered that. The Outer Region didn't seem all that bad, but I tried not to think about what the demons who lived there had to do to earn their place. The psychological torment over what they had to do to their fellow men, a hundred or maybe a thousand times over, would torture their hearts as the Circles would have tortured their bodies.

Adrianna shrugged and smiled as if she hadn't relived her brother's death and what she was forced to do to Kiran. "Are you ready for dessert?"

I was so taken aback by her sudden change in demeanor, it took me a moment before I realized what she was asking. "Sure," I replied weakly.

Adrianna hopped up from her seat and left the room. I downed my second glass of juice and gave myself a refill. My head swam a little. Adrianna returned with a large bowl full of strawberries. They were possibly the best strawberries I'd ever seen. They fit in the palm of my hand perfectly, and they were bright red with no sign of any bad spots. Adrianna had cut off the stems.

After taking another gulp of my juice, I grabbed a strawberry and popped it into my mouth. It was like it had been dipped in sugar. It was so sweet my face pinched as I ate it.

My head swam again, and I had to steady myself on the couch. I felt like I had been spinning in a chair.

"What's wrong?" Adrianna's voice seemed far away.

"I'm feeling a little woozy that's all." I took another long sip of the juice.

"Ow—sorry! You probably shouldn't drink any more of that." Adrianna took the glass from my hand. "I should have said something. I keep forgetting you are human."

"Why? What's in it?" I asked.

"Peach schnapps."

"Oh." I was very dizzy. Adrianna grabbed my arm, probably to stop me from slipping off the couch. "It's not because I'm human," I tried to explain to her. "It's because I don't drink."

"I'm so sorry," she said. "You should lie down. Here." She grabbed a pillow and placed it against the arm of the couch. Before I knew what was happening, my head was against the pillow.

"I'm alright," I said. "Just a little dizzy." I sat back up.

"I'll get you some water."

Two Adriannas walked back into the living room each holding a glass of water. As they got closer, they became one.

I took the glass from her and sipped. My world stopped spinning. "I'm okay," I said.

"Are you sure?" Adrianna asked.

I nodded. I didn't like being like this in front of her. I wanted to be alone in my dizzy misery. Drinking wasn't for me.

"I shouldn't have served that to you. What was I thinking? Nash is going to be so mad."

I took a deep breath. Why was Adrianna nervous about Nash suddenly? "It's okay. I won't say anything to Nash." I hoped to avoid him for the rest of the day which shouldn't be too difficult as he had decided to go sneaking about the Outer Region.

"I should get you back home," Adrianna said.

I didn't argue.

She helped me to a standing position.

"I'm fine," I said. "I can walk."

She backed away from me but kept her hands out, ready to catch me if I fell. I must have looked wobbly. I made it to the car. I felt better. At least, my head had stopped spinning.

Adrianna started the car and pulled out of the driveway. I watched the houses and buildings as she drove. I was glad Adrianna drove like a normal person. I don't think I could have held my strawberries and sandwiches down if she drove like Nash or Bob.

The streets were monotonous: plain, white buildings, a handful of deserted shops. No one walked outside, and mist swept the area. But something caught my eye.

As we passed the Angel District, I saw a familiar vehicle parked outside. Nash's car. What was Nash doing in the Angel District?

"Hey, is that Nash's car?" I asked.

Adrianna looked over out the passenger window. "I don't know. There are lots of cars like that."

I looked over at her. "I've never seen another car like that. It's Nash. He's up to something."

Adrianna shrugged. "Nash would tell us if something was up."

Were we talking about the same guy? Even Lucifer had started to get suspicious of him. Adrianna might be willing to let it go, but I was not.

nine

ADRIANNA stopped the car outside Nash's house and turned off the ignition. "Here we are." She looked over at me, and her expression grew serious. "I'm sorry about the peach schnapps."

"It's not a big deal. I'm not feeling it anymore." My head felt funny, but I could walk without wobbling. As I reached for the door handle, Adrianna grabbed my arm.

"This thing between you and Nash," she said, "you're just stressed. We all are. It's this war we're fighting. I've seen it before. It can make friends look like enemies. Nash cares about you. He can be stupid sometimes. What man isn't a little thoughtless from time to time, right?"

"Sure," I said. She didn't understand. Nash was hiding something big from me. I knew it. It was just a matter of finding out what. This wasn't him being stupid or thoughtless. This was him being cruel. Nash wasn't a stupid man, but he could be a malicious one.

"Whatever Nash did," Adrianna said, "I'm sure he didn't do it on purpose."

I frowned. How could you sleep with someone by accident?

"Just give him a chance to show you that," she said.

I smiled. I was learning a lot from Adrianna already, like how not to be as naïve as she was. "Alright," I said. "This was fun. I hope we can do it again."

"Yeah, me to." She let go of my arm, and I got out of the car.

When I got to the door, I turned and waved to Adrianna. I grinned like nothing was wrong in the world. She smiled back and started the engine. As she drove away, I opened the door and stepped inside.

I breathed a sigh. I couldn't trust Adrianna. Nash must have asked her to keep me company while he completed his tasks. He knew I would leave. I glanced outside the window. Adrianna was gone. Nash had not yet returned. I wasn't sure how long I had.

I raced to the library and pulled down books and opened drawers, looking for anything that might explain what Nash was up to. After tearing apart the library and finding nothing, I leaned against the shelves and slumped to the floor.

Who could I turn to? My friends were my enemies. Chandra hated me from the start. Nash lied to me. Adrianna kept me busy while Nash was doing God-knows-what. Tom and Kiran held secreted conversations on the training field and in empty hallways. I caught them whispering between each other more than a few times, but always in private when they thought no one else was listening.

I picked up my head. Nash wouldn't keep anything in plain sight. Standing, I rushed back to the main entrance. I took the steps two at a time. Reaching Nash's door, I tried the handle. It was locked. Nash didn't even keep his front door locked. There was something in there that he didn't want me to see. I didn't have a key.

Wait! I did have a key. Lots of keys. Keys Nash wasn't supposed to know were missing.

I turned, ready to race back to my room.

"What are you up to?"

I spun. Tom stood in the hallway. If I couldn't trust Adrianna, I was certain I couldn't trust Tom. Nash had let Tom in on everything, even down to hunting the wrong angels.

"You want to tell me who destroyed the library?" he asked.

"I was looking for something," I said.

Tom reached for one of my hands. I flinched, but he easily captured my wrist. He inspected my hand like it was a newly discovered specimen.

"What are you doing?" I asked.

"Well, it doesn't seem your hands have turned into massive, clumsy pinchers. Dainty and delicate as always."

I snatched my hand away from him. "I'll clean it up."

"What were you looking for?" he asked.

I thought fast. "It was a book I was reading."

"Must have been a damn good book."

"Yeah, it was alright. I thought Nash might have taken it."

"It is *his* book if you got it from *his* library."

"Well, he's not here. So, I was just going to borrow it for a while like you do."

"Since I didn't come here for the venom, I'll head back downstairs." He meandered down the hall.

I looked back at Nash's door. I had the key. But it wouldn't be wise for me to forage through Nash's room with Tom here.

Good thing I stole the Hundred Keys.

Nash probably had the real key on himself anyway. I would have had to get close enough to lift it off him. The thought gave me a curious mix of feelings I didn't want to dissect.

TOM read in the library. *Oh, just leave already.* I wished Caiduc was there. He could teleport me into Nash's room, and I would be out before I was ever discovered. But I hadn't seen Caiduc in over a week.

Maybe he got bored of me.

I laid out on the training field and stared up at the rip Michael left in the sky.

"You shouldn't stare at that. You could go blind."

Adriel stood above me. The light glowed around his head. I hadn't heard him approach. I hadn't felt his feet disturb the grass. I was normally so good at hearing things others could barely perceive.

He sat next to me.

"You stopped visiting me for a while," I said. "Where were you?"

"I'm sorry," Adriel said. "I watched from afar. I didn't want to disturb your healing."

"Did you just lie to me?" I turned, propping myself up on my elbow to look at him.

"I did."

I frowned. "Why?"

"Nash didn't want me to stay," Adriel said.

"I figured that, but why would you lie about it?"

Adriel searched the ground. "Because I want you to believe that nothing can force me away from you."

"Except Nash."

"It's no secret Nash and I don't get along. But I don't think he means you harm. I felt I could trust him with you."

"If that were true, you wouldn't have felt the need to watch me from afar."

"I hadn't thought of it that way. I couldn't bear not to be alert when you were wounded. I've tried to give you privacy, but when you got hurt, I couldn't stay away."

"You shouldn't trust Nash."

Adriel looked at me. "Why not?"

"Because he's been talking to Lucifer. I think it's him you should be watching."

Adriel searched my eyes. "You don't trust Nash. Neither do I." He said it like it was a math equation.

"You only trusted Nash because of me?"

Adriel nodded. "He's no better than a demon now, and demons are capable of cruel things. But he seemed to be protecting you. I felt the same sense of duty from him as when he was protecting the Throne, but he broke that vow too."

"Can you trail him?" I asked. If there was anyone who was good at watching, it was Adriel.

"Trailing him would mean taking my eyes off you. I couldn't do that, now that I know he might be a danger to you."

"But if you're watching him, I'll be fine. He won't be able to do anything to me unless you see it first."

Adriel looked down at me. "Many other enemies are at your back. How can I leave you for a second?"

"If you find out what he's up to, I might have a hell of a lot less enemies at my back." I needed him to do this. I wasn't going to be somebody's pawn, not even Nash's.

I peered into the library. Empty. Tom decided to leave. If his house was so much bigger than Nash's why didn't he take his books and go back home?

I guess big houses aren't everything.

Grabbing the bannister, I raced up the stairs to my bedroom and tore open the closet door. I unzipped my backpack and grabbed the keys.

I glanced around the corner before jogging past the stairs. I stopped at Nash's door.

Fiddling with the chain, I tried to think of an organized way to do this. *It's got to be one of these damn keys.* Clang!

I dropped the keys.

Clenching my teeth, I glanced down the hall. I waited for someone to come running up the stairs to find out what the sound was. No one came.

I picked up the keys. They were heavy, making it difficult to try each in the lock. I had more adrenaline last time and barely noticed the weight of the keys. I wished this time was like last time.

More than half the keys were on the other side of the chain before I found the right one. I turned the key and slid the door open.

My arms were heavy as I closed the door behind me. At first glance, the room appeared as it had the first time I entered, but one thing was different. *Don Quixote* was open to the middle of the book, revealing its hollowed center.

So, he knew.

I dropped the keys on the bed.

What was he hiding this time?

I searched under the bed and tore open the drawer of the bedside tables. Maybe he only locked it because he found out someone had taken the keys. But he wouldn't have locked it if there was nothing else to find.

What was new about the room?

Nothing.

I pulled open the closet door. I pushed the clothes on their hangers aside like I was peeking behind a curtain. Continuing down the line, I was met with bare white walls until I got to the corner.

Bingo!

Leaning in the corner of the closet behind the clothes was a staff with intricate carvings etched into the steel. He had me train with that staff. Why wasn't he keeping it in the armory with the rest of the weapons?

"What are you doing?"

I spun around.

Nash stood in the doorway.

Oh, shit!

"I . . ."

Nash held up the keys. "I was looking for these. What on earth have you been using them for?"

"Nothing. I . . ."

Nash cocked his head.

He blocked my only way out. The walls closed in on me. If I was getting out of here, it would be through him.

"I wasn't doing anything," I said. "I heard a crash. I came in here to see what was up. The door was unlocked. The keys were on the bed."

Nash narrowed his eyes.

Stop looking at me like that.

"I know you didn't come in here to check on me." He approached.

I pulled back as if he was a snake ready to strike. No, I wouldn't let him frighten me. I stood straight and stepped forward, meeting him in the middle.

"You didn't think you'd find me in the closet," Nash said. "You came looking for something, and you found it."

"What's so important about that staff?" I asked.

"It's important because I have it, and Lucifer doesn't know about it."

So, he was lying to Lucifer.

"Why are you keeping it from her?"

Nash's lips curled into a smile. "It's dangerous to have all that power. Lucifer has far too much of it."

His lips were inches from mine.

"Nash." My eyes watered. "What is that weapon?"

Nash cradled the side of my face in one hand. His thumb ran over my lips.

My breath caught.

Dread filled me as he said, "It's Endbringer, the Angel Killing Staff."

Ten

d ARKNESS encased the world. A steady drip echoed like a leaky faucet in the next room. I was alone in the darkness.

I stepped tentatively, oddly seeing my hands in front of me despite the gloom. Light managed to glow on me, but not around me. I was the only color in a dark world.

I couldn't be lied to in this world of color and darkness because I would know the truth.

The world is a piano, and its music is light.

The sound of scratching mingled with the drip. I knew that scratching, like fingernails on bark. A creature crouched in the midnight world. His outline perceivable.

I touched him, and his body suffused with light.

"Caiduc?"

He turned, low to the ground, still scratching his wrist. "Hello," he said.

"Where is this place?" I asked.

Caiduc glanced around. "It's a dungeon."

"Why are you here?"

"I am being punished."

"For what?"

Caiduc touched his earring. "For something I shouldn't have done." Caiduc looked up at me. "But I had to."

I swallowed. "How do I get you out of here?"

Caiduc looked up and pointed.

All I saw was darkness.

His gaze returned to mine. "You can't."

"But what will happen to you?"

"Bad things."

Darkness swallowed Caiduc.

I jolted up from bed.

Was it a dream? Was Caiduc in that shadowy place?

I stared at the wall. "Caiduc?"

He crouched at the end of my bed, veiled in the darkness, unmoving.

I sat up in bed. My eyes pierced the spot where he huddled. I moved to the end of the bed and waved my hand in front of me.

Nothing.

I sighed.

Caiduc hadn't come in weeks. It wasn't like him. Sure, he would watch me while I slept, but he'd never hide from me.

Something had happened to him. But who could harm a Jinn? I doubted, with their ability to teleport, that even the Pit would scare them.

But everything scared Caiduc.

I didn't want to imagine him alone in the dark.

Lucifer controlled everything in Sheol. What if she found out about Caiduc and locked him up like she did my mother and that angel? I wouldn't let her slice away parts of him.

I didn't know much about Jinni. Maybe they could be hurt in a way I never thought of.

My bare feet padded along the cold, marble floor. Dull light flooded in as I pushed aside the blackout curtains. The light stung my eyes.

Every day was brighter as if the wound Michael left in the sky kept tearing at the edges, opening wider and wider. How many angels could pass through that rip at once? Thirty, fifty, a hundred?

I wasn't safe in Sheol anymore. I was never safe here. Those I thought were my friends were lying to me. About what, I still didn't know.

But I cared about them even after the lies. They were my family. I'd save them despite themselves.

I needed to find out what happened to Caiduc. Whoever made him disappear would be sorry they did.

We're Not Gonna Take It blared through my earbuds as I pulled on my jeans and boots. I nodded to the music while I tugged my laces tight.

All my life, I tried to convince myself that the horrible things I saw in dark corners weren't real. I hid, turned away from them, but one thing I never did was confront them, fight them. I would fight them now.

I slid my door shut. Nash stood across the hall. He locked his door and pocketed the key.

He kept it locked because of that staff, Endbringer. A chill ran through me. What had he done to get that weapon, the weapon that could kill angels?

What was an angel death? Nothingness? The Pit?

Nash glanced at me before jogging down the stairs with his hands in his pockets.

I stared down the hall. The door seemed to grow. I turned toward my room and closed the door.

I couldn't begin to talk to Nash about how much that staff unnerved me. But why? It was a weapon that could kill Raphael.

Not just take his Grace, but kill him. But it was also a weapon that could kill Adriel.

Nash wouldn't do that. Would he?

He couldn't hate Adriel that much. But then, why hadn't he told him about the Staff? Why hadn't he told any of us?

I sat on my bed with my head in my hands. I opened the drawer to my nightstand. The tea leaves from the Third Circle were inside in a plastic bag. I had washed the mud from them.

Removing one leaf from the bag, I sniffed it. I pulled it away from my nose. It smelled like old socks.

How could such an unpleasant smelling thing grant you eternal life?

I pressed the leaf to my mouth and tried not to breathe in its awful smell. It was rough against my lips. Sufferers crushed the leaves into their mouths.

I could eat it. I'd live forever, and I wouldn't have to worry about ending up in Hell. Defeating Raphael would be easy because I couldn't die.

I stared down at the leaf. I couldn't. *If I eat this leaf, I'll never see Mom and Dad again.* I might find a way to get out of my contract with Lucifer, but this would mean forever.

I shoved the leaf back into the bag with the others and shoved the bag into the drawer. These leaves were for Jiao. If I ate them, it might be a waste anyway. I had no idea how to prepare them. If they didn't need to be prepared, they would have worked on the people in the Third Circle. They would have lived again, not just dead spirits trapped with Cerberus.

Pushing the curtain back, I glanced outside. Nash's car left the driveway. I slumped down the side of the bed and hit the back of my head against the mattress.

Maybe he wasn't going to Lucifer. Would he go back to that bar and talk to the demon with the gross, yellow boils? What did he want with him?

Only one way to find out.

I peered out the window. *Follow him!*

Jumping up, I raced out the door and onto the street. Nash's car sped around the corner. My shoulders slumped.

You're not faster than a speeding car, Lia.

Lucifer's skyscraper was in the opposite direction, so Nash wasn't leaving to see her. What was he up to? Did he have the keys with him?

He would be more careful now. I was reckless. I forgot to put the keys back, and I was caught in his room. I was possibly the worst spy on the planet.

A man strolled on the sidewalk opposite Nash's house. He wore a long coat. His hands were in his pockets.

Great! I lowered my head, trying to peer at the man without letting him see my face. He might look like a man, but he was a demon, and if he saw that I was human, he might try to possess me.

From what I learned with Sam and Delilah, possession was sort of a pageant. A ritual had to be done, and although I'd never seen it performed to completion, knock on wood, what I did witness seemed to take quite a lot of time. Maybe enough time to get myself out of it if it ever happened again.

I sighed. I shouldn't let myself get caught up in the situation to begin with.

The man passed me. I watched his back as he continued down the sidewalk.

Something was strange about him. He walked alone, and his gait was awkward, like a baby deer taking its first steps.

I crossed the street and followed him.

His body was shaped like a man's, but something was wrong with his feet. I looked more closely as I walked. They weren't feet. They were hooves, like cow hooves, black and bulky. They made clunky sounds every time they hit the pavement.

Had I lifted his Veil? No, if I had lifted the Veil, that would explain the hooves, but it wouldn't explain the awkward movements.

The Veil was like a painting overlapping the truth. If this demon had hooves for feet, he would be walking on them much more naturally. That only left one possibility.

This creature wasn't used to walking on legs, and I'd bet that if he crafted human feet for himself, he would still have trouble with those.

Rushing closer, I grabbed his shoulder and whirled him around.

His eyes were black, like an animal's, with no white to be seen. His mouth was human, but too small for his face. Now, it was unmistakable. A Jinn stood before me.

His too-small mouth formed a round circle, and his hands shook.

"Do you know Caiduc?" I asked.

"H-how do you know Caiduc?" His voice trembled like he was in a snowstorm.

If Jinn were so powerful and mysterious, why were they so frightened of everything all the time?

"Never mind that. Do you know where he is?"

He wasn't looking upon me in fascination like Caiduc always had. This Jinn was afraid, afraid of me. "W-what a-are you?" The side of his cheek twitched. I had to make sure he wouldn't teleport out of my hands at any second.

"Someone that could track you down no matter where you go," I said. "Now, tell me where Caiduc is."

The Jinn seemed to believe me because he didn't flash away from my grasp.

"Caiduc broke the rules," he said.

"Which rules?" I asked.

"He helped a human without offering the Exclusive Promise."

I narrowed my eyes. *Exclusive Promise?* It sounded like wedding vows. "What are you talking about?"

"Caiduc didn't give the Siphon his earring," the Jinn said.

I glanced up. An earring made of a string of beads and bones dangled from the Jinn's ear. Caiduc had one like it.

Reaching up, I yanked the earring from the Jinn's ear, ripping the earlobe. I think it flinched more out of fear than pain.

I clenched the earring in my fist and held it up to the Jinn's face. "Take me to him."

The Jinn pushed his chin into his neck and gave his head a subtle shake. "I can't do that. He is in our world."

The Jinni have a separate world?

"What's your name?" I asked.

"Queduc."

"Take me there, Queduc, and you'll get this back." I pocketed the earring.

His eyes darted.

"As you wish." The Jinn grasped my arm.

My vision blurred, light flashed as my feet left the ground. I waited for the splash, but it never came. Instead, I was hit with another sensation. Spinning.

I spun head over feet. It wasn't a falling spin, but more like I was suspended in the air by cables that were spinning me upside down and right side up again.

Glad I didn't have breakfast this morning, I tried to fight against the head rush. My ears popped.

A dreadful thought crossed my mind. Caiduc said that the form he chose wasn't his true form. Jinni were puffs of smoke. And this was their home world. What if I couldn't breathe here? What if I couldn't perceive things the way they did, and I couldn't find the Jinn who brought me here to bring me back?

But that thought along with all others left my head as I looked around me. The sky was violet. The color deepened at the horizon.

Was it spinning?

I blinked.

My head swam, and I vomited.

"Humans are not meant to travel to our world." Queduc stood in front of me. "That is why you suffer."

The ground where I knelt was cerulean blue, the same blue as the water in a swimming pool. It felt cushiony like a memory foam mattress.

No buildings rose from the ground. Instead, patches of shrubbery grew across the land in a mix of violets, blues, and reds. No sun shone above, the orange moss that covered the ground and stones glowed, providing adequate light.

I took in a deep gulp of air. I could breathe fine. Apparently, oxygen was important to Jinni too.

Despite the dark, violet sky, the colors below were bright like overexposed film. The brightness only made me dizzier.

Trying to stand, I stumbled. It felt like someone rammed into the side of me. My legs shook as I got to my feet on the soft ground.

The Jinn stood with his hands clasped, and his head was low like a child who knew he deserved a timeout.

I felt bad for doing this to him. Would he get into trouble for helping me? But I had to save Caiduc. He had helped, and it would be wrong of me to turn my back on him.

"Take me to Caiduc," I said.

The Jinn pointed toward a hill.

"You're coming with me," I said. "You first."

The Jinn stepped in front of me and led the way. His hooved feet made impressions in the soft ground as he walked, but those impressions disappeared seconds after he left them.

Like the infomercials on television. Now, let's jump and see if the glass of wine tips. I wondered if the details of this world were borrowed. Jinni sample from things they liked. Maybe they liked memory foam mattresses.

We were within a few feet of the hill where the ground was steeper. It isn't easy to climb a memory foam mattress. My feet dug into the ground. If it was real foam, I think it would have torn under the pressure as I struggled to climb. I was on my hands and knees, sinking my fingers into the ground.

The Jinn didn't seem to have any problem climbing the hill. His legs had morphed into powerful pistons, much like the back legs of a horse. The pants he wore had ripped over the massive muscled appendages.

The ground evened out, and I stood. As I rose, I was met with a crowd of Jinni. Puffs of smoke mixed with a variety of different creatures. Each were parts of animals, humans, angels, and demons in a grotesque collage of limbs, heads, and torsos.

Did Jinn not realize how creepy they all looked?

The hill was wide and flat, more like a plateau with sloped sides. The ground had stained my hands blue. I tried to wipe them on my pants, but the color was deep under the skin.

Orange moss grew on the rocks, giving off an evening-like glow.

A Jinn stood alone in the center, scratching his wrists and looking down like a chastised child.

Caiduc!

Thankfully, I walked among the crowd unnoticed. They probably thought I was an imitation of a human.

Queduc followed close behind me. Doubtless worried I wouldn't keep my promise of returning his precious earring. What was so valuable about bits of wood and bone anyway?

On the hilltop was a podium with three tall seats behind a lectern. At each seat sat a Jinn. One was a puff of smoke, his true form, while two others were a hodgepodge of human and animal features.

"Who are they?" I asked.

"The Assembly," the Jinn said. "Dailuc, Iriduc, and Jeriduc. They are here to judge Caiduc for his misdeeds."

Iriduc shuffled in his seat. He wore the features of a lizard. His skin was gray, and his eyes were glassy. He kept moving around as if he couldn't get comfortable.

The Jinn Dailuc pointed to Caiduc. His face was a mix of features from different animals. He had the beak of a bird and the ears of a fox. "Caiduc."

Caiduc looked up.

"You are on trial for disobeying the laws of the Jinni," Dailuc said.

"Why are they doing this?" I asked. "Caiduc didn't do anything wrong."

"They must let him speak while he has a mouth to do so," Queduc said.

"What?"

"They might decide to take his energy. If they do that, he will no longer have the strength to maintain this body."

He'll be a puff of smoke, and puffs of smoke didn't have mouths.

I pushed through the crowd.

Caiduc knelt before the Council. Seeing him behind the crowd was difficult, but I caught glimpses of him between the bodies of Jinni. His head was low to the ground. What were they going to do to him?

I looked up to the podium.

Jeriduc, the Jinn who was in his true body, glowed. The mist that formed his true body became opaque. From the haze formed a face, a human face, but the imitation was slightly off.

The spacing was too wide between the eyes and the nose and mouth. It looked like a caricature of a human face.

Jeriduc leaned forward, his human-like face encased in the glow of the orange lights. "You have aided a human without offering the Exclusive Promise. How do you answer this charge?"

Jeriduc transformed back into his true body. He only changed to give himself the power of speech.

Dailuc's beak opened. "Is this true?"

Caiduc lifted his head.

Unlike the demons at trials Lucifer presided over, the Jinni did not make noise or laugh. They waited for Caiduc to speak.

Caiduc scratched his wrist. Flakes of bark floated to the ground. He opened his mouth to speak.

He was going to tell the truth and suffer the consequences. I wouldn't let that happen.

I pushed through the first row of Jinni, passing through one of the smoke clouds. A few gasps rose around me. I coughed away the smoke.

"He did offer me the Exclusive Promise," I announced. *What did I just say?*

The gasps were echoed.

Caiduc turned his head toward me. "Lia?"

The heads of the two councilmembers who weren't in their true form turned to me as well, and though I couldn't see it with my own eyes, I'm sure the attention of their transparent co-councilor was on me too.

I had to think of something fast. Caiduc's life depended on it. I reached into my pocket. I still had Queduc's earring. *Sorry Queduc.*

"That earring is a counterfeit," I said. "This is his real earring." I held up Queduc's earring. "And as you can see I have it, so Caiduc hasn't broken any of your laws."

Iriduc stared down at me. "Who has brought a human to our home?"

Oh shit! Don't you dare say anything, Queduc.

"When you pulled Caiduc away, he was in the middle of transporting me. He gripped my arm as he was pulled into this world." I hoped that was how it worked.

"You've been here for sixteen days?" Iriduc asked.

I nodded.

Iriduc raised an eyebrow. "Why would you ask Caiduc to dishonor himself with a lie?"

Yeah, why had I done that?

"I asked Caiduc to wear the fake earring so that no one would know he was helping me. Jinni aren't trusted in Sheol."

Iriduc pursed his lizard lips. His arm extended to an impossible length, and his palm opened to receive the earring.

I placed it in his hand, and he drew back his arm. He held the earring to his eyes.

I think that was the first time I prayed.

Was there some way Iriduc would know it wasn't Caiduc's earring?

A hush went through the crowd as Iriduc inspected the earring. He reached back up over the lectern and dropped the earring into my hand. "The Promise has been made," he said. "Caiduc may return to Sheol to serve his Siphon."

eleven

I stared at the earring dangling from Caiduc's furry ear. We were back in my room and away from the crazy Jinni council.

"What's so special about that earring?" I asked.

Caiduc touched the earring. "Jinni magic is very powerful," he said. "That is why we can only aid one being at a time, be it human, demon, or angel."

"Are you helping someone else?" I asked.

Caiduc shook his head.

"Then why not give me your earring?"

Caiduc lowered his head. "If a Jinn helps another being, part of that being's life force is taken by the Jinn through the earring when the Jinn puts it back on. It increases the Jinn's power. That is the purpose of giving the earring. Immortal beings pay in strength. Humans pay in life years. That is why I didn't give you mine. I don't think of you as a Siphon but as a friend."

"That's sorta nice, I guess. So, how did they find out about us?"

Caiduc scratched his wrist. "They saw you in between worlds. You were here and you were there at the same time. You were in the Shielded Glade."

I furrowed my brow.

"That is where Queduc brought you."

"Your home world."

"Yes."

"It is made up of . . ."

". . . all the most beautiful things." Caiduc nodded.

"What happens to Jinni when they die?"

Caiduc shook his head. His earring swayed back and forth. "Jinni can't die. Jinni can only transfer power, but they will always have a small amount to themselves."

"What happens when a Jinn uses a Siphon?"

"The Jinn's power increases."

"You said that. But what does that mean? What could a Jinn do with all that power?"

"Jinni magic has no limit, but every time we use the energy, it goes away. That's why we must store vast amounts of it. The Assembly taxes us and stores the energy in a giant vault."

"So, without a Siphon, you have to use up your stored energy to pay the Assembly?"

"Yes."

"Plus, you use the energy when you transport me?"

"Yes."

"Why didn't you tell me? How much do you have left?"

"I have enough."

I gave him a narrow smile. My eyes tensed.

A knock came at my door. "Coming! Caiduc, you have to—"

He was gone.

I walked to the door and slid it open.

Tom leaned in the doorframe. "I've got a demon-hunting mission for you."

"I'm not hunting demons today," I said.

Tom smiled wryly. "Sorry, but you've exhausted your vacation days. If you don't get out there, you'll be soft as a kitten's belly by the time Raphael comes for you."

I glared at him. "Fine." I walked out into the hall with him, sliding the door to my room shut.

He looked down at my sword in its sheath. "You slept with that on?"

No, I tried to follow Nash and thought I might need protection. "Yeah, I have to. Too many enemies at my back. Don't know who to trust."

"Me neither," Tom said. "That's why I sleep with a hacksaw next to my bed."

I rolled my eyes.

"No, I do," Tom said. "You can never be too careful."

We walked to the bottom of the stairs and out the front door. Nash put his sword in the trunk of his car.

"Where is everyone else?" I asked Tom.

"While you were sleeping it all off, they had to fight a Gorgon. Nash thought it best they take a break. You two will be able to handle this one just fine."

"What about you?"

"I'd love to join you." Tom retreated to the front door. "But I have to do some Azazel stuff."

I had forgotten about Azazel, the angel who tempted his fellow angels to have children with human women. Lucifer wanted us to find him. He was supposed to be tied up somewhere in the desert.

I shot Tom a look of betrayal, but Tom only smiled at my expression and rushed back into the house.

Nash slammed the trunk shut.

I sighed. This was going to be a long drive.

I slumped into the passenger's seat and pulled the door closed. Nash didn't look at me as he started the ignition.

He didn't tell Adriel about this hunt. Adriel would have come, knowing my suspicions about Nash. I hadn't spoken to Adriel in a few days. Was he watching him like I had asked?

"Where are we going?" I asked.

"We have to open the portal a couple blocks away." Nash's eyes were pinned to the road.

I folded my arms and settled deeper into the seat.

Nash pulled into a deserted parking lot outside a grocery store. He drove around to the back of the store. He lifted his wrist to his lips and spoke into the communicator.

"Tom. This is Nash. Is this the right location?"

Static.

"Yep." Tom's voice buzzed. "You're good."

Nash stepped out of the car. I unbuckled my seatbelt and followed him. He opened a portal.

I climbed through.

Ever rode a drop tower? It's one of those rides that bring you up to the top, normally up fifty feet or more, and drops you fast, so fast you think you'll end up splattered on the concrete. That's how I felt climbing through the portal. Every time I passed through got worse.

Trying to steady myself, my hand landed against a wall. Yellow paint colored the wall. On one side of the room was a bed. Pictures of the moon, planets, spaceships, and stars covered the blue comforter. And tucked, asleep, under the covers was a little boy.

Nash climbed through the portal.

"Nash!" I hissed and pointed to the boy.

Nash gestured with his head towards the closet. He withdrew his sword.

I glanced towards the boy. He was still asleep under his space-themed comforter.

Nash nodded, signaling for me to open the closet door. I nodded back that I understood and put my hand on the doorknob. I yanked the door open.

The closet was empty.

Rustling came from the opposite side of the room.

Long, thin arms curved from beneath the boy's bed as the demon pulled itself from the darkness. Its skin was ashy. Black, oily hair grew to its tailbone. Its body was impossibly long, reaching the ceiling.

The long face let out a scream.

Nash spun.

Before the creature ran, he grabbed its long, thin arm, easily wrapping his hand around it above the elbow. He yanked the demon back.

"Who's there?" The little boy sat up in bed. He was maybe five or six.

Nash and the demon struggled in the center of the room.

I backed up and ran into something. A dresser.

Crash!

A snow globe fell from the dresser and shattered. Liquid and confetti stars spilled on the floor.

Nash pinned the demon's arms behind its body and moved to the open window. He opened the portal at the window.

I remembered the fear in my chest when I first saw Nash, Adrianna, and Kiran, right after an angel attacked me. I was sixteen, and it scared me more than I was willing to admit. This boy was only five.

"It's okay," I said to the boy. "My friend is just helping with the Bogeyman."

"What?" the boy asked. "What friend? All's I see is you."

Damn it. That's right. Nash and the demon could Veil themselves. Could make themselves invisible if they wanted to. Only I could see through that.

"Lia, let's go." Nash climbed through the portal with the demon.

The door to the bedroom opened. A woman burst into the room.

"Billy." The woman rushed to the young boy and wrapped her arms around him.

"Mommy, the lady told me the monster is real." The boy pointed at me. "Why are her clothes so dirty?"

The woman looked at me with wide eyes. "Who are you?"

The portal glowed at the window, but soon it would blink out of existence, and I would be stranded in the little boy's bedroom.

"I—I'm sorry."

"Get out of my house. Ronald, call the police!" The woman shouted.

I ran to the window and climbed into the portal.

Twelve

THE blood rushed to my head as I came out of the portal and onto the other side. Nash held the arm of the demon as she struggled, but she no longer looked the way she did when she crawled from beneath the little boy's bed.

Her skin was medium brown, her eyes gray-green. Highlighted toffee-colored hair grew past her shoulders. She was nearly as tall as Nash. She wore a black dress that was low and high in places I wouldn't dare show off.

The scenery was as motionless as a painting. We were the only beings that moved within it. We were what was wrong about it.

"Let's go." Nash yanked the woman forward.

I cringed. Did he have to treat her that way? She was a demon, but she didn't look like one anymore. *You don't always see them the way you should, Lia.* They're monsters. I had to remember that.

The demon righted herself after Nash's harsh jerk. Her pale, pink lips curled into a smile.

We walked a couple blocks before we arrived back at the car behind the grocery store. Nash shoved the demon into the back seat. Her arms were manacled behind her.

I watched her from the rearview mirror as Nash slumped down into his seat. He turned the ignition.

"Don't waste your time," the woman said. "I'll get back out. I'm very resourceful."

Not resourceful enough to find a better hiding place than underneath a five-year-old's bed.

Nash ignored her and drove to the front of the store.

The demon kicked his seat. "I've never been captured by a man like you. So handsome. You probably don't really look like that, but I can get past it."

She didn't know Nash was a fallen angel. Maybe she was new to this. That would explain why Nash thought he'd only need me for backup.

"And you," the demon said. "What do you look like? Are you all boils and wrinkled skin underneath?"

I opened my mouth to say something, but Nash put a hand on my shoulder. He pinned me with his eyes.

"Not the talkative types," the woman said. "I'm great at reading body language. Let me guess, you two like each other, but there's something unspoken about it. Or you *have* spoken about it, but for one reason or another it's become hush-hush. So, who's been unfaithful?" One perfect eyebrow arched.

Nash's mouth formed a hard line. He slammed on the brakes. "We're here."

Nash parked the car outside the castle surrounded by seven walls. Limbo. He pulled the demon out of the car and marched her toward the castle.

I watched from the car.

An overweight man with a clipboard stood next to a tall, wide door. He stopped Nash and the demon. They talked.

The man waved Nash and the demon through as the large door opened. Nash was gone for a few minutes.

I leaned my head back against the seat and stared at the ceiling of the car.

The car door slammed.

Without a word, Nash started the car. Nash's eyes were fastened to the road as he sped along.

"You can say it," I said. "You're wondering if I'll tell Lucifer about the Staff. It's been bothering you since you found me in your room."

Nash didn't look at me. "I wasn't wondering that at all. I assumed you *wouldn't* tell Lucifer about the Staff."

"Well," I said. "I might be able to use the knowledge as leverage to get my soul out of her hands again."

"You could," Nash said. "But you won't."

"How do you know what I would and wouldn't do?"

Nash stabbed me with his eyes. "Because you know things that you're too smart to mention."

What did he mean by that?

I pulled my eyes away from him. "Nash!"

Nash slammed on his brakes.

Bob stood in front of the car. He wore a wide grin on his face.

"What the hell!" I screamed.

Bob walked around to Nash's side. He pulled open the door and yanked Nash out of the driver's seat. "Right on time." He slammed Nash against the brick wall of a building.

I opened the door and raced around the car to where Bob had Nash pinned against the wall.

Nash was eye level with Bob, but that was only because Bob had lifted him five inches off the ground. He tossed Nash out of the car like his body was filled with feathers.

Bob's wide grin made it look like the corners of his lips had been stitched to his ears. "Poor angel. Not even one seventh as strong as we are."

Bob's voice was layered, multiple voices speaking at the same time. The way Lucifer's had been once. "You think you can disrespect me because to you, I'm not her. But I am her. We all are."

"Let him go." I pointed my sword at Bob. "Or you won't have a hand to keep that shiny watch on your wrist."

Bob turned his head with the grin plastered to his face. He dropped Nash. "You need to stop fighting other people's battles, sweetheart, and try fighting your own."

Bob turned and sank his hands into his pockets. He whistled as he strolled away.

"You want to tell me what's going on?" I rounded the car and pulled the passenger's side door open.

Nash slid into the driver's seat and slammed the door shut. He rubbed his neck.

"What was that all about?" I sat.

"Nothing." Nash's neck was red with Bob's handprints.

"You can lie to me about a lot of things, but I'm not stupid. Why did Bob attack you?"

Nash shook his head. He was deciding if this lie was worth it. "I saw him open a portal," Nash said.

"I did too," I said. "He's the Redeemer, Nash, and he's trying to kill you."

Nash shook his head. "I—He's not authorized to own a portal."

"What?"

"He stole one," Nash said.

"I didn't know a portal was something you could steal like a gold watch or a fancy purse."

"Lucifer doesn't allow Bob to have a portal. She doesn't allow any of the Seven Princes to have one, not even herself."

"Why?"

"Because she can't trust herself."

"So, Bob's mad that you saw him?" I said.

"He's mad that I threatened to tell Lucifer," Nash said.

"But you didn't?"

"No. But I guess this makes it clear what I have to do."

"You're going to tell her?"

Nash's hands gripped the wheel.

"Nash?"

"No," he ground out.

"Why not? Why wouldn't you tell Lucifer, the woman you're *sleeping* with—"

His glare stopped me.

"You didn't know I knew that."

Nash stopped the car on the bridge. He got out and walked over to the railing, wrapping his hand around it.

I stood behind him.

Nash shook his head. His eyes locked on mine. "What do you think was the price for freeing Adriel from the Angel District?"

"You're giving yourself up to Lucifer for Adriel?"

Nash narrowed his eyes. He tore himself away from the railing. "Not for Adriel. For you."

My hands rolled into fists. "I didn't ask you to do something like that for me."

Nash stood in front of me now. "If I had known that you sacrificed your own soul for your mother's, I would have bartered for that too." His dark eyes had the look of a lion staring down its prey.

I had the sudden urge to move away from him. I took a step back, but Nash only stepped closer.

"I did it all for you, Lia," he said. "And you don't care."

"I didn't know," I said. "And I didn't ask for any of it, just like I didn't ask to be here."

"Then, go," Nash said. "The angels think you're here. They'll still come to find you. It would be better if you go."

"I have to save my mother," I said.

"You shouldn't be here." He was so close now, his breath was on my face. He smelled like coffee. I'd bet the taste of it was still on his tongue. I shook the thought from my head.

This man had lied to me, and now he stared at me like he wanted to rip me apart. If he so desperately wanted me to leave Sheol, why didn't he toss me into a portal and be done with it?

I wasn't worried about getting back. I had Caiduc.

"I'll go if you tell me everything," I said.

Nash raised his eyebrow. "What's everything?"

"I don't know," I said. "Everything you've been keeping from me."

Nash's mouth formed a hard line.

"Tell me why you won't out Bob?"

Nash hesitated, probably thinking of how he wanted to lie to me. "Because he'll tell Lucifer things about me, things I don't want her to know."

"Things you don't want *me* to know?"

"Things you can't understand."

"I understand more than you think." I walked away from him.

A few blocks past the bridge, I turned back, but Nash hadn't followed. When I faced forward, Caiduc stood in front of me. I jumped.

"If you're going to do that teleportation thing, you should consider doing it a bit farther away and approach someone like a normal person," I said.

"But I am not a person," Caiduc said.

I looked at his little nose, the only thing human about him besides his speech. "I guess not, but still, you're going to give me a heart attack at eighteen."

"I will try to be better."

"Hey," I said, slowly. "I didn't mean to yell at you. I'm high-strung right now. That's all."

Caiduc studied me, his head cocked sideways.

"I'm not telling you about it," I said. "I'm not going to turn into the Jinni version of reality T.V."

Puzzled, he looked at me.

"Would you stop staring at me like that?"

Caiduc lowered his head. "I am sorry."

I sighed. "I need to go somewhere, and it's important."

"Anywhere you wish."

"I need you to take me back to Jiao's. It's time to find out how badass I really am."

Thirteen

HE cobblestones were slippery from the rain, and darkness veiled the deserted street. Street lanterns glowed against the dark, but could not master it.

I had become used to the darkness. It was a comfort.

"I wanted to thank you," Caiduc said.

I turned to him. "Thank me?" His form wavered in the misty street, his hand scratched his wrist.

"For saving me. For lying to the Assembly on my behalf. It was wrong, but it was also right. I wanted to thank you properly as a human would." He folded his branchy arms around me. The soft fur on his head tickled my chin.

I patted his shoulders as he embraced me. "Okay, okay."

He released me.

"I owed you anyway. You're the best Jinni taxi service in town, and you don't charge. There's really no need to thank me."

"So, the exchange was mutual?"

"Well, you owe me maybe a few more free rides."

"You did not want to tell me why you were upset," Caiduc said. "But it is because of your friend, Nash."

"I don't know if he's my friend anymore. I don't know what he is to me."

"Why the confusion?"

"Because he's lying to me."

Caiduc cocked his head. "Perhaps his lies are to protect you?"

"Maybe," I said. "But that still doesn't give him the right to do it."

"I don't understand."

"It doesn't matter," I said. "He wants me gone. At least, he's honest about that part."

"Maybe you think that way because you convinced yourself that he should not want you."

Did I convince myself of that? Nash used to be an angel, a warrior of God. Even fallen, he's the best demon hunter in Sheol. Why *would* he want me?

We stopped outside the tea house. I glanced over my shoulder. Caiduc had disappeared.

I knocked.

The door opened. Jiao stood in the frame. "You." She went to close the door, but I pushed back.

"Wait!" I said. "I need your help."

"You got my help," Jiao said. "And far too much of it."

"Please, I need you to train me."

Jiao laughed. "I don't take apprentices." She attempted to shut the door again.

I slammed my hand on the wood. "I drank angel blood!"

Jiao's eyes were wide. She paused at the door.

"That's how I got my magic, and I have no idea how to control it."

"You won't learn anything here." She didn't try to slam the door shut this time.

"I can pay." I reached into my pocket and showed her the Void Mortem leaves. "With this."

"Come in," Jiao hissed.

Warmth pushed out the cold inside the tea house. The cherry blossom's delicate flowers littered the ground.

"Give me that." Jiao snatched the bag of tea leaves from me. "What is this?"

"Void Mortem."

Jiao narrowed her eyes at me. She reached into the bag and grabbed a few leaves, bringing them to her nose. She sniffed and shoved them back into the bag. She threw the bag at me. "That isn't Void Mortem."

"Yes, it is," I said. "I went to the Third Circle of Hell to get them. I fought Cerberus."

"What you have there," Jiao said, "is a perverted imitation of the real leaves. I suppose they are meant to make the dead wish for something they can't have. The real leaves can only be found in Arcadia."

"Why did you want to know so much about Hell?" I asked.

"You thought I wanted to learn about Hell so I could obtain the immortal leaves?" Jiao laughed. "I wanted to know about Hell because it will be my residence one day. I never hoped to get my hands on Void Mortem. The demon blood that runs through my veins destines me to the fire. I wanted to know how badly it would burn."

"So, it's no good."

Jiao shook her head. "I never thought for a second it was the real thing. But I am impressed by the lengths to which you would go to obtain it only to give it to me."

"You'll help me?"

"Only to satisfy my own curiosity. But you'll not tell a soul about it."

"No. I won't."

"You want tea?"

I had at least three abilities I knew about, besides making angels fall. I could heal, force-push, and have psychic dreams. These things made me strong, but I had no idea how to control them. Jiao was the closest thing to what I was. She drank demon blood that gave her special powers. I drank angel blood that gave me special powers. I needed to find out what Jiao knew because it could save my life.

"Water's fine," I said. "I don't really know tea."

"Well, stick with me long enough," Jiao said, "and you'll know tea. Sit."

I sat opposite Jiao at the low, wooden table.

Jiao poured hot water into a cup. "You have a lot to learn. I can teach you some techniques and exercises, but what you have isn't like witchcraft. There are no incantations, no spells."

"Isn't that easier?" I asked. "It would be harder to learn all kinds of spells and stuff. Plus, I don't know Latin."

"The power doesn't come from the words." Jiao passed me the cup of hot water. "The words guide. A long time ago, witches used power without words. But the power was unruly. They crafted the incantations as a way of directing their powers."

"But now they can't perform magic without the spells, right?"

"They can, but it is more difficult and far more dangerous," Jiao said.

I picked up the cup. Why had she given me hot water and not cold? "So, no one has written words for my magic?"

"No one has your magic, and I'm no scribe. So, you're going to have to learn to control your powers without the aid of words. It won't be easy."

"I'm in much more danger if I don't learn to control them," I said. "Angels are after me, and one of them killed my—"

Jiao lifted a hand to stop me. "Let's make a deal. I don't tell you about my life, and you don't tell me about yours."

"Okay," I said, slowly.

Jiao placed a metal ball on the table. The ball was small enough to fit in the palm of her hand. "First lesson," she said. "Move the ball."

"I can't. I don't know what to do."

Jiao folded her arms. "You haven't tried."

I closed my eyes and focused. Something fluttered on the edges, like a memory I couldn't grasp. "I can't."

"Yes, you can. What did you search for when you used your power the other times?"

"I didn't search for anything."

"Yes, you did. You wanted to feel something. Something you didn't feel, but knew you should."

I shook my head. I should feel pain. For all the shitty things I did, and the noble things I failed to do. For making innocent angels fall, for trusting people I shouldn't, for not saving my parents.

My eyes widened.

Power that pushed the limits of possible. It was like discovering a pile of diamonds, glistening and bright in the sun.

The ball jetted across the room, shattering the glass panels of a cabinet.

"I—"

"Good." Jiao grabbed my hand. She picked up a penknife and slashed my palm.

"Ouch." I pulled my hand back. A long, red cut oozed blood. "Why did you do that?"

"Heal it." Jiao folded her arms.

I frowned. "Couldn't I have started with a paper cut?" I reached for the glittering source of power. It sparkled in different hues and levels of brightness. Different powers. I grasped for one.

The cut closed up. The blood remained, but the skin was smooth and unscarred.

"I don't understand. How was I doing it before?" I stared at my hand.

Jiao stood. "Before you were doing it instinctively. Now, you are doing it with purpose. You are telling the magic what to do."

"So, that's it."

"Well, it's not like buttering bread," Jiao said. "You'll have to come back. There's still more to learn, and you need to practice."

THE damp air was heavy on my skin. It increased with a splash before becoming dry. Too dry, too still, so unnatural.

I struggled to breathe in this air.

The world is a piano with broken keys, and its music fights for life.

I was small in the vastness of the plain. I was tiny in the face of the depths.

The Pit was a black hole filling my vision, not allowing me to look away, for there was nowhere else to look.

His back was to me. Adriel's featherless wings were spread like the branches of a burned tree. He stood so close, so close to the Pit. Was he thinking of jumping?

My heart clenched.

I rushed forward and wrapped my arms around his waist, anchoring him to me.

"Lia." His breath trailed my name into the air.

"Please don't leave me," I said.

He loosened my arms from around his waist. He turned around and cradled my face in his hands. Warmth ran through my body so fast I forgot the chill of Sheol.

"I would give anything to feel the light of Heaven again," he said. He lowered his mouth to mine, and his kiss lulled on my lips. "I feel that light when I touch you."

fourteen

THE crayon snapped.

My hand hit the picture as waxy particles smeared the image of my dad. It was perfect. Me, Momma, Daddy.

I pushed the drawing aside and threw the crayon box. The box slammed against the wall with a satisfying thump.

"What happened?" Momma walked into the kitchen, her hair tied in a messy bun, strands fuzzed around her face.

"I don't want to draw anymore." I folded my arms. "Where's Daddy?"

Momma sighed and walked to the sink. She plugged the sink and poured water from a bucket into it. "Daddy has work. He'll be gone for a while."

"That's what you said before. You're a liar!"

Momma pinned me with her eyes. "We don't say that, Rachel!"

I stood. "You're a liar! You're a liar! You're a liar!"

Momma turned from the sink. She walked towards me and tripped over the open dishwasher door.

"I'm gonna go find Daddy!" I ran.

Turning the knob to the front door, I raced across the yard and into the street.

"Rachel!" Momma called.

I didn't care. She was a liar.

A horn blared.

I was pulled back.

The car sped down the street. The smell of rubber stung my nose. Bright arms cradled me while I cried.

I looked up, and a warm face greeted me. She smiled. Her golden hair matched her eyes. I touched the soft curls.

"Rachel." Momma ran across the yard to where I sat and hugged me.

The woman who saved me stood by the fence. She had wings. Beautiful, white feathered wings.

"Look, Momma." Tears choked my voice. I pointed.

Momma turned, not releasing me from her embrace. "There's nothing there, baby." She scooped me up and carried me back to the house.

The woman smiled at me.

"Not there." I nestled my head into my mother's arms. "Not there."

The world is a guitar with no strings, and its music is silent whispers no one hears.

My heart pounded as I jolted awake. I pulled my arms up to my chest and sobbed.

greed and gluttony

BOB picked a golden cup from the horde.

"Don't touch it!" Mammon snatched the goblet from him. His bony fingers crept along the cup in reverence.

Makes sense, Bob thought. It is gold, but Mammon would have acted the same if it was plastic.

"I like what you've done with the place." Bob stepped around piles of clothes, trinkets, and coins. "The horde is bigger than I remember."

"That was twenty years ago," Mammon said. "Of course, my collection has grown."

"Do you know what's in these piles?" Bob asked.

"If you have come to criticize me, Gluttony, your company *is* something I've had *enough* of."

"That is because it is so rich and decadent," Bob said. "It's sickly sweet."

"Bah." Mammon waved his hands. "You are wasteful."

Bob grinned. He stepped around a pile of spoiled food. The rotten smell stung his nose. "That's the difference between you and me, Mammon. I may be excessive, but I am never wasteful."

"I do not waste. I save," Mammon spat back.

Bob glanced over Mammon's rail-thin body. "And you never enjoy."

"I'll enjoy soon." Mammon returned an apple to the pile. "While everyone else is without, I will have saved for the winter."

"Winter never comes to Sheol."

Bob strolled into another room. The rooms in Mammon's house had no purpose other than storage. The piles in this room were stacked to the ceiling.

"Would you stop walking through my house!" Mammon screamed.

Bob turned. "I'm surprised you let me in. You must know what I came for."

"I have an idea." Mammon didn't just hoard things. He hoarded information. "I talked to Bell. He seemed to like what you have planned, but he doesn't want to do anything about it."

"You know we have to be together on this."

"And the girl Bell told me about?" Mammon asked.

"She would be a figurehead, a mere formality." Bob's eyes were pinned to a gold watch among the pile.

"Don't even think about it." Mammon seized the watch. "I don't even want your eyes on my things." Mammon put the watch in the pocket of his worn clothes. All those fashionable clothes he gathered, and he wouldn't even wear them. What a waste!

Bob wore a new suit every day. Always the same style, but a different one. All black with silk lapels and a blood red, satin tie. "We used to balance each other."

"While the days of that are over," Mammon said. "We are separate now."

"And that's a good thing." Bob looked down at Mammon. "We can't let Pride overcome us. You understand that."

"Leviathan will understand better."

"Your greed shades with envy," Bob said. "Leviathan is on their way. They have broken through the ice of the Ninth Circle."

Mammon hugged the golden goblet to his chest. "Then, it has begun."

part two

aeonian

fifteen

I tried not to trip as I walked in the dress. The garment compressed my waist and fell to the floor in layers that made it difficult to get the dress on without stepping on them. I'd worn fancy dresses like this to dinner, but never out of Nash's house. Walking in them had remained a challenge I couldn't master. I felt silly in the dresses like I was a monkey in a business suit.

Adrianna insisted on doing my hair, which she curled and pinned behind each ear. The scarlet locks matched the red dress.

"You'll stick out more if you don't get dolled up," Adrianna said. "People like to show off at this party. Trust me."

She showed me how to put in colored contact lenses. "They'll mask your light. That way demons won't know you are human."

The lenses were one shade deeper than my natural eye color and made my eyes jet black.

"Like your own little Veil," she said.

She begged me to take out my nose ring. I obliged because I couldn't bear to see her grovel like that over a piece of jewelry. I even let her do my makeup. By the end of it, I didn't recognize the person in the mirror.

Maybe she was Rachel, but I was still Lia.

I still wore my dad's cross and the locket with my parents' pictures encased inside.

I could avenge them. Now, if I wanted to. I had Caiduc. I had taken lessons from Jiao and awakened my powers.

So, why didn't I?

I still had more to learn. I needed to practice before I faced Raphael. But that wasn't all. Nash might be lying to me, but he was in trouble. Bob wanted him dead.

According to my instincts, this wasn't a fight I could win. But I had to stay. I had to know I'd tried. If I didn't, I'd regret it forever. And I wanted Nash to prove me wrong. Whatever he was up to, it couldn't be terrible. He couldn't be terrible.

He waited by the car, opening the door for me as I ambled over.

"You don't have to do that," I said.

"You look like you were having more than enough trouble getting over here," Nash said. "I think getting the door was the least I could do."

"You could have refused the invitation to this party." I pulled the dress skirt into the car. "And you certainly didn't have to bring me along."

"But I didn't want Lucifer to catch me alone for obvious reasons." He shut the door.

I frowned. How long was he going to let Lucifer use him like that?

Nash settled into the driver's seat.

"You could have taken Adrianna or Chandra. They're better at stuff like this."

"Adrianna and Chandra hate these parties," Nash said.

"And you don't?"

"Of course I hate them, but Lucifer insisted I attend this year. You pick your battles with the Queen of Darkness."

"There are no battles with Lucifer."

"You don't know the half of it."

NASH pulled up to a massive building with lights shining from its many windows. I craned my neck to see the top of the building. Not quite as tall as Lucifer's skyscraper, but getting there. Stone hawks looked down at me from the eaves.

I jumped.

A man opened my door and offered me his hand. He wore a crimson red vest. Another man wearing a similar vest took the keys from Nash.

I waved the man off and got out of the car myself, slipping on my skirt twice before I managed to forfeit the car seat.

I glared at Nash like it was his fault I had embarrassed myself. It was his fault. He wanted me to come to this frivolous event.

"Pick up your skirt a little," he said. "You won't trip, and it'll save the hem from getting dirty."

I fisted the sides of my skirt and lifted it as I walked. I passed men in suits and women in gowns. Why did I feel their eyes burning into me? They weren't looking at me. But still, I felt like a lizard trying to balance an elephant in that dress. While their movements were elegant, they were all monsters underneath.

I ground my teeth as I stepped forward. The other guests pooled into the main hall. Music played as if through surround sound speakers. Violin strings mingled with piano keys. The harmony washed over me, pulling the anxiety away in one long, calming breath. Until I looked around.

People stared at me like they knew I was an imposter, like they knew I was human.

The Veil lifted. Their eyes were solid black.

Not there. Not there.

"Lia, what's wrong?" Nash asked.

They can't see you. All they see is another young demon. They wouldn't know if they'd seen me before. As far as they know, I can Veil myself like they can.

"Nothing," I said. "I'm fine."

The hall was six or seven stories high. The area encompassing the marble flooring was massive, several times bigger than the first floor of Nash's mansion. Windows stretched from the floor to the ceiling. Columns held up a large balcony in the back of the room. Beneath the balcony were glass tables and chairs. More tables were above the smattering below.

Nash must have followed my eyes. "Lucifer will be up there. It's best we stay away."

"But how will she know you came?" I asked.

"She will see me, but I doubt she'd approach me. She'd expect me to approach her."

I found the source of the music. A band played in the corner of the room. The ceiling above them was sloped, making the sound bounce off the walls, magnifying it.

"You want to dance?" Nash asked.

I tore my eyes away from the band. "What? No."

Against the opposite wall was a banquet table lined with platters of food. People chatted around it, picking food from the platters.

"Let's just sit," I said. "I want to get this over with as soon as possible."

"Sitting around and dreading it, won't make time pass any faster," Nash said.

I marched across the floor and slumped down at one of the tables. Nash pulled the chair across from me.

"You shouldn't sit like that," he said.

Couples and groups of demons laughed and talked around us. A few of them nodded and gestured towards me.

I straightened in the chair. "You're telling me how to sit now?"

A set of marble steps led to the balcony. Lucifer hadn't arrived. I hoped I didn't have to see her, but of course she would come to her own party.

Couples danced to the slow music. I found myself envious of the women who moved gracefully in their bulky dresses. Men chatted in the corners. Others danced with the women. Laughter and dance.

Did they ever think about what they had to do to get it? Did they care?

A few miles from the party, demons tortured people in the Circles, and these people drank and laughed like nothing was wrong in the world.

"Are you hungry?" Nash asked.

I couldn't eat. I kept clenching and unclenching my hands. But it was awkward sitting across the table from Nash. "Sure," I said.

Nash unhinged himself from the chair, almost too eager to leave me alone.

What did he expect when he brought me here? Nash and I hadn't had a real conversation since that day on the bridge, and he expected me to act normal around him at this fancy party?

"Care to dance?"

I looked up.

A man stood at my table. He looked young, my age. He had dark skin and clear, gray eyes. His good looks made my voice shake more. "I'm with someone." I thumbed over my shoulder, not knowing what direction Nash had gone.

"That's okay." He smiled.

That was polite for a demon.

The man walked away.

"That's going to keep happening." Nash set a plate of food in front of me and sat across from me.

"No, it won't. Not as long as you're here." I moved the food around with my fork.

"If we don't dance," Nash said. "They'll assume we're friends or that we just met."

"We *are* just friends," I said. "Isn't that extraordinarily polite for demons?"

"Not really," Nash said. "After their contracts are done, pretending to be normal is the only way they won't go insane."

"Isn't that insane though? Being normal after something like that?"

"I didn't say they *are* normal."

Veils, bogus trials, pretenses. Everything was fake.

"You want to dance," I said, "so, *we* can pretend to be normal."

"I didn't say that either."

"You don't seem to be having a good time," I said.

"Why would I be?" Nash asked. "I was coerced into coming."

I folded my arms. "I just wish you hadn't dragged me into your bad time." My eyes drifted to the balcony opposite the tables.

Lucifer had arrived. Her long, black hair was like silk. She wore a red dress with dazzling golden embroidery. I couldn't help but compare her dress to my plainer one.

"Maybe I will dance with the next man who asks," I said. "At least then I won't have to sit at this table with you."

"The next man who asks?"

"Yes."

"Alright then. Lia," he said, "will you dance with me?"

I wanted to wipe that smug smile off his face, but at the same time, the corner of my lips twitched into a smile. That was clever of him.

He offered his hand, and I took it. He led me to the dance floor where other couples swayed. Clasping one hand in his, he swept the other hand to the small of my back.

He danced in time to the music. I danced to his rhythm despite myself.

"Lia." My name pulled from his lips.

"Hmm?"

"You need to leave Sheol."

"Why?"

"It's not safe here."

"It's never been safe in Hell, Nash."

"You have to go."

I shook my head. "No. I'm the only thing keeping you from the Pit. I'm your only way of defeating Raphael."

"No, you're not."

Endbringer. That's why Nash hid the weapon. He wanted to kill Raphael so I wouldn't have to.

But I wanted to.

"Nash, I'm not going anywhere. I can't."

"You have to trust me."

"How can I when you've been lying to me?"

"I have good reasons."

"Do you always have good reasons for your bad deeds?"

Someone tapped on Nash's shoulder right above my head.

Lucifer stood before us. "Nash, I wanted to invite you to enjoy this evening's festivities in the back room."

What was she talking about? We were enjoying the festivities. Did she mean—? My jaw dropped.

Nash pulled away from me.

"I'll go too," I said.

Lucifer shook her head slowly. "I don't think you want to do that."

"I'll be fine," I said to Nash.

"No, Lia. Please, just stay here." His eyes were sharp as knives.

I pressed my lips together.

Nash followed Lucifer to the stairwell, and they ascended to the balcony, walking through a door in the back. The door closed behind them.

I gritted my teeth. My dagger was bound to my leg. Lucifer wouldn't force Nash to do anything while I was here.

The room had thinned out.

I stormed to the balcony, climbed the steps, and slipped through the back door. The hallway was in shadows. I tried to push up my skirt to reach my dagger, but the billowy fabric was heavy and kept getting in my face.

To hell with it!

I ripped the dress down the side, pulling my dagger from my thigh holster. I followed the dark hallway. It opened to a large room. Screams echoed off the cavernous walls.

People blocked my view. They observed something in the center of the room. I pushed through the crowd.

Men and women knelt to the floor. Whips ripped into the flesh on their backs and turned it to gory ribbons. They screamed.

Blood made the floor so slick, they slipped in it, but the demons continued to whip them while the crowd laughed and cheered. Lucifer leered, wielding one of the whips herself.

The sufferers, they were people, humans.

I froze.

"Lia," Nash hissed.

I hadn't seen him approach. He pulled me back through the crowd.

"Put that away," he whispered.

I had my dagger raised. "Why are they doing that to those people?"

"Lucifer holds these parties every night."

"Every night?"

"She likes to torture the people she sends to the Circles herself first. A real send off."

"But why? They're going to be tortured forever anyway."

"She's the Devil. She'll drain them dry before she sends them to the slaughter. No one is safe in this world, Lia. Do you think that she shows *compassion* for souls like Tom's? He's here because of doubt, not of God, but of himself. He didn't kill anybody or cheat or steal. And yet he had to spend hundreds of years terrorizing and sacrificing other souls to save himself an eternity of pain. No one wins."

Nash's fists clenched. "This needs to be stopped," he ground out. I was struck by his fervor. He might be a fallen angel, but Nash was as disgusted by all this as I was.

"Why did you bring me here?" I whispered, dropping the knife to my side.

"I wanted you to see this, to see the depths of Lucifer's depravity," Nash said. "I wanted you to know the motivation behind what I'm about to do."

Sixteen

THE plate crashed against the wall.

I covered my head and ducked, hoping to avoid the next one Jiao threw at me. Glass shattered.

"Hey, do you have to throw them at my head?" I asked.

Jiao's mouth screwed up into a determined frown, and she hummed another one.

I crouched lower to the floor. "This isn't working."

"Push them away."

The plate sent bits of glass around me. If Jiao kept this up, soon I would be ankle deep in tiny bits of ceramic and crystal.

"I'm trying."

"No, you're not."

"Yes, I am." I yanked my sword from its sheath. The blade sliced clean through the ceramic plate. Either side crashed to the floor.

"Put that weapon away," Jiao said.

"It's been two weeks, and all you can do is throw plates at me? Nash got me further than this in fourteen days."

"Go train with Nash then." Jiao poured the tea. "I'm sure a fallen angel knows more about magic than a two-hundred-year-old witch."

I raised an eyebrow.

"Sarcasm," Jiao said. "Fallen angels are running on fumes. They can't give magic to anyone much less know how to use it. Why are humans so impatient?"

"Well, I don't have magic tea I can drink whenever I want to add a few decades to my life."

As Jiao sipped the tea, her wrinkles faded. "You don't need the tea, not yet anyway. You'll live plenty more years than a normal human."

"Because I'm living in Sheol right now?"

"No, because you drank angel blood. The blood heals, although not as perfectly as an angel's since it's mixed with your messy human blood."

"How do you know so much?" I asked.

"That's not important." Jiao's hand trembled as she set down her teacup.

I furrowed my brow. I was getting better at picking out liars.

"You keep going back to square one," Jiao said, "because you keep forgetting the most important thing: remember your pain."

"Why is that so important?"

"Angels are bound to their duties. The only time they feel true pain is when they stray from those duties."

"When they become fallen?"

Jiao nodded. "The pain awakens the blood. Excites it to action. That's what you need it to do. That's when you can reach inside yourself and pull it out."

"What can you do with your magic?"

"I practice tea magic. Everything I do is confined to the teas."

"But you're a witch, right? So, you can do magic with incantations?"

"No." She sipped the tea.

"I don't understand—"

"Did you want to train or do you want to pry into my personal business?" Jiao asked.

I pressed my lips shut.

I had to learn from Jiao. It was time I took matters into my own hands. Nash wouldn't save me. He couldn't afford to. That's why he told me to leave Sheol.

He knew I would follow him and Lucifer and see the horrible things she did to people for fun. Hell wasn't punishment. It was torture for the sake of torture. He wanted it to disgust me so I would leave, but it only made me want to fight harder. I couldn't let any more people end up down there. I couldn't be the reason people were forced into the Circles or the Pit.

The gray hairs disappeared from Jiao's head. She threw the cup at me.

I forced the cup back.

Jiao caught it in her outstretched hand. "Good. I like this cup."

"Then why did you throw it at me?"

"I can tell by that frown you were thinking about something that brings you pain."

That's all I had to do: relive horrible things in exchange for power.

"IS it a bit irresponsible to force such imperfect and unenlightened beings to make a decision of an eternity?" Tom abandoned his book.

"God deserts no one until they have reached a final decision to reject Him," Adriel said. "He is just."

I put *A Tale of Two Cities* on the table beside me and sipped my hot chocolate. I'd come to the library, hoping to get some reading in, but I guessed that won't be happening. *Didn't these two ever stop?*

Tom leaned forward. "What would be the right conditions? Right after a person dies? That split-second between life and death, when your brain decides, and you find yourself in the intake office in Limbo."

"Is that really how it works?" I asked.

"Yep," Tom said. "You die, and then you decide. There is no moment of clarity. All the feelings and emotions you might have had before death are still with you: the fear, the regret, depression, carelessness. Yet, you are meant to make a decision without knowing that you are making one. And all that time voices shout in your head, telling you things that make you doubt, that make you waver, that condemn you."

I cringed. Nash was right. People deserved to be punished for their bad deeds, but Lucifer went too far. She chucked people into Hell that didn't belong there and contracted demons to gather souls.

Adriel stood. "It has to be in your heart. Those who go to Hell know they belong there, not because of God, but because of the marks on their souls. Without such, there would be no reason for doubt."

But even if evil intent was in your heart, would you deserve eternal punishment? I shook my head. What right did I have to decide that? I'd been hurt by someone, and I wanted him to rot in Hell forever.

Tom's eyes shaded to solid black. Angels could see past the Veil. *What does Adriel see?* Tom's true form must be hideous for Adriel to turn his lips up every time he saw him. Or maybe it was Tom's personality that gave Adriel such distaste.

Tom stood. "Is Nash home?"

I shrugged. "His car was gone this morning. Why?"

"I need to talk to him. I might know where Azazel is."

"That angel Lucifer wants us to bring to Sheol?"

"Azazel is not an angel," Adriel said.

"Fallen angel turned Archdemon." Tom held a book in his hands.

Another Archdemon. I didn't do so well against the last one. "But Lucifer thinks he may still be an angel."

"It's possible," Tom said. "But many believe he demonized his soul."

"Lucifer would know about that," I said. "Wouldn't he have to bow to her?"

"Oh, he could have bowed to her without Lucifer knowing."

I raised my eyebrow.

"He could have pledged himself to another of the Seven Princes. That's effectively the same thing as bowing to Lucifer."

Andromeda demonized her soul. She became a monster. What had Azazel become?

"Nash will want to go tonight." Tom slid the library door open. "Hope you two are ready." He left.

I sat on the table next to where Adriel stood. He put the book he held back on the shelf.

"Are you ever going to read one of those?" I asked.

Adriel looked down.

"You've looked through dozens. But you always put them back. At least one must have piqued your interest by now."

He shook his head still looking at the ground. "I can't read."

My eyes grew wide. "You can't read!"

"Does that surprise you?"

"Yes! You've been around so long. I thought you'd know hundreds of languages or something."

"I know over a thousand languages. Some of which are no longer spoken. But just because I can speak them doesn't mean I can read them."

"You never wanted to learn?"

"My duty was to guard the Throne. Angels are not permitted to own anything other than their weapons. There are no books in Heaven. I did not come to Earth until Sydriel went missing."

No books. Maybe Heaven would have been a Hell to Tom anyway.

"I could teach you," I said.

"I would like that."

"Have you been following Nash?"

"I have as you suggested," he said.

"Well, what did you find out?"

Adriel shook his head.

"Nothing?" I knitted my brows in confusion.

"He frequents Lucifer's building and various bars."

"That's it. That's all you know!"

Adriel nodded.

"You're not a very good spy."

"I don't like to spy on my brother. I did it only because you asked." Adriel grimaced.

I shook my head. "You're right. I shouldn't have asked you to do that."

"Whatever Nasriel might be up to, he's doing what he thinks is right."

"I thought you hated Nash."

"I don't hate him. He makes bad decisions for the right reasons."

I strapped on my arm bracers and placed my sword and dagger in the sheaths on my belt. Closing the door to my bedroom, I walked down the hall to the stairs. My hand froze on the bannister.

Across the hall, Kiran grabbed Tom's wrist, pinning his hand to the wall. What were they up to now? Were they fighting? Over what?

Kiran leaned forward and . . . kissed him.

They were locked together, Tom staring wide-eyed. Kiran stepped forward, tangling his legs in Tom's, his hand cradling the side of Tom's face.

Tom's eyes settled into a look of comfort. The tension left his shoulders as Kiran leaned further into the kiss. He eased back and whispered something against Tom's lips.

Kiran embraced him, and Tom's hands fisted the back of Kiran's shirt.

I hurried down the steps. Kiran and Tom!

What about Adrianna? Did she know about this?

"Lia?" Nash stood at the bottom of the stairs. "Have you seen Kiran and Tom?"

"What?" I froze. "Why would you ask about that?"

"We have to leave," Nash said.

"Oh," I said. "No, I haven't seen them. Maybe they're in the library. Or, um, maybe Tom's in the library and Kiran is out back practicing his stances. That's right. Kiran's never in the library. That would be silly."

"Lia, you're talking fast."

"Am I? Must be the coffee."

"Hey, Li, what's up?" Adrianna appeared from the living room.

"Nothing," I choked. "I'm going to wait in the car. I don't want to be the hold up."

I pushed past them and out the door. I slammed the car door shut and sighed.

"What are you thinking?"

My skin jumped. I glanced in the rearview mirror. Caiduc sat in the back, scratching his wrists.

"I don't know. Your popping up like that wiped all thought from my mind. It's creepy."

Caiduc lowered his head.

I did have to stop abusing him. He was so sensitive.

"I wasn't thinking anything interesting anyway. I was thinking about how rude it is to cheat on people."

"That sounds like a very interesting thing to think about."

"Yeah, well it's not. It's a very depressing thing to think about."

Caiduc shuffled in the back seat.

"You can't be here right now anyway. Nash will see you."

"Why are you worried about Nash seeing me?"

"Because Nash doesn't like Jinni."

"Why?" he asked.

"Because he doesn't like creatures who don't follow any rules."

"But we do follow rules."

"Not ones that he knows about," I said.

But Nash had used Jinni. He used them to find angels. The wrong angels.

The car door opened.

I turned in my seat. Caiduc was gone.

Chandra slipped into the seat. "What are you looking at?"

I slumped back. Nash opened the driver's side door and sat. Adriel sat in the back with Chandra.

I peered into the rearview mirror. Tom got into Kiran's car. Adrianna sat in the back. I should tell her. We were friends. But Tom, Kiran, and I were friends too. Friends don't let friends cheat on other friends.

The engine roared.

I turned the knob on the car radio. A loud blare issued from the speakers. I turned the knob more, trying to discover a station that played music, trying to take my mind off Kiran, Tom, and Adrianna.

Chandra covered her ears. "What are you doing? Turn it off."

Nash yanked the knob to the left, stifling the sound.

"Sorry," I said. "I was trying to find a station. Didn't you say it would be a long drive?"

"It will be," Nash said. "Two and a half hours."

"There are no stations in Sheol," Chandra said. "Only loud, terrible static."

Two and a half hours with no music! That was hell. I should have brought my MP3 player.

If we opened the portal anywhere else, we'd have to travel on Earth. Travel through Sheol was faster. But sometimes the Circles got in the way, and we didn't have a choice.

If Nash would use Jinni to find angels, why wouldn't he use them for transport. They were way more efficient than the portals. Of course, you had to sacrifice your life-force to use them.

Who was the Siphon for Nash's Jinni? I never noticed an earring in Nash's ear. Nor had I seen one on Adrianna, Chandra, Kiran, or Tom.

It was an odd concept anyway. Human Siphons were more understandable. The Jinn serves, and you lose years off your life. Simple. But demon and angel Siphons lost strength.

Couldn't they build that strength back up again?

Jiao said that Nash ran on fumes. That meant Nash's strength wasn't capable of growing, but only exhausting itself. He would run out. A Jinn would drain him faster.

I glanced over at Nash and checked for an earring. He didn't have one. I would have noticed.

So, he was either using someone else as a Siphon, or he was lying about using Jinni. If I had to place my bet, I'd put it on the latter.

Seventeen

I struggled to breathe in the dry, hot air. My lungs felt like someone had poured cinnamon into them. The sky was shades of blue-violet, and the land was tan and gray. Sand surrounded the rocky plateaus.

Nash stepped through the portal, and it zipped closed. Adrianna talked with Chandra. Adriel ran his hands through the sand.

Tom and Kiran stood a few feet away from each other, but kept changing their distance and posture as if trying to negotiate what would seem more natural.

"Where are we?" I asked.

"East Jerusalem," Tom said.

"Well, I hope you know where we're going." The lack of humidity tortured my esophagus.

"It's not far." Tom led the way.

"Does Michael really hate this angel so much?" I asked.

"Michael hates what he considers impure and imperfect," Nash said.

"He is doing his duty." Adriel was in step alongside me. "He is the Commander of the Army of God, and he weighs the souls at judgment."

"So, he decides whether a soul is fit for Heaven?"

"Yes."

Even if Lucifer renewed her deal with me, there was no chance I would make it into Heaven with Michael in charge.

"Here." Tom opened a portal in the ground.

I furrowed my brow. "You expect us to go through another portal, back into Hell?"

"What is the meaning of this?" Kiran asked.

The portal glowed in the ground. I peered inside, but all was mist and shadows.

"You said you found him," Nash said.

"Trust me." Tom jumped into the portal.

Chandra shook her head and jumped in after him followed by Adrianna and Kiran. Adriel looked to me and Nash. Nash nodded. Adriel leapt into the glowing circle.

My eyes anchored to Nash. I'd never climbed through a portal in the ground. It was strange. Tom had been wrong so many times before.

"Go," Nash said.

I nodded, pressing my lips together, and dropped.

The wind rushed in my ears, making them pop. Colors swirled around me as I fell. What is this place?

I tumbled into the mist. Water crashed against the rocks below.

Oh, no!

I fell head first toward one of the jagged rocks peeking from the water. I could sense the pain. The moment of impact, my head splitting against the stone.

I pushed my hands out in front of me, a poor shield for such a collision. Closing my eyes, I waited to hit the rocks. I should have died a long time ago. This is it. I'll have to fight Raphael from the grave, but I'll never stop.

The air stopped rushing. I still felt it fly past me, but it became a soft breeze instead of a roar. I opened my eyes.

My descent slowed. I bit my lip, pulling the energy from the depths of my body like glittering diamonds. My eyes sparkled, and the glow rose to my energy. I thrust myself back away from the jagged rocks.

I hit the water with a splash. The waves swept over my head as I struggled to remain above the spray.

The sky was dark as were the waves that crashed around me. Despite the darkness, I managed to find a flat rock among the waves. I swam to it.

I pulled myself up onto the plateau and coughed the water from my lungs.

"Nash! Adriel!"

The clouds swirled. Something was strange about them. They didn't drift across the sky like ordinary clouds. They rose like smoke from the water, mingling together in hues of gray, black, forest green, and navy.

The rocky plateau where I lay was connected to a larger, flat rock. Water lapped over the edges. My clothes clung to me. Hair matted my face.

Rising from the rocks were three stone faces with crowns on their heads. They had to be fifty feet above the waves. I looked closer. The crowns were buildings, like ancient Greek buildings with pointed tops. From each face hung arched bridges, and a long staircase led up to the main face.

"Anybody!" I screamed.

That fall was treacherous. What if they died? What if they broke all their bones hitting the waves?

Was this place part of Sheol? Did it still count? Or would they go to the Pit?

"Lia!" Tom ambled over to me. "You're the last one I thought would make it through that. I guess that means the others are probably okay too."

"Tom, what the hell? You send us through a portal into this?"

Tom put his hands up. "I didn't know it would be like this."

"What is this place?"

Points of light, like suspended flakes of glittering confetti, glowed from the two smaller heads. Birds with black feathers flew around the massive stone faces.

"Dudael."

"Huh?"

Adriel pulled himself up onto the rocks. I breathed a sigh of relief. What was wrong with his left wing? The bones looked bent.

"Tom, you have some explaining to do." Chandra grimaced. She tossed her wet ponytail back.

Nash and Kiran followed close behind her.

"We're in Dudael." Tom was unable to wipe the grin from his face.

"You still haven't explained what that is," I said.

"Dudael is the place Michael ordered Raphael to bring Azazel. He ordered Raphael to bring him to the center of the desert, to make an opening, and to chain him to the rocks until the Day of Judgment."

"Maybe the scripture was being hyperbolic." Kiran flicked his sword.

"No," Tom said.

"But we're in Sheol," I said. "Couldn't we have walked instead of portal hopping?"

"That's the exciting part." Tom gestured to the sky and the rocks bordering the waters in the distance. "This is set apart from the rest of Sheol. You couldn't get to it from the Outer Region."

"So, this whole place is for one guy?" I asked.

"Wasteful, isn't it?" Tom wrung out the length of his shirt. "He should be chained to one of these rocks. But I don't think that was meant to be there." Tom pointed to the three faces.

"We should look inside," Nash said.

"Wait! Where's Adrianna?" I asked.

"She'll be alright." Nash stepped toward the staircase.

"What if she's lost in the waves?" I asked. "She might have broken something and can't make it to the surface."

"She'll heal," Nash said.

How could he be so careless? What if the waves pushed her too far down? By the time she heals, she would drown, be revived, and die all over again. Forever.

"Adrianna!" I called as we approached the stairs.

Chandra echoed my call. "Adrianna!"

Kiran didn't even seem worried that Adrianna was missing. If she never turned up, he could continue to have his affair and never have to tell her. *Has it gotten that sour between the two of them?* They spent forever together.

I glanced at Nash. Good thing we drifted apart. It was better to be tossed aside now than a thousand years from now.

Nash climbed the stairs. I followed and looked up to the top, the giant face. I sighed. This would be like climbing the steps of a ten-floor building.

I looked behind me. No sign of Adrianna. What if she *did* get lost in the waves? Nash wasn't going to leave her, was he?

But he didn't look back.

My feet dragged as I climbed. The ground was small below me, and the face had become larger. Mist trailed from the faces and puffed around them.

The mouth of the face formed an archway, unguarded.

I stepped through. Ivy grew along the stone walls. Columns, capped in intricate designs, rose from the ground. Two staircases curled up to a loft.

More stairs!

"Nice place," Chandra said. "I thought you said no one lives here but an angel tied to a rock."

Tom climbed the stairs.

I sighed, but followed the others. We entered a room with a large pool in the center. At each corner were stone vases. The winds tore outside the arched doorway, open to the elements.

We walked onto a rope bridge, crossing over to one of the smaller faces. The bridge twisted in the wind.

"We're not really going to cross this thing?" I didn't know if I had it in me to use my powers. Invoking them was as easy as training a sloth to outrun a cheetah.

"It won't be so bad," Tom said. "Just don't look down."

Nash led the way across the bridge. Adriel walked behind me.

The bridge swayed. I did look down. Rocks, jagged from the water below, waited to skewer us if we fell.

The wind beat at us.

How strange. This place was part of Sheol but did not hold the same stillness. The waves and air were alive and ready to batter.

I gripped the ropes connecting the bridge to the two faces. The mist made the rope damp and the wooden planks slippery.

My boots became slick. I fell. I tightened my grip on the rope as I dangled over the edge. The wind caused my body to twist like a flag in a hurricane.

Something flew with the birds. Black smoke surrounded the gray-skinned creature. But the clouds looked like smoke. Were my eyes playing tricks on me?

A hand grasped my forearm. Adriel pulled me back onto the bridge. I clung to him tighter than I had to the rope.

"Thank you." My voice shuttered.

I sighed in relief when we made it to the other side of the bridge. We walked through the mouth of the second face.

"Well, well, now. I have guests." A man sat at a stone table with ten chairs surrounding it.

The man's long, stringy hair covered one side of his face. Pale skin peeked from beneath. A large, metal arm bracer covered his shoulder to his wrist. Over his shoulders were a set of black, feathered wings.

I never saw an angel with black wings before.

"Sit," he said. "The meal was just prepared."

I eyed the man. He must be Azazel.

"I thought you said he was chained to a rock," Chandra hissed in Tom's ear.

Tom smiled and approached the table. "Was hard getting here. My muscles are sore already."

"Please, be my guest." Azazel motioned to one of the chairs.

I sat with the others, none of us sitting too close to Azazel.

Clunking echoed through the room.

"What's that?" I blurted out.

"Oh, that's Raphie."

A goat ambled in. His large, brown horns curved over his head. His fur was cream-colored. His eyes were yellow. The goat walked over to Azazel.

Azazel petted its head below the horns.

"Raphie? Like Raphael," Chandra said.

"Yes." Azazel stroked the goat's back. "Had to do something to thank him for giving me this wonderful home. Three faces. Two for my brothers and one for me."

Azazel lifted his hand as if he were picking up a piece of lint. Tilting his hand, his head followed like he had taken a sip of something. But nothing rose to his lips. "They were so helpful, my brothers. I'm so glad, they were blamed for none of it. Although the three of us are the reason I am here."

"You don't have to stay here," Nash said. "We've been asked to take you back with us."

"Oh, Nasriel, is it?" Azazel said. "I didn't recognize you. Your eyes used to be gold. Now they're like ink. And where are your wings?"

"We don't have much time," Nash said.

"And Adriel. You've changed too. I'm flattered to be in the presence of the Seraph, Protectors of the Throne. The winds must have torn away your feathers. Sorry for that. Can't control the weather."

He glanced around the room and blinked. "I don't recognize the rest of you."

Raphie clunked over to me and nuzzled his head in my lap.

"We'd better eat," Azazel said, "before it gets cold." He lifted his hand and brought it to the side of his mouth. He chewed.

The stone table was bare. No food, no drinks, not even platters and plates.

I glanced at Nash.

Raphie strolled over to the wall and ate the ivy growing from the ceiling. At least the goat knew what real food was.

Nash stood. "We were sent to get you out of this place, Azazel."

Azazel's lips curled into a smile. "How nice of you."

"So, you'll come with us?" Nash asked.

Azazel made a motion like he was wiping his mouth with a napkin. He walked around the table and stood in front of Nash.

"You mutilated yourself, Nasriel?" Azazel asked.

"Yes."

"Shame." Azazel's hand rose to the side of his head and twirled in the air. "We do what we think is right, and the moment doubt crawls in, we turn to ash. It's unfair really. Not knowing perfection until you've stepped outside of it."

In what must have been half a second, Azazel pulled his head back and rammed Nash in the temple.

Nash staggered back, holding his hand to his head.

"We are but His servants," Azazel said. "But sometimes we know not how to serve. I will not go to your she-devil. You will not take me from the home I have built."

I rose, pulling my sword from its sheath.

Azazel rushed to the stairs. "Meet me in the tempest." He went through the doors into the driving winds.

Nash pulled his sword. We raced up the stairs and outside. The top of the second face was a crown of ruin. The stone columns crumbled under the force of the gales. Ivy tied rocks to the ground.

Azazel stood at the opposite edge, his arms and wings spread to the sky. The wind tore away the black feathers. He held a sword. The steel was black, its hilt silver. His angel weapon.

"Let us do great battle among the chaos." Azazel pointed his sword at us.

Behind us, smoke rose. The mist bore pale faces with blackened lips and sharp teeth.

"Furies." Nash's voice was a whisper on the wind.

The creatures flew at us. One toppled me to the ground. I struggled beneath it. The smoke veiled its eyes. A pale chest, face, and black-lipped mouth was all it was.

I reached for my dagger and plunged it into the heart of the Fury. The wind tore the shriek from its mouth.

Three Furies surrounded Nash. Chandra beat one in the face with her brass knuckles. Kiran and Tom fought back to back. Azazel laughed. Adriel ran towards Azazel, but two Furies blocked his path.

I stood. A Fury yelled and swooped for me. I tore my blade through its flesh. Black blood dotted the ground. The Fury I stabbed through the heart sputtered on the ground. Would it heal? This was still Sheol.

The Fury's pale, crooked arms appeared from beneath the smoke.

Nash cut through the three Furies. He marched toward Azazel, cutting down Adriel's second Fury as he approached.

Adriel's blade went through the belly of the remaining Fury. Azazel smiled.

Hot pain rippled down my back. I spun. The Fury drew back its long, yellow nails. I hacked at the arm those nails belonged to. My back stung as the wind battered the fresh cuts.

I looked to the sky. Hundreds of Furies hovered within the swirling clouds. They dove.

Five of them were on me. My arms became heavy from swinging my sword. I aimed for maiming them. It seemed they could heal faster internally than externally.

I cut off the fingers of one as it tried to slash me. Too many surrounded me. My arms, back, and legs burned from their cuts.

The Fury pinched the skin of my lacerated back between its nails and pulled. I screamed. The creature let go.

I whirled around.

The beast lay on the ground. Adrianna cocked a smile at me. "Were you gonna leave me to the waves?"

I slashed into the Fury who landed at her side. Adrianna boxed with her daggers, sending rapid cuts into the flesh of the Furies.

Nash fought Azazel. Alone.

They struggled, sword against sword.

Nash's feet inched towards the edge.

He stepped back. Azazel advanced.

Nash swung his sword. And Azazel blocked it.

Nash turned. Azazel's back was to the cliff now.

My muscles ached. My back burned with a sharper pain. I swung at another Fury.

Metal zinged.

Nash and Azazel locked blades, Azazel bearing down on Nash.

Black blood wet Nash's shirt. Was he injured?

So much blood spilled around me, the scent stung my nose, like charcoal mixed with copper. I could taste the saltiness of it in the air.

A loud, guttural sound stilled me. My eyes shot towards Nash and Azazel.

Nash was on the ground. He held one hand to his bloodied abdomen.

Azazel's sword pointed down at Nash, aiming for his neck.

My blood was ice in my veins. But that ice fast became fire.

I charged forward, forgetting the Furies around me. They sunk their nails into my skin, but I barely felt the pain.

Azazel bore his eyes into Nash's.

I reached out and touched him, grabbing a fistful of black feathers. The feathers came away easily. They didn't burn.

"What?" The word pulled from my lips, a whisper on the wind.

The feathers weren't his. He pasted them on the bones. Crows cawed in the distance.

"Li—" Nash could barely get the word out. Black blood leaked from the corner of his lips.

Azazel turned to me and swung his blade at my stomach.

I jumped back, gripping my own blade in shaking hands.

I had to do away with him fast. Nash needed my help.

My grip became stronger. My blade met Azazel's and shattered.

No!

Nash's sword lay on the ground beside him. It was less alloy, more Arcadian Steel, but even if I could reach it, I couldn't lift it. It was too heavy.

Azazel lifted his blade.

And I pushed.

The air in front of me vibrated like guitar strings and forced Azazel off the edge. He plummeted to the water below. False feathers flew in the wind.

He wouldn't die, not in Sheol, but it would be quite some time before he could climb up again.

I knelt beside Nash. He was bleeding. Bad.

The others were locked in battle with the Furies.

He wouldn't die. He can't. This is still Sheol, right? But what if the rules here were different? He wasn't healing.

"Nash."

His eyes trembled. Did he, too, doubt he would recover?

Adriel couldn't heal him like he did after the fight with Uriel. He was fallen now.

Wait! If Adriel could heal, did that mean I could too because of the angel blood?

I pressed my hand down on the wound in Nash's stomach. He grunted in pain. I focused, driving the memory of my parents into my brain.

The world is an organ, and its music is pain and dread.

"Come on. Come on." Tears squeezed from my eyes. "Don't do this to me, Nash," I said through my teeth. "You're a bastard if you do this to me. You can't toss me aside. You can't protect me with hate. I'm not letting go just because you want me to!"

My skin glowed, and that glow suffused into Nash.

eighteen

DRIEL set the book aside. "It doesn't surprise me that we weren't able to capture Azazel."

Adriel had been through two books now. I thought he would pick up on reading quickly. By the time, I started to help him, he could recognize most of the letters from memorizing them himself. I taught sounds, he already knew meanings.

"Why?" I asked. "We thought we were going to liberate an angel from a rock and, instead, had to fight a fallen angel and a couple hundred Furies. How could you have predicted that?"

Adriel pushed his chair inches from mine. My feet dangled, his were planted firmly on the ground. He looked ridiculously big in that little chair.

"God doesn't want us fighting our brethren. That is why I'm trying to make amends with Nash."

God. How did Adriel know what He wanted? Even Azazel, in his mad ravings, admitted that God's desires were a mystery.

"What are you thinking about?" Adriel asked.

"God," I said. "I don't understand Him. Why does He let His angels run everything? He's so . . . hands-off."

"That is why He made us," Adriel said.

"I don't get why you're not mad at Him."

"Mad at Him? He is my creator. He gave me everything."

"And then, He took everything from you."

"He didn't—"

"I know," I said. "But He made the rules, didn't He? Concepts like sin and wrongdoing didn't exist before Him. Someone had to lay the groundwork."

"Are you saying that morals are not innate?"

"If they are, and there was nothing before Him, then he created them. So, He created a system of rules, arbitrary at the time, and He punishes those who break them though it is in our very nature to do so."

"You should not speak of God in such a way," Adriel said.

I paused. "Have you seen Him?"

"What? No," Adriel said.

"Has anyone seen God?"

"Michael has seen God."

"I know, and Metatron. So, one Archangel, one half-angel, and no one else."

"I don't like what you're suggesting," Adriel said. "You must have faith."

"I used to," I said. "But now all these other things have come out and shown their faces: angels, demons, Nephilim, Jinni. Everything's falling apart, and you're telling me that God just sits back and watches?"

"He works through His creations."

I frowned. "I'm sorry. I've been hanging out with Tom too much."

"Perhaps I have been too harsh," Adriel said. "You don't know God as I do, but one day you will grow to know Him."

"My soul is destined for Hell, Adriel."

Adriel shook his head. "God will pardon what you have done. Like an angel, you believe what you are doing is right. You want to save people. That can only be right."

He looked into my eyes. I was suddenly aware of how close he sat. Barely an inch of air whisked between our knees as he leaned forward in his chair, his forearms resting on his legs.

He tried so hard to be civil with me though I challenged his god. He would have walked out on Tom.

I wanted to kiss him. But I was about to test his patience again.

"I saw my father, my birth father."

"How did you do that?"

"A Jinn."

Adriel frowned. "Jinni are dangerous, and their aid comes at a price."

"I'm not wearing his earring." I pushed my hair behind my ear. "See. No price."

Adriel narrowed his eyes. "A Jinn is helping you without the earring?"

I nodded. "His name's Caiduc. He's very *curious* about me. I guess that's why he doesn't charge me."

Adriel's frown deepened.

"What?"

"That is very strange that the Jinn would make such a sacrifice. They rely on their earrings for power."

I shrugged. "It's not that big of a deal, is it? So, he'll get a little weaker while he's with me. He can always pick up a Siphon later."

Adriel shook his head. "Jinni magic runs out very quickly, and once it is all used up, the Jinn will become a speck, unable to communicate or transform itself."

"So, it stays like that forever?"

"Once the Jinn loses all its power, it can no longer hold an earring, can no longer enter into a contract with another being to be its Siphon."

So, it's like the Pit. An endless nothing. An existent non-existence. I didn't want that to happen to Caiduc.

"How do you know so much about Jinni?" I asked.

Adriel lowered his head. "I had to do a lot of things I'm not proud of in my attempts to find Sydriel."

"You used a Jinn?"

"Yes. For a few years before I realized that it could not help me."

CHANDRA knocked me to the grass. I stood, twisting my sword in my hand. I lunged at her. She sidestepped me, and I barreled towards the ground.

"This isn't fair to me." Chandra blew on her fingernails. "If you don't put up more of a challenge, I won't improve."

I swung. She parried the blow.

"It's like swatting a fly with broken wings." Chandra battered my knuckles with the flat of her blade. I dropped my sword.

Chandra rolled her eyes. She was so much like Felicia, demeaning, narcissistic. Chandra slapped my cheek. And she always made me look like an ass.

I glanced over at Kiran. He shook his head. He didn't think I was trying. He thought I was losing to Chandra on purpose, so I wouldn't have to fight him and admit I was ready for Raphael.

I might not have the years of training that Chandra has, but I have one thing she doesn't. I reached inside myself and pulled the power. It strengthened my arms and legs. It pushed at Chandra.

Chandra's movements slowed. I brought my sword down on her. I whipped around and hit her again. This time, Chandra's sword matched mine. I shoved. She staggered. I slapped her cheek.

"Best two out of three," I said.

Chandra narrowed her eyes.

I dropped my sword and selected a new one, broader, heavier. "Kiran!" I yelled across the field to where he fought with Tom. "I'm ready to take you on."

Kiran stopped mid-swing.

Nash and Adriel stopped sparring and looked my way.

Adrianna gasped.

Tom grinned, gesturing for Kiran to make his way over to me. "You've shaken my bones enough for one day."

Kiran stepped up to me. "You know what this will mean."

"It will mean I've beaten the best swordsman." I held up my weapon. Normally, I would have trouble with a sword with this mass. I was used to my long, thin sword, nearly weightless. My powers gave me the extra strength I needed to wield the weapon without looking like a klutz.

Kiran brought his weapon forward and swung. Even dampening his speed with my powers, he was still fast. He cleaved me in the leg, the arm, the side of the neck, the chest. I fell.

I didn't even get a swing on him.

Kiran smiled. "Now, you're trying." He offered me his hand.

I grinned. "Next time, *I'll* be offering *you* a hand up."

I waited in the alleyway where Bob opened his portal. My warm jacket protected me from the chill. I popped in the contacts Adrianna gave me. With the contacts in, I wouldn't have to worry about demons discovering I was human.

I had gone through nearly ten songs on my MP3 player, but I would wait all night if I had to.

Bob rounded the corner. He wore his slim, black suit and blood-red tie.

I unhinged myself from the wall.

Bob smiled as he approached me. Did *anything* surprise him?

His lips twitched. So, he was surprised. He just didn't want to show it. "Didn't think you were the type to hang out in alleys, sweetheart."

"Oh, yeah, and what *type* is that?"

Bob smirked. "Angry at me for putting Nash against the wall?"

"More than angry." My hand was on the hilt of my dagger. "You want him dead, and you almost succeeded." Nash might have died if I hadn't used my angel magic on him. Bob freed the Furies from the Circles, and Ono or Bob or whoever brought them to Dudael.

"I'm not going to let Nash die," I said. "Whatever you're up to, Nash won't get in the way." *But I might.*

"He already has," Bob said.

"Well, not anymore. So, stop sending demons and fallen angels to kill him."

"What about my key?"

I thought he might ask about it. I reached into my pocket and planted the large key into his hand. "I don't want it anyway." *Neither do you, Beelzebub, you just like to have the upper hand. Everyone knows you don't have that with Lucifer.*

"I can't make any guarantees," Bob said. "Not if Nash keeps stepping out of line."

What was out of line *to Bob? What had Nash done?* I didn't ask. I wanted Bob to think I knew more than I did. Maybe then he would leave us alone. "Why does Lucifer need all the locks anyway?"

"She had to put in extra security because someone went up to her floor and went where they weren't supposed to."

When I unlocked the door and saw the one-winged angel? No, Lucifer was on alert before that.

"I saw what she does to people at her parties," I said.

"She's doing her job, sweetheart. She's just not very good at it."

"Nash doesn't seem to think so either."

"You need to stop trusting Nash. Do you know who he is?"

"He's a fallen angel, former Seraph."

"Sounds like you don't know the details."

"I know he was part of the original Fall."

"Part? That's understating things." Bob flashed me a sly smile.

I slammed my hands down on the table.

Tom jumped.

"Tell me about Nash, everything." I slumped into the chair across from him.

Tom stared at me from the other side of the desk. We were alone in the library.

"Stop staring at me, and tell me what I want to know."

"What do you want to know?"

"What happened before he fell?" I folded my arms. "Who was he? Lucifer's lead general? How did she implicate him in all this?"

"*Lucifer* implicate *Nash*?" Tom pinned me with his eyes. "It was Nash's idea to rebel."

"What? Why would he do that?"

Tom had a pained look on his face. "The story says the angels' jealousy of humans caused the rebellion, but that's not true. Doubt made Nash rebel. He didn't believe in God. So, he convinced Lucifer, and with her powers of persuasion they influenced the other angels to fight. They fell to Michael and his army."

"But if Nash was the one who started the rebellion, why isn't he the ruler of Hell?"

"Because Nash was in love with her."

nineteen

I wore the black dress. It wasn't the nicest one in my closet, but it was the most practical. Not that any of them were very practical, but this one happened to be more so than the others. The dress was low in the front, but the skirt was less poufy than many of the others. It would be easier to remove my dagger from the holster around my thigh.

Waylon was making me a new sword, but it wasn't ready yet. This one would be a stronger alloy like Nash's. I wished Waylon would make me one of pure Arcadian Steel. My sword was short and thin. I'm sure he could manage.

Beneath the dress, I wore jeans and boots. No one would see. The skirt trailed to the ground.

As I approached the building, I took a deep breath. A car pulled up. I ducked alongside it, pretending as if I had gotten out the back seat. I nodded to the valet and joined the other party-goers as they walked up the steps to the main entrance.

Everyone in Hell was taller than me. I guess that's what happens when you get to choose what you look like. Most of the guests probably wondered why I would choose this Veil. Short, my hair dye fading at the tips, and eyes so narrow, they made me look like an anime character when I smiled.

If only I could balance in heels. At least then, I wouldn't be so short!

I wore the contacts in my eyes. I didn't like them. They made me look young and doe-eyed. But I needed to keep them in or the demons would know I don't belong.

My body zinged with nervous energy. Was I actually excited to do this? To call Lucifer out on her shit?

I stepped into the main hall. The band played in the back of the room. Classical. Did Lucifer know music had progressed past the eighteenth century?

I headed for one of the tables across from the balcony. I needed to see when Lucifer decided to go to the back room for the *after-dinner entertainment.*

I scanned the balcony. Lucifer had not yet arrived. Would she be late like she had been the night before?

"Care to dance?" A man approached my table, offering his hand.

Dance? With me? Adrianna hadn't even done my makeup, and I hadn't brushed my hair.

"No, thank you," I said. "I'm waiting for someone."

Why had I told that lie? Now, when hours pass and no one shows up for me, he'll wonder why I said that.

Who cares, Lia? Hopefully, you're not here for hours. Once Lucifer comes, you can get on with it and—

A chair screeched across the floor. I jumped.

"This seat taken?" Bob sat across from me.

"What if I said it is?"

"May I ask why you're here? I thought you and Nash were staying out of my way."

"I didn't realize going to a party for a fun night out would be getting in your way."

Bob smiled.

I looked toward the balcony. "Don't you have someplace better to be?" I asked.

"Lucifer isn't coming tonight, sweetheart."

"What? You're lying."

"I'm afraid not."

"Why *not?*"

Bob shrugged. "She doesn't come to all of them, you know."

"So, who will be hosting tonight's *events?*"

"Oh, you're here for the beatings. That will be handled by the Archdemons. I won't be attending myself. Excessive violence is one thing I can have enough of."

I rolled my eyes. *Why did Bob insist on sitting next to me?*

Bob ogled the buffet like he wanted to eat the whole thing, and he probably would before the night was out. He wouldn't care about leaving some for anybody else. Yet, his body was long and slim. *Where did he store it all?*

A man eyed me as he passed, but he didn't ask me to dance. He wouldn't, not with a Prince of Hell at my table. At least Beelzebub warded off any would-be suitors.

"Where are the other Princes of Hell?" I asked.

Bob grinned. "Mammon, Ash, Bell, Lucifer, and I live in the Outer Region. Leviathan and Satan are in the Circles."

"Why are two of you in the Circles while the others are here?"

Bob leaned forward. "Do you really want to know, sweetheart?"

I glared at him. "Yes."

"Leviathan is much too large to enjoy the Outer Region. They live under the waters of the Fifth Circle."

"They?"

"Leviathan is a plurality, genderless."

"What about Satan? I thought that was just another name for Lucifer?"

"All our names are other names of Lucifer. We are her. We are parts of her fragmented soul."

The concept was hard to wrap my head around. All the Princes of Hell were Lucifer in different bodies, each with a different consciousness.

"Satan is in the Ninth Circle, half-frozen beneath a sheet of ice."

"He's a prisoner there?"

"You could say that. Lucifer fears Satan the most."

"She fears a part of herself?"

"She fears parts of herself she can't control. That's why she tore us apart."

The demons on the balcony gathered at the door. I stood. "I have to go."

"And just when I thought we were having a pleasant little conversation."

I marched to the stairs. By the time I reached the top, the demons had paraded inside. Beelzebub winked at me from below. I slipped through the door.

I wandered down the dark hallway. I found a dim corner and hiked up my skirt, pulling my dagger from its sheath. I tiptoed down the hall, keeping my head low. Demons passed, gossiping, arm-in-arm. I kept my dagger at my side, lost in the folds of my dress.

Screams echoed down the hall.

I was close.

I stepped into the room. The demons' backs were to me. I couldn't see over their heads. I pushed through the crowd to the center.

A man screamed.

His arms were gone, leaving only bloody stumps. A demon with curved horns above his brows, sawed at the screaming man's leg with a rip saw.

The howls that came from the man were inhuman, high-pitched wails. His leg fell in a bloody mess, mingled with his dismembered arms.

In the corner of the room, people watched in terror behind the bars of a steel cage. One woman huddled in the corner of the cage. She rocked back and forth probably wishing it all away.

The demons hooted and cheered as the man flailed around, speckling blood on the faces of the onlookers. The demon raised the rip saw and pulled the man's remaining leg. The man wildly shook his head, trying to roll off the table.

I grimaced. *This must be stopped.*

"That's enough!" I stepped forward.

The demon with the rip saw paused. His eyes shot toward me. The room grew quiet. I held up my dagger.

His massive feet were thunderous as he marched toward me. I held my hand out. I was going to throw him back against the room, liberate the people from their cages, and cut into a few demons.

Nothing happened.

The demon's shadow engulfed me. He stood seven feet tall. His body was muscles. The horns curved behind him.

What do I do? My powers weren't working.

The demon reached out. I sank my dagger into his leg. He howled, his massive hand coming down as I yanked my hand away.

Hands held me down. I sliced at fingers. Turning, I cut through the crowd into the hallway. I raced to a door at the end of the hall.

Adramelech stood inside. The new Chancellor of Hell pulled back its lips on its massive mule head.

Run!

But I froze. Two demons shot towards me. They wore ball gowns. Their eyes were black.

"I'll give you a head start!" Adramelech said in her deep voice.

I scrambled to my feet. Fear tingled through me. I had to summon the pain. I might need it. I dashed down the nearest corridor, not sure if the building had a back exit. I could be running into a dead end.

Lucifer might not want Adramelech to kill me, but I had made her fall. I was the reason she turned into a monster. She would kill me if she caught me.

Must get out of here!

I shot down the hallway and hit something hard.

A dark figure stood over me. His eyes were solid black. That demon close-lined me!

I peered down the hall.

Adramelech strode lazily toward me. Was she teasing me or was it difficult to walk on those hawk feet?

I stood.

The demon grabbed my arms, pinning them behind my back.

Adramelech's steps were evenly paced. She took her sweet time about it. But when she reached me, she would tear me apart.

I pushed.

The demon flew against the back wall.

I ran to the nearest room. No one gathered in this room. A table was set with golden dinnerware.

Adramelech burst through the door.

Instead of going around the massive table, I climbed over it, sliding onto the other side and bringing plates and utensils with me. They crashed to the floor.

Adramelech lunged her massive spear at me. "Nowhere to run now."

I glanced around the room. Adramelech blocked the door. I looked up, and dodged the spear as she thrust it at my face.

I can't stay here. I'll die.

Adramelech stabbed at me with the dagger again. I grabbed a plate. The metal glanced off the golden platter.

Adramelech smiled.

I moved around the table, carrying the platter as a shield. I needed to get to the door.

Demons crowded the doorway.

Shit! So much for that.

Adramelech sank her spear into my side. I cursed myself for taking my eyes off her. What was I doing?

Adramelech pulled the spear from my body, and warm blood pooled onto the floor.

I was screwed.

Blood gushed between my fingers as I held my hand to my side. I was more than dead. I was double dead. Adramelech would make sure I ended up in the Pit.

I reached inside me and healed the wound. I couldn't seal it all the way. I needed to focus on getting out of here. As difficult as it was, I cut myself off. Blood still dripped, but the wound was shallower now.

Demons poured into the room.

No way out!

My eyes darted across the room. Floor to ceiling windows lined one wall. I jumped onto the end of the table and ran. I leapt, shielding my face with my arms and using my force-push ability, as I crashed through the glass.

I hurled into the air and fell into the darkness. Before impact, I pushed myself away from the ground, slowing my descent. I still hit the ground hard.

Scrambling to my feet, I clenched my side. I had to find a place to heal up. The blood loss made me dizzy.

Something slammed into the ground. Adramelech. She jumped. She lay in a crumpled mess on the floor.

Crack!

Her neck snapped back into place. Her bones were crackling all over as she got to her feet. Her kneecap popped back into place. Her arm cracked back, bending at the elbow. I watched as she popped and crackled like bubble wrap.

With one final crack of the neck, she smiled.

I ran as best I could with the burning ache in my side. I turned a corner, seeking a place I could stop and hide my wound.

Hide!

I wrapped around a corner and pinned myself to the wall. Closing my eyes, I waited with baited breath. She wouldn't find me. She couldn't. If she did, I was dead.

Crackle.

I raced down the alleyway and into the shadows. Reaching the back of the alley, I stopped. The fence blocking my escape had space underneath. Could I fit?

I jerked my head back.

Adramelech's long shadow flooded into the alley.

I had to try.

Getting low to the ground, I attempted to crawl beneath the fence. I turned my head sideways to make it through. The concrete scraped my cheek.

I pulled myself up on the other side. Holding my side, I ran. I slumped behind a grouping of metal garbage cans.

My breath came in short, rapid gasps. Blood was sticky on my hands. I focused. My parents. The pain. The wound sealed up.

The dress was ruined. Adramelech's spear left a jagged cut in the side. If Caiduc didn't show up, I'd have to walk back to Nash's. I didn't want to do that in a long ball gown anyway.

I stood and ripped the gown where the ragged cut started. The skirt tore away from the top of the dress. I tossed the skirt over the garbage cans.

I looked down. Not bad. My new makeshift shirt stopped above the hem of the jeans. The ends were jagged and uneven, but I doubt any demon would look twice.

The blood was the real problem. It caked my side and stained the hip of my jeans. I flaked the blood off my skin. Good thing I wore black jeans. Maybe no one would see the color change. The skies were darker in this part of the Outer Region.

What I hoped more than anything was that Nash wouldn't see it.

My cheek burned. I reached up and touched the side of my face. The scrape was still there. Huh. I managed to focus my power so well I only healed my side. If I could evoke it as well as I could focus it, I bet even Jiao would give me a gold star.

I sighed. *Guess Caiduc isn't coming.* I couldn't yell out his name. Adramelech might hear me. I tucked my dagger in the sheath around my thigh and walked out into the dark street.

Where was I?

I turned the corner. Lucifer's skyscraper rose in the distance. I wished she had been at the party tonight. I could have made my point in front of her. What could she do to me? She had my soul. She could torture me like she does to the people at her parties. She could refuse to give me a contract.

Shots sounded.

I jumped.

Fireworks?

The sky broke into flashes of light. The light darted down across the gloomy sky of Sheol. In the distance, like shooting stars, the lights soared.

Oh, hell. The angels had come for me.

Twenty

I raced through the empty street and ducked down another alleyway. The angels came down miles from where I stood as I watched their descent, but I had run miles. I was barely out of breath. I burst out onto the street.

Angels and demons battled on the wide, gray street. My eyes swept the masses. I spotted a familiar face.

Nash fought an angel with shining hair and a long broadsword.

Michael!

Michael swung his sword.

Nash backed away from the blade.

Michael flew and landed with a thump in front of Nash. "Where is she?"

Nash dashed to the side as Michael's blade came down. He cursed as Michael bore down on him. He leapt backward. Another angel swung his blade at Nash. He ran his sword through the angel's stomach, and silver blood pooled out.

Michael attacked from behind, but Nash turned to meet his blade.

Nash plunged back into the fight with Michael.

I held out my dagger and sank it between the shoulder blades of an angel. He screamed and tried to turn. I grasped fistfuls of his white feathers. He howled. He burned like a torch.

Michael's eyes anchored to me. He pushed against his sword, forcing Nash back. He marched toward me.

Nash turned and ran through the clogged street.

He was leaving me to fight Michael alone?

My dagger held in front of me, I stood my ground. Let him come. I'll make him fall.

But I doubted my dagger was a match against his broadsword.

"Lia!" Someone pushed me out of the way before Michael struck. I landed hard on my side.

Adrianna helped me to my feet. "Sorry about that," she said.

Michael's eyes followed me like a hungry lion's follows a gazelle.

Feet stampeded toward him.

Michael whirled around.

Nash returned and raced toward Michael with Endbringer, the angel killing staff.

Nash jabbed, and Michael dodged. Nash grinned like a kid pouring salt on a snail. He eyed Michael as the Archangel's face twisted in rage.

The battle became more congested as demons clogged the street. The demons outnumbered the angels three to one, but still the street bled with inky blood.

Demons and angels collapsed in the street. Heat rose from the ground. An odd feeling in the cool air of Sheol.

Nash dashed forward with Endbringer. He thrust, striking at Michael. Michael dodged and swung his broadsword.

Nash jumped back, avoiding the weapon. With the butt of the staff, he jabbed Michael.

Michael stumbled. He grimaced and shot into the air.

Nash leapt to meet him. The staff glanced off the broadsword. Nash dropped to the ground.

Another angel approached Nash from behind. He had a war axe, ready to cleave Nash. I rushed forward, but Nash turned. He pulled back Endbringer and sank the staff into the angel's gut.

Fire burned around the staff where it entered the angel's body. Smoke rose around the wound. The flames continued to burn a circle radiating outward. The angel's mouth opened to scream, but he continued. The flames ate their way through his vocal cords. He became smoke and ash and nothing more.

Adriel fought an angel farther away from us. Unlike Nash, he didn't fight to kill but to push back. His eyes met the angels as if he heard the silent scream. His face paled as the flames consumed his brethren.

Nash turned to Michael.

Michael grimaced. He had two angel killers to worry about. He charged at Nash.

The streets were chaos. Demons fought, fled, and perished. But more demons came. Many of those who clotted the streets when I arrived, bled on the ground. The demons who had "died" would be back, but not for many days and they would never be the same after that. They would feel the pain of their wounds forever and maybe go crazy from it.

A rip sounded, like paper tearing but a thousand times louder. I glanced to the sky. White lights sailed down. Angels hit the ground and stood where they knelt.

Among them was their leader. His light hair was tied back. He carried a staff. His blue eyes held a glint of silver.

He was beautiful, but he was a monster.

I lurched, gripping my dagger.

"Lia!" Adriel grabbed my arm. He pushed me into the alley and pressed my back against the brick wall. "You can't go after him. You'll die."

How could he do this? He was like Nash. "You don't understand, do you? I *have* to do this for Mom and Dad. For me."

"But, I don't want you to end up here." Concern flooded Adriel's eyes. He cared about me.

I grabbed a fistful of his shirt and pulled his lips down to mine. I kissed him as if I was trying to steal his breath. I took everything from him and gave nothing back.

I let go of his shirt. "I might not be able to do that again." I took off, charging back into the battle.

As I approached Raphael, images of my parents' bodies dangling from their seatbelts flashed in my mind. My body warmed with the power flowing through my veins.

He stood with Gabriel.

I raced towards them.

Gabriel's eyes were pinned on me. He rose his silver horn to his lips. Chandra ran forward and busted him in the mouth with her brass knuckles laced in Arcadian Steel. Gabriel's head twisted away from his horn. Silver blood flew from his mouth.

I rushed at Raphael, my dagger raised. Raphael swung his staff, battering me in the side. I fell to the ground and felt like a bull had rammed me.

Too strong.

I gritted my teeth.

Raphael approached me. He shook his head. He was so strong. His face was so beautiful. He placed the blunt end of the staff against my chest and pinned me to the ground.

"You think I would let you get near me," he asked, "knowing your power?"

I struggled beneath the staff, hands trying to push it off me. But he didn't know my power. I reached inside and pulled them out, fistfuls of diamonds. I pushed.

The staff jolted back.

I rolled from under it.

I stood. Raphael was too fast. His staff hit the side of my head. My world fuzzed and wavered. Raphael jabbed the staff into my stomach.

I bent over, feeling like I might puke. Tears came to my eyes. I staggered backward and slumped against a brick wall. My head throbbed.

He's too strong. Adriel was right. What was I thinking coming out here to fight him alone?

But, no, I needed to do this. "You killed my parents," I screamed.

I stood and rushed him.

Raphael flew backward. He stood atop the building across the street.

An angel hovered above the ground. I grabbed him. He screamed as he flew, feathers burning, but I held on despite the heat burning my face. I let him go and dropped onto the flat roofed building.

Raphael grinned.

He moved closer to me with even, unhurried steps.

I held out my dagger, paling in comparison to his silver staff of pure Arcadian Steel.

"I didn't want it to come to this," he said. "But it looks like I'll have to maim you to bring you with me." He swung his staff so quickly I didn't have time to move. The weapon hit the side of my knee, and the kneecap shattered.

I fell to the ground with a scream and dropped my dagger.

He backed away from me.

Pain trapped my mind. All I could see was white as I howled in agony.

But the pain lessened, and my screams quieted. I was healing myself. My knee crackled. It was sore, but not the eye-popping anguish that was there before.

Raphael eyed me from where he stood. He was five or six feet away from where I sat.

I stood, my legs shaky, my knee popping.

"Stay down, young one," Raphael said. "Your purpose is greater than you can comprehend."

"You're a murderer!" I screamed. "The only thing I can't understand is why you haven't fallen like the scum you are!"

Mom and Dad's faces flashed in my mind along with images of us having breakfast, laughing in the car, talking over dinner. And with the joy came the pain, the pain of knowing I would never see them again.

I screamed as the power pulled from me. I threw Raphael forward, barreling towards me, but I didn't move. I wanted him to come.

He crashed into me. I pressed my fingertips into the exposed skin on his face. Heat flared. Raphael cried out. His scream was dull in my ears.

His eyes were wide with terror. His wings burst into flames, ash trailing behind him as my power pushed us through the air.

As we neared the edge of the building, I threw myself from him and rolled across the flat-topped roof. I gasped. My head swam in a mire.

I staggered as I stood, but I had to make sure. I ambled to the edge of the building and looked down. Raphael lay on the concrete below in a mess of bruises and broken bones. The feathers of his wings were gone. Only blackened bones remained.

Breath pushed out of my lungs. I did it. I made the angel who killed my parents fall.

His broken bones would mend, but he would spend an eternity paying for what he had done. In that moment, the permanence of Hell didn't seem so unfair to me.

My leg hurt, but it couldn't be more than a fracture. I was too mentally and physically exhausted to focus on healing it completely.

Screams and the clash of metal came from the streets below. I limped to the other side of the building and leaned over the edge.

Angels and demons fought in a clotted mass, but there was no sign of Gabriel. He must have seen what I had done to his leader and left the fight.

Kiran plunged his blade into the stomach of the angel attacking him. Chandra fought beside Adrianna. Tom held his shoulder as he ambled towards an alley.

Nash jabbed at Michael. Michael dodged, floating inches above the ground. He flew towards Nash. Nash ducked Michael's blade as he swept it over Nash's head.

Nash crashed into Michael. Endbringer barred in front of Nash.

A trail of silver blood ran down Michael's face. Michael was on the ground.

Nash raised Endbringer above him, ready to bring it down into Michael's chest, to end him. But Adriel jumped between them. Endbringer sank into Adriel's body.

"No!" I screamed.

The point of the staff was inches from Michael's face, but it hadn't harmed him. Nash paled.

The fire ate around the Staff. But instead of smoke, light burst from Adriel's body. I looked away until the light dimmed.

I could no longer see Adriel. He was a white torch, the light blotting him out. Two white feathered wings rose from the light and stretched out to the sky. The light was sucked in as if a strong gravitational pull brought it to the center.

The light grew smaller and brighter. Adriel appeared beneath it. His skin glowed. His hair was no longer ashy. His eyes were golden.

In his hand was the Twinblade.

Adriel snapped the iron collar from his neck. He pulled the staff from his body and dropped it to the ground. The light closed up inside him.

Nash staggered back, eyes wide.

The street became quiet. The fighting stopped. The angels turned and kicked off the ground darting back into the heavens. Only Michael remained.

Adriel turned and faced Michael. His newly feathered wings glowed. He tucked them back. Fog curled around the two angels. I leaned over the ledge of the building.

Michael stood, his broadsword in hand. "Welcome back, brother."

Adriel raised the Twinblade.

"Do you want to fall again?" Michael gripped his blade.

"I am doing what is right. You cannot damn someone for her potential to sin, but for the actions only."

Tom had gotten to him.

Michael snorted in distain. "She *has* taken the Grace of our brethren. Can't you see that I am doing what is right?"

They met swords. Adriel pushed his leg forward leaning into his thrust, but Michael held him back. They sparred, matching each other as if each could see into the immediate future. They both knew the rhythm of the fight. They danced along in harmony. If Adriel wanted to win, he had to blunt that melody.

Michael lunged, and Adriel parried the blow with his steel arm brace. The blade clashed against the metal in glowing sparks. He swung at Michael, and Michael sidestepped the blade.

Adriel kicked Michael in the chest. Michael staggered, but rushed to right himself. The blow opened him up for another attack. Adriel swung his blade. It sliced into Michael's cheek, and left a long cut from the corner of his lips to the side of his face. Silver blood painted his jaw and neck.

The demons watched in stunned silence. They had never seen two angels fight before, much less a Seraph and an Archangel.

Michael growled. He rushed Adriel, his broadsword before him. The large sword seemed weightless in Michael's hands. The flat of the blade battered Adriel's head.

Adriel knelt.

No!

The shadow of the massive sword was upon Adriel.

Nash, get up and help him!

Nash rose, staff in hand and raced towards Michael. Michael brought his sword down on the Staff, stopping Nash's pursuit. Nash jerked the Staff up.

Michael kicked off the ground, and Adriel followed him into the sky.

Twenty-One

THE demon downed his drink in the time it takes a mouse to scurry away from a cat. He leaned the cup back and smacked his lips. "You want to know where Raphael is? It'll cost you."

I fingered the coins in my pockets. My drink was untouched, I only ordered it to seem natural. "How much?"

"What have you got?" He wore a tan, leather jacket with a blue shirt underneath. His brown hair was swept back.

"How much?" I repeated. He thought I was another demon like him. The colored contacts covered what I really was.

He grinned. "Show me what you have in your pocket."

I grabbed a handful of coins and slammed them onto the bar.

He spread the coins out. "I'll want double what you have here."

I snatched the coins from the table. "No deal." I stood.

"Wait, wait." His hands were up. His voice was complacent.

I searched the Angel District for Raphael. I wanted to see what had become of my parents' murderer.

The demon waved me back to him. "I'll tell you this for what you have there."

I nodded.

"Raphael is in the Angel District, but you have to search low, not high, if you know what I mean."

I raised an eyebrow. "Thanks." I tossed the coins onto the bar and left.

I put my hands in my pockets as I walked out into the cold street. I'd walk to the Angel District. I didn't want Caiduc to use his energy. His powers were finite, and every time he teleported me, he used some of that limited energy. I didn't want to be responsible for turning him into a speck of smoke. I decided to only use him when I needed to. I could get to the Angel District on my own.

Winks and his twin brother stood at the gates. I was becoming a regular. They opened the gates for me, and I tossed Winks a golden coin to share with his sibling.

I felt a little guilty stealing from Nash, but it wasn't like he would *give* me the money, and I had no other way to get it. Well, I guess I could get a demon job, but that seemed a bit risky even with my shielded contacts.

Following the path to the city, I reflected on what I learned from the demon. *You have to search low, not high.* I looked in the wrong place. Low must mean below as in below the ground. Sheol had a complex sewer system. The Angel District got fairly crowded. It made sense that Lucifer would expand into the sewers.

The music got louder as I entered the city. Demons chained angels up and whipped them. Angels groveled for money tossed on the ground. Angels were forced to engage in lewd scenes with demons.

The first few times I came to the Angel District, I was outraged by these conditions and couldn't look at the atrocities.

But now, I passed and realized I hadn't brimmed with anger and disgust. I still didn't like the practices, but my rage over them had cooled.

There might be a more formal entrance to the sewers, but I was not sure how long it would take for me to find it, I decided instead to seek out a manhole cover. I searched the alleyway and the streets. I found one between two buildings.

Sticking my fingers in the holes, I tried to lift the cover, but it was too heavy. I stepped back and closed my eyes. I focused on the diamonds, the power within me, but was blinded to it. I brought myself back to my parents' deaths. The diamonds were dim, but they were there. I reached for them, but they were difficult to grasp.

The manhole cover lifted and fell, jumping along the edges. I tried again. I evoked the memory, reaching for the pain. Had the pain dulled? But I still loved my parents. Why didn't it hurt so much anymore?

I gritted my teeth. The cover flipped back and hit the cement with a clang. I clamped my teeth together so tightly, my jaw was sore.

Placing my hands on either side of the manhole, I dropped down. I was ankle deep in water. I swashed through it down the tunnel.

Voices mingled with screams. I turned the corner. Angels knelt in the water. One was being maimed by a demon. The demon sawed at the angel's bony, featherless wings. Another drowned an angel in the murky water. Angels hung in chains from the walls of the sewers.

I had to look at them. I needed to know if another one of them was Raphael. But he wasn't there.

I continued down the tunnel. Every second turn or so, more demons tortured angels. I swallowed back vomit as a demon flayed an angel's skin. Black blood darkened the water at the angel's feet, and loud plops of flesh splashed the liquid around him.

After checking for Raphael, I left quickly. My legs were heavy as I walked. The metallic smell in the tunnels made me nauseous.

The groupings of angels and demons became sparse the further I walked.

I stopped.

Chained to a metal grate at the back of the tunnel was a fallen angel. His arms were stretched wide, his ankles bound under the water. His featherless wings were crushed behind him.

He lifted his head as I approached.

Raphael!

His once-blue eyes were black. His blond hair was dull, the color cast in gray. "You." His lips were cracked, and dark blood crusted in the corners.

"Have you come to watch them torture me?" He grinned.

"It looks like they already did."

My parents' murderer chained in a stinking sewer, and my blood was cold. I thought I'd have the desire to rip into him with my dagger. I brought it for the purpose, and yet the longing wasn't there. I *had* killed him. I had destroyed him, and nothing was left to torment.

Adriel was like that.

His Grace had been restored, and he had not returned to Sheol. I couldn't blame him. He didn't want to be anywhere near me, not when I could take what had been given back to him.

"You don't know what you have done." Raphael's eyes stabbed me.

"I've stopped you," I said.

"Stopped me from finding the truth. Stopped me from stopping Michael."

I furrowed my brow. "What are you talking about?"

"You don't know, do you?" Raphael laughed.

"I know I stopped my parents' murderer from closing the gates of Heaven."

Raphael narrowed his eyes. "That's what you think?"

I stepped up to him, my face inches from his. "That's what I know."

Raphael smirked. "I'm not trying to close Heaven's gates. I was trying to start a war with Michael. He thinks he's God. He's the one you should have made fall."

"Why Michael?"

"No one's seen God," Raphael said. "Not Michael, not me, not the damned Prince of the Countenance."

"You were trying to call out God?"

"If there is a god."

Raphael doesn't believe in God?

"Michael lies to everyone. Let me show you."

Was Raphael lying to me? But why? He had nothing left to lose.

"Close your eyes. Take my memories." Raphael's eyes were closed. A long, dark scar wrapped around his neck. Raphael loved humans. He fought with Michael during the rebellion in Heaven. He's never been the same.

I focused, pulling at my powers. I felt like my mind was being sucked through a straw.

Wind whipped around me. I floated in the air. The ground was below the clouds. I looked down at my hands and saw nothing. I was there and yet not there.

Steel clashed against steel.

Michael and Raphael fought in the distance, their wings spread, weapons raised against each other. They weaved and dodged in the wind, the swirling storm beneath them.

Raphael ground his teeth and darted at Michael. His staff glanced off Michael's armor. The thunder roared. The lightning cut the clouds.

Michael swung his broadsword at Raphael. Raphael dodged, twisting in the wind. Staff met broadsword. The angels pushed.

Raphael staggered back. He hovered then darted towards Michael. They met blow for blow, parrying each other. They had trained together, fought together.

But Michael was a liar.

The rage had a utilitarian quality to it. It wasn't pure hate or anger. It was purposeful.

I felt what Raphael felt.

They were locked together, a whirlwind of their own. Sparks lit their weapons. My consciousness was linked to Raphael. When he moved, I moved. I was tethered to him by an invisible cord.

Michael lurched forward and pushed against Raphael's staff. "You're mad. Do I have to try to behead you again?"

What? Michael did that to Raphael? But why?

Raphael gritted his teeth. "I'll shine a light on your lies."

Michael laughed. "You think I'm afraid of a little girl?"

"She'll make them listen. She has the power."

Michael's face screwed up. "She is an abomination."

"And she will be a savior." Raphael pushed Michael away.

"She's arrived. You better get to her before I do." Michael jolted up.

Raphael looked down. Through the passing clouds, a car drove down the road below.

Crash!

Michael slammed into Raphael from above. Raphael fell, unable to control himself in the twisting, violent winds.

I sailed through the air with him.

Lightning struck.

Raphael hit the car like a bullet. His staff sank into the engine. He stared at the terrified faces of Micah and Alexandria Hebert. Another version of me was in the back. Younger. More naïve. And very, very afraid.

The car flipped. I tried to run to them. I could save them. I had power. But I was pulled through the sky.

Twenty- Two

I tapped the desk as the secretary phoned Bob. Her hair was pinned back. I guessed the smile made her jaw ache, but she continued to do it like she was tied to a rope above a pit of snapping alligators and one little frown would lower her closer to the pit.

I sighed. "I've been here three times in the past four days."

"I'm sorry." The secretary placed the phone back on the receiver. "The Morning Star is busy at the moment. Why don't you try again tomorrow?"

"No." I slammed my hand onto the desk. "I want to see her now. We have a deal, and I need to make sure she holds up her end."

"I'm sorry but—"

"I'm going to see Beelzebub." I marched to the elevator. I didn't want to see Bob, but I hoped he was at his post today. He had been absent more and more lately.

"I don't think that's a good idea." The secretary's voice called to me as I pressed the button for the elevator.

"Well, I don't care." I walked into the elevator. The doors closed, and I jabbed the button to Bob's floor.

The elevator lurched up.

I could have asked Caiduc to bring me up to Lucifer. But I didn't want Lucifer to become suspicious that I had a Jinn transporting me around Sheol. I also wanted to limit the number of times I asked Caiduc to do that. He used enough energy bringing me back and forth from Jiao's.

I did what Lucifer wanted. I made Raphael fall. I cringed. He wasn't the one responsible for my parents' deaths. It was Michael. Michael tried to kill me. He was the cause of the car wreck.

The elevator doors opened. I stepped out and walked down the hallway lined with statues of Cherubs.

"Bob!" I called through cupped hands. I walked into the dining room. The table was set but the ten chairs were vacant.

The adjoining room had a sofa and ornate rug. Soft music played throughout the room and the connecting hallway.

I followed the music down the hall. The music grew louder. The hall opened to a room with hardwood floors and white couches. Water fell from a slit in the ceiling into a fountain that acted as a divider.

I walked past the fountain. Bob chatted on the couch with a woman who wore a burgundy red dress. They laughed, holding wine glasses in their hands.

The woman pointed her dark eyes at me. Her red lips smiled.

"Oh, Lia." Bob turned his head. "You like Chopin?" He gestured with his wine glass to the record player on a table in the corner of the room.

"I need to see Lucifer." My hands were on my hips.

Bob smacked his lips. "All business, no fun this one. Opposite of you, my dear."

The woman playfully clutched Bob's arm. She whispered something in his ear, and he smiled. She fielded me with her eyes.

"I don't think so." Bob grinned. "Lia, I don't think you've met Ash."

Ash stood and approached me, offering her hand.

"You said you were wondering where the Seven Princes of Hell were. Well, Ash is one of them."

I took Ash's hand. "You're not really a *prince* though."

Ash's hand grew in mine.

I glanced up.

She was he. His black hair was short and combed back. He wore a white shirt and black pants. "Pleasure." He brought my hand up to his lips and kissed it.

I jerked my hand back. "You . . . you changed." I didn't know demons could Veil across genders.

"I can be whatever you want me to be," Ash said.

"I don't want you to be anything. I just want to see Lucifer."

Ash laughed and looked back at Bob. "Well, technically you're seeing her. We're all Lucifer. But Pride chose the official title."

"Don't tease her, Ash." Bob smirked. "Lucifer doesn't want to see you, sweetheart. You crashed her party five nights ago."

"And who told her about that?"

"Well, all the demons you ran into that night, including the Chancellor. You made quite a scene."

"Lucifer owes me," I said. "I made Raphael fall. Now, she has to let my mother go."

"Is this the mother that sold your soul or the other one?" Bob asked. "I get so confused."

"If you don't bring me up to see her, I might pass along information about your *extracurricular activities*."

"Oh, you learned much from Nash. But remember what I said to him?"

"You don't have anything on me, Bob," I said, "and if you kill me, I'm sure Lucifer wouldn't be very happy about that."

Bob whistled the air from his lungs. "Whoa. Who said anything about killing you? You're dark, sweetheart. You should probably talk to a professional about that."

I narrowed my eyes at him.

"Oh, alright," he said, "since you asked so nicely." He kissed Ash on the cheek. "I'll be right back, my dear."

"I'll change into something nice for you." Although her appearance was that of a man's, something in the way she smiled remained the same.

I followed Bob to the elevator.

Once upstairs, he rapped on the door to Lucifer's office.

"Come in," Lucifer called.

Bob opened the door. "Lia tells me she has information on Azazel that might be of interest to you."

"No, I—"

Bob patted me on the back hard and grinned. *He wanted me to lie for him!*

"Fine." Lucifer waved me in.

Bob closed the door, and his footsteps faded down the hall.

"What about Azazel?" she asked.

"I lied to him." I slumped in the chair across from Lucifer. A desk was the only thing separating me from the Queen of Hell. "I made Raphael fall."

"That you did."

"What about my mother?"

"I think you're forgetting the details of our deal," Lucifer said. "The deal is that you make Raphael and all his *followers* fall, and I'd release your mother's soul to Heaven. You still have quite a list to work on."

I folded my arms. "You can't do it, can you?"

"Pardon?"

I shook my head and let out a short, exasperated chuckle. "I should have seen this coming. You can't do any of it. Because you don't make the decisions. You can't just send people up to Heaven."

Lucifer smiled. "Maybe not."

"Definitely not!"

"Sorry to disappoint, but I've never been known for my truthfulness."

I gazed at her. "You haven't won. I know a way to bring angels back. I've seen it done."

Lucifer's lips curled into a smile. "How do you know it will work again?"

Lucifer didn't know about Endbringer. None of the demons, except Nash, knew what the weapon could do. For all they knew, Nash might have speared Adriel with any weapon. Something else happened that day. Something none of us understood.

"WHO are you? Get out of here!" The man on the bed yelled. He must have been five or six hundred pounds.

"He can see you but not us," Adrianna said.

Tom stood in front of the five of us, chanting in a language that might have been Latin. Ever heard of a demon performing an exorcism?

"So, this demon," I whispered to Adrianna, not wanting to interrupt the exorcism, "it possesses people because it has no mouth?"

"Pretas possess people because they eat through them. Without a mouth, they can neither eat nor drink so they indulge through their hosts. The problem is, they've been denied so long, they don't know when to stop."

The large man tilted on the bed as if he was trying to get up. I felt sorry for him as I watched him struggle.

"Get out of my house!" he screamed. "You filthy hobo."

Hobo? I wore clothes from Nash's closet. I was worried I'd overdressed for a demon hunt.

"How much longer?" I asked.

Adrianna shrugged.

"Get out of my—" The man screamed and grabbed his chest. His mouth gaped open.

His body moved, and a large lump rose in his throat. Long, gray fingers came out of his mouth. They wrapped around the side of his face, pressing down into his cheeks as if something was pulling itself from inside the man.

Nash withdrew his blade followed by Kiran. I held mine, hoping I was ready for whatever this thing was.

A bald, gray head emerged followed by a long, thin body. It fell out on the man's stomach as it was birthed. A thin layer of slimy liquid covered its body.

It looked up. It had big, bulbous red eyes and no mouth. It scrambled away and into the horde of pizza boxes and candy wrappers.

Chandra rushed forward, kicking over the boxes. "Where the hell did it go?"

Nash shoved a pile of clothes aside. A long, thin slit ran down the wall. "Check the rest of the house. Tom stay here in case it comes back out."

Tom closed his book, tucked it away in his satchel, and drew his sword.

Time for a little demon hide-and-seek.

"Is that guy going to be okay?" I asked.

The man's chin was slumped on his chest. Thick drool dripped from his lips.

"He'll be fine," Chandra said. "Having a pretas birth itself from your mouth can be quite an ordeal. He'll come to in a couple hours."

I doubted Chandra or any of the others waited a couple hours to check on the host, nor would I believe they would come back to see if he was okay.

"Lia, come with me," Nash ordered.

Great.

I followed Nash down the hall. Adrianna and Chandra went one way. Kiran took the other. The house was packed with stuff. Boxes and boxes of who-knows-what. Discarded paper napkins, chip bags, and empty food containers littered the floor.

"Did the demon make him a hoarder too?" I asked.

"No." Nash opened the door to one of the rooms and peered inside. "He was probably a hoarder before. Pretas tend to possess people who are loners and already adhere to a particular lifestyle. The preta may have increased his bad habits but it didn't create them."

I checked the door to the right. Nash checked the left.

"Lucifer lied," I said. "She can't save my mother from Hell."

"Sorry about that." Nash looked at me.

"I am too." I checked the next room. "I shouldn't have been so gullible. I was stupid to believe her. I should have listened to you."

Did I just admit that?

"I'm worried about Adriel. Why hasn't he returned?"

Nash frowned.

"What?" I asked.

"His grace is restored. Adriel will protect Michael. He'll think it was God's will."

That's couldn't be true. Adriel would return. He would never side with Michael. But why had he stopped Nash from killing him?

I pulled the door handle, attempting to close it when Nash's hand slammed on the door.

"There," he said.

The demon crawled alongside the baseboards. He crept between piles of trash toward a dirty mattress in the corner of the room.

Nash stepped inside. He rushed for the creature, bringing his sword down. The demon scrambled away. Nash's blade sank into the floor.

"Lia, catch it!"

The demon scurried for the hallway. I threw myself to the ground, grabbing its long, skinny body. It wriggled like a snake. Before it could slip out of my hand, I reached down and grabbed my dagger.

I stabbed the creature over and over again. Black blood speckled my face and arms. I stabbed until all I stabbed was wooden floorboards. The demon had disappeared, vanished to the Pit.

I stared at where the demon had been. Now, it was an inky black stain on the floorboards. "I hate her, Nash."

Nash offered me his hand. "She has become something that should have never been."

Then someone should undo it.

I stared at the vase, but couldn't pull at my power.

Lucifer would pay for lying to me. She got me to do what she wanted with nothing in return. My hands balled into fists.

"Calm down," Jiao said. "You have to summon pain, not anger."

"That's too bad," I said through gritted teeth. "Because I have a lot of anger right now."

"I don't care about your problems." Jiao stood, abandoning her tea on the table. "Focus on the pain."

I could do it if I wanted to. Although I feared years had dulled the pain, Raphael had made my parents' death fresh in my mind. But the anger overwhelmed that. I didn't need to summon the pain. I needed to dampen the anger.

I reached in and found one diamond dim in the darkness surrounding the void. I grabbed it, and the vase tipped, but did not fall from its pedestal.

Jiao stood, a scowl on her face. She held out her hand, and the vase flew against the wall, shattering to pieces.

"You have to stop doing it by accident." Jiao knelt.

I grabbed her arm. "Are you okay?"

"To have power, you must reach for what moves you," Jiao yelled. "You can't let that pain go."

To have power, I had to relive my parents' deaths over and over again.

"How did you do that?" I asked.

"I'm a witch."

"I didn't hear an incantation."

Jiao sighed.

"You have angel magic," I said, slowly. "How?"

Jiao had been hiding something.

Jiao pushed herself up. "Your angel friend."

"Adriel?" I shook my head. "He would never—"

"He needed help," Jiao said. "He was looking for someone. Another angel."

Sydriel.

"That was our deal." Jiao's legs shook. "His blood for my assistance. But it didn't work."

I narrowed my eyes. "What do you mean?"

"Angel blood fights the demon blood. I was a witch before Adriel offered me his blood. Neither of us knew what would happen. I was willing to take the risk, but I never imagine I'd lose everything."

Everything? Did Jiao have a family or did she outlive all her relatives?

"That's why I practice tea magic. The tea acts as a medium to enhance my power. I drink a special tea to make me stronger, but the power still drains me. If not for the tea, I would have no power at all."

If Adriel did all this to find Sydriel, he must have been in love with her. *And Adriel thought Jiao could help if she was like me, but how?*

"Jiao, do you know how my psychic power works?"

"If you try to read my mind, this apprenticeship is over."

I eyed her. "No, I just want to understand it better." *I saw things when I was with certain people, Raphael, my mother, Adriel.*

When I rescued Adriel from the Pit, I saw a vision of a cage and silver blood. Oh, no! Did Adriel have something to do with that?

"You see the memories and feel the emotions of the person," Jiao said. "Very strong psychics can read present thoughts."

"Can the memories ever lie?" I asked. *Maybe Raphael's memory had lied to me about Michael. He wanted me to kill Michael, and that way, it would be easy for his followers to take over Heaven. Perhaps his plot wasn't over. But what's more, it would mean that what I saw with Adriel wasn't true either.*

"Memories cannot lie," Jiao said. "They are easier to read than thoughts because they are more like recordings. Sometimes a psychic can see a memory more clearly than the person who created it."

The man in the room, maybe it wasn't Bob.

Adriel was desperate to find Sydriel. He let a witch drink his blood. If he was in love with her, how far would he have gone?

Twenty-Three

WHO was the man in the room: Bob or Adriel?
My mother killed an angel, and someone helped her to do that. He called himself the Redeemer.

I stood on the balcony overlooking the training field. *The Unforgiven II* bellowed through my earbuds. I had done horrible things. How could I blame Adriel for the terrible things he had done to save the one he loved?

Why didn't it change the way I felt about him? It should, shouldn't it? Maybe I understood him and why he did it.

He didn't abandon me when I made angels fall. I had brought so many angels to that horrible place where they were beat, whipped, and flayed. And yet, he stayed beside me.

Had we both sinned?

But Adriel's sin had been erased. He earned his Grace back. Would he join Michael for fear he would lose it again?

A flash of light streaked the sky.

I yanked the earbuds from my ears, ran from the balcony, and rushed down the stairs. "Nash!" I withdrew my sword, running out onto the field.

The ground rippled beneath me as the angel landed with a thump on the ground. He knelt, head down. The air rushed into my face.

The angel stood. His golden eyes pierced me.

Adriel!

"Lia."

I dropped my sword and stared at him. He was beautiful. His skin glowed, and his hair held its black luster.

The light from the tears in the sky shone down on him. The brightness brought life to the grass which was greener. The tears threatened to rip Sheol like a page from a book.

"Lia!" Nash's voice rang out behind me. His feet slowed.

"I've returned," Adriel said, Twinblade at his side. "I trust you, Nash. I want to help you finish this fight."

"SO, you're a full angel now?" Adrianna asked.

Adriel nodded. He bit into the buttered dinner roll.

I sat next to him. Nash was at the head of the table and Adrianna, Kiran, and Tom sat across from us. Chandra was on the opposite end.

Nash narrowed his eyes at Adriel.

"I thought angels didn't feel the pain of hunger." Adrianna watched as Adriel chewed.

He swallowed and wiped his lips with the napkin. "I don't, but I like food now."

Instead of a dress, I wore a long-sleeved shirt and a pair of gloves. The gloves made it more difficult to eat, but it was a necessary precaution. If I touched Adriel, I'd make him fallen again.

After the meal, we helped Nash clean up. I found Adriel in the library with a book open: *A Tale of Two Cities*.

He looked up when I entered and smiled.

"You like that one?" I asked.

Adriel nodded. "Such unfettered sacrifice. It's beautiful."

Like the sacrifice you made for Sydriel.

"You came back to fight with us," I said. "Aren't you afraid to lose your Grace again?"

Adriel frowned. "You can't kill Michael, Lia. It's wrong. God restored my grace because I protected Michael. It is His Will."

I stepped back. "Nash was right. You're on Michael's side now."

"No," Adriel said. "I'm on your side. Michael can be stopped and still live."

Could he though?

Adriel shook his head. "It's the right thing to do."

"Adriel, did you . . ." I trailed off.

"Yes?"

". . . did you offer your blood to Jiao to find Sydriel?"

Adriel placed the book back on the shelf and bowed his head. "How did you know that?"

"What else did you do to find her?" Tears welled in my eyes. "Were you the one who did this to me?"

Adriel looked at me, alarm on his face. "No, of course not. How would doing that to you help me find Sydriel? And if it could, I would never hurt someone else, not even to help Sydriel."

"You hurt Michael to help me. Turning a little girl into an Angel Killer, won't that be the most beautiful sacrifice."

"It would be your sacrifice, not mine. I would never do something like that. Lia, you have to believe me."

I wiped my tears with my gloved hands.

He reached for me. His hand coming up to caress my face. I jerked away from his touch. "Adriel, no!"

He yanked his hand back. "I don't know what came over me."

"You can't," I said. "You shouldn't be around me. I can undo this miracle, and I don't want to."

I rushed out of the room and up the stairs. Closing the door, I plopped down on my bed. I continued to wipe the tears away, but they kept coming.

"Why are you crying?"

I looked up.

Caiduc perched on the end of my bed.

"It's nothing." I wiped my tears one last time.

Caiduc eyed me curiously. The fur on his chest was missing.

"What happened to your fur?"

Caiduc bowed his head. "I had to let go of my lion."

"You no longer had the energy to maintain your form?"

"Not all of it, no. But I still have my touch of humanity." He tapped his nose.

Caiduc was using all his energy on me with nothing in return. Soon, he would be a single molecule, unable to use his powers.

"Give me your earring." I held out my hand.

"I—"

I gestured more forcefully. "Give me the earring. I'm going to need you, and I don't want you wasting away on me."

Caiduc cautiously brought his hand up to his ear and removed his earring. He placed it in my open palm.

I pressed the needle of the earring into my ear. It stung. I never wore earrings before. Too bad it wasn't a nose ring.

"There," I said.

Caiduc looked up at me. "Are we friends?" He scratched his wrist.

I stopped his hand. "Of course, we are."

Caiduc threw his arms around me. I patted his back. The lion's fur grew between us.

SHOUTING came from downstairs. I peered over the railing on the second floor.

Adrianna pointed a finger at Kiran's chest. "How long has it been going on?"

"This is what I want. You're smothering me. You've always smothered me."

"I gave you everything." Adrianna's lips quivered.

"You gave me a war to lose and a place in Hell," Kiran said. "I don't want to be with you anymore. You suck the life out of anything you touch."

Adrianna raised an eyebrow. "I've been nothing but good to you. You wanted that sword. You won that battle. You know the stakes, the price. I thought we got past that."

"We did. This has nothing to do with that."

"Huh. Really? I don't think that's true." She turned and walked out the front door.

"Damn." Tom walked up to me. "I didn't think he would tell her."

I jabbed him with my eyes. "This is your fault."

"Fault? It has nothing to do with fault. It was doubt. The doubt would have existed even if I did not."

"Do you blame doubt for everything?"

"Yes. Because it is to blame for everything. Indecision is the worse sin of them all. It leads to broken hearts, lack of progress, and failure to survive. That's why animals don't have doubt, only humans do."

I pushed away from the glass railing.

"Have you chosen yet?" Tom asked.

"Chosen what?"

"Between Nash and Adriel."

I narrowed my eyes. "I'm not choosing between Nash and Adriel."

"Because you doubt which would be the better man?"

"Because there's no choice to be made."

"Why are you still here? Raphael is fallen. Your contract with Lucifer is complete, your side anyway. What have you left to do but choose?" Tom's lips curled into a smile.

I parried the blow with my metal arm bracer as Nash swung the long, silver sword down on me. My sword deflected his next blow.

"Lean into your blows." Nash's blade met mine.

"I know how to fight, Nash." The metal sparked on our dull blades.

"Then you would lean in."

I dropped my sword. "Why did you really bring me to this private training session?"

"To train." Nash swung his sword at me, and I dodged, a hair's breadth between me and the blade. "If you insist on staying here to fight demons, you'll train like the rest of us."

I spun, avoiding his jab. I sensed his moves before he made them, not always, but I was getting better. "You still have Endbringer?"

"Why do you insist on talking about the Staff?"

"Why do you insist on keeping it? You have more angels to kill?"

Nash frowned.

I furrowed my brow. "You think the Staff might do to you what it did to Adriel?"

"I'm not sure. The Staff is supposed to kill angels. It's effects on fallen angels may be another matter."

"It brings back their Grace?"

"It brought Adriel's Grace back. There's no telling if it would work a second time."

"Why not?" I asked.

"It might have been more to do with the situation than the Staff itself."

"You mean that Adriel saved Michael?"

Nash nodded. "The Staff would have killed Michael. Adriel stepped in front of him, not knowing what the Staff would do to him. Probably assuming it would kill him. Because of all that, he regained his Grace."

"That's why it wouldn't work again, not on someone who knows the Staff won't kill him. Even if he does jump in front of someone to save him, it won't be a sacrifice."

"Michael will return. He won't allow a weapon like the Staff to exist."

"So, he's coming back for the weapon? That means he's probably coming back for me too."

"He wouldn't find you if you weren't in Sheol."

"Like Raphael didn't find me?" I dodged his next blow. "Angels attacked me in my bedroom. They attacked me at my uncle's house."

"I'll handle Michael when he comes for Endbringer. He can't chase you after he goes against me." Nash ducked as I swung my sword at his head.

"I'm not going anywhere, Nash. You're stuck with me." My blade zinged against his.

He struck down, and my sword dropped to my side. Nash rushed forward, holding me in his arms, his breath was on my lips. "Why are you still here, Lia?"

My heartbeat quickened. It beat against Nash's chest. I became very self-conscious of it. I knew he felt it too.

The world is a cornet, and its music rouses the serpent.

"To kill Lucifer."

Nash pushed me away. I staggered back. Nash held his hand out. A rip echoed behind me. Nash dropped his sword, and shoved me through the portal.

endbringer

THE bar smelled of alcohol and smoke. Demons sat around tables, played cards, and drank liquor. Patrons mindlessly eyed the bartender as he served other customers.

Nash weaved around tightly packed tables and chairs to the back of the room. He stopped at the pool table where a group of demons chalked their cue sticks. One demon, with a cigarette hanging from the side of his mouth, racked the balls. He wore a leather jacket and dark shirt beneath.

"You're gonna lose, Reed." The cigarette bobbed as the demon spoke.

"I want to lose." The demon at the end of the table set the chalk down. A scar ran down his left cheek. "I've already won fifty-six thousand times."

"Fifty-six thousand. Aw, that's nothing." The demon finished racking the balls.

Nash approached him. "Are you Mephistopheles?"

"Who's asking?" Belial inhaled smoke.

"I need information."

Mephistopheles pointed to Nash. "You and me both. But as you see, I have a game underway. Now, if you want to play, maybe we could talk while our partners shoot?"

"Or we could talk while *your* partner shoots?"

"Aw, but see, that wouldn't be fair. You'd be distracting me while the other team would both get to study the table. Maybe shout advice while his partner shoots. This way we're both accompanied."

"I have my partner," Reed said.

Mephistopheles pulled a dagger from his side.

Nash was quick to draw his blade.

But Mephistopheles turned and sliced the neck of the guy behind him. Blood spilled from the wound. "Hep is out. Looks like you need a new partner, Reed."

"I'm not taking an amateur," Reed said.

Mephistopheles patted Nash on the shoulder. "He's no amateur."

"I'll break." Reed dropped his shoulder and walked around the table.

"He'll get over it," Mephistopheles said. "Now, what information do you need?"

"I'm looking for Belphegor."

"Oh, yeah, what for?"

"I came to you for information, not sharing."

"Stripes." Reed lined up his next shot.

"You have to give a little to get a little." Mephistopheles slapped Nash in the chest and laughed. "I'm up."

Mephistopheles used his cue stick to angle his shot. The ball sank into the corner pocket. He managed to sink two more balls before no shots were left to be had. "Bad break, Reed." He leaned back against the wall. "So, what do you say, you wanna tell me why you're so interested in finding one of the Seven Princes?"

"He owes me." Nash took his shot. He landed three balls into the pockets.

"Owes you? For what? Belphegor barely gets out of bed. He's too lazy to ask for favors. That's why he hasn't been home in weeks. Ashmedai has been coming around. She's a looker, isn't she? I mean, when she's not a man. Damn beautiful. Belphegor doesn't want to handle all that, if you know what I mean?"

Nash looked away from Mephistopheles as he spoke.

"You've seen Ashmedai before, haven't you? What did she look like for you?"

Nash lulled his head toward Mephistopheles. "Your mother."

Mephistopheles slapped the wall and laughed. "That's a good one."

"Meph? Are you still in this game?" Reed called from the other side of the pool table.

"Yeah, yeah. Hold your horses, Reed. You'd think this game was the only thing between you and a pretty lady. And with your ugly, old mug, we both know that's not the case. You do know you could have picked any face you wanted, right? Can't understand why you went with the one plastered on you when you died."

Mephistopheles stepped forward. "Oh, man, look at this table. How are we losing this bad, Sal?"

Sal shrugged and grunted. His shoulders were half as wide as his cue stick.

Mephistopheles hit two more balls into the pockets. "That's better." He threw himself back against the wall. "I'll tell you what, you have three shots to win this game. You win, I'll tell you where you can find Belphegor."

Nash unhinged himself from the wall. He popped the remaining two stripes into the pockets. All that remained was the eight ball.

"Don't scratch," Mephistopheles called from against the wall.

Nash leaned forward. "Corner pocket." He tapped the table, indicating where he would put the ball. He hit the ball hard, bouncing it against the rail. It sank into the corner pocket.

"Fifty-six thousand, and one," Reed announced.

Nash tossed his pool stick on the table.

"Good shot." Mephistopheles lit another cigarette. He blew smoke from his lips. "Belphegor is in the Angel District. He figures Ashmedai won't find him there because of his open disdain for the place."

NASH stood outside the gates of the Angel District. He leaned against the side of his car. Belphegor was in the city somewhere. But where would he go?

Nash approached the gates of the city. The twin giants stood at their posts.

"Hey, Nash." Stubs shifted his belt. "Couldn't stay away, could ya?"

Nash smiled. "Meeting someone today."

"Oh, hope she's pretty," Bill said.

Nash laughed. "The pretty ones will break your heart, boys."

"They're all Veils anyway," Stubs said. "You gotta see what's underneath first."

Bill chuckled and punched his brother's arm.

As they laughed, they opened the gates to Nash.

"Have fun with your ugly date," Stubs said.

Nash smiled, shaking his head. Stubs and Bill never knew the truth of why he visited the Angel District so often. He approached the city.

Mist passed through the trees and curled into the alleyway that led to the street. The loud music and bright light accosted his senses. He missed when his senses were sharper, and yet he never became nauseous from the enhanced sights and sounds.

Adriel's Grace had been restored. Of course, it had. Adriel was always the better brother, the more devoted follower.

Nash marched through the streets. Where would a lazy demon like Belphegor hide?

Lights flashed in the sky. Rising above the buildings was a neon sign that read: Double Star Motel. The sign blinked on and off in orange and blue lights.

Well, that would be a good spot to rest for a lethargic demon.

Nash passed crowds of demons hooting at fallen angels as they were tortured and chained. *Lucifer could have put me here*, he thought. *She had more than enough reason to, but she didn't.*

She knew you would hate yourself more that you didn't have an excuse to suffer with the others. Nash cringed. He sounded like Adriel. Always criticizing himself. Maybe he needed to be like Adriel. He had gotten his Grace back.

Nash pushed through the crowd into the alleyway. The alley cut across to the motel. Nash walked inside with his hands in his pockets.

Ornate columns held up the twenty-foot-high ceiling. Red carpet led up to a mahogany desk where the clerk stood, waiting for customers.

The other Princes of Hell didn't have the same taste for modern decor as Lucifer. They preferred the baroque.

Wide, golden arches ran along the side of the main entrance, leading to equally ornate rooms. The ceiling was painted with angels, fully feathered, lounging on clouds.

How ironic!

Nash approached the clerk. "I would like a room, please."

"Of course." The clerk reached behind the desk and produced a key. He wore a black suit, and his blond hair was neatly parted at the side. He smiled. "Can I help you with anything else, sir?"

"When was this place built?"

"Oh, I can't answer that." His voice was breathy and lightly accented. "It was well before my time, I'm afraid."

"I've never seen this place here before." Nash slowly took the key from him, not taking his eyes off the man.

"Oh, of course, you must mean the motel. I'm sorry. The building has been here for ages. It was renovated only recently. The sign was put up only yesterday."

"Why is it called a motel?" Nash asked, glancing at the rich decor. "That's a bit misleading."

"I suppose you're right. The owner's choice, not sure why the misnomer, but I apologize for any confusion all the same."

"No need."

"Well, it seems I already have." The man clapped his hands together once.

"Who's the owner?" Nash asked.

"You know the funny thing is, I don't know."

"Who hired you?"

"A gentleman I met on the street. He called himself Mick."

"How many rooms are in the building?"

"One thousand fifteen including fifty-two suites. Would you like to upgrade to a suite? We have two available."

Nash paid the clerk and walked to the elevator.

"Have a pleasant stay, sir." The clerk waved to him.

This was Belphegor's hotel. A mysterious owner and the hotel popping up only a few days ago. It was the best way for Belphegor to laze about in the Angel District. Extravagant, but not above a Prince of Hell.

Nineteen buttons ran along the elevator. The golden letters next to the second-floor button read: Bar and Lounge. Nash pressed it. *Maybe if I mingle a little, I can find out where in the hotel Belphegor is staying.*

The doors of the elevator opened, and Nash stepped into the open room. A man wore a long-sleeved white button-down with a black, silk vest. He stood next to a rack of black suit jackets.

"Jacket, sir?"

"Please."

The man pulled a jacket from the rack and helped Nash into it. The jacket had silk lapels and fit nicely.

"Very sharp, sir."

"Thank you." Nash walked through the door and into the lounge area. Red curtains covered the walls. A mirror was set into the wall with shelves crossing it. The shelves were lined with amber, green, brown, and blue bottles. Candles in stout glass holders sat along the marble bar top.

Bar patrons talked, laughed, and sipped their drinks. They wore suits and long cocktail dresses.

Tables ran against the walls with four cushioned chairs at each. Every ten feet or so a plush couch was filled with guests who chatted.

Mid-tempo music played from speakers in the corners of the room. Chandeliers hung over the dance floor between the bar and the tables. Demons swayed with their partners.

Nash approached the bar. He leaned one arm on the bar top.

"What are you having?" The bartender wiped down a glass.

"I'm seeking information," Nash said. "I'm looking for the room Belphegor is staying in."

"Sorry, mate. Not allowed to say which rooms our guests are staying in. Especially not a bloody Prince of Hell."

Stupid! Oh course, Belphegor would have told the bartender to keep that information private. *My only chance is to find out from one of the guests.*

Nash scanned the room.

"Hello?" Someone tapped his back.

Nash turned.

"Lia!"

She wore a red dress. Her brown hair ended in burgundy curls. The nose ring sparkled on her left nostril. Her red lips smiled. She was perfect.

I pushed her through a portal. Not very nice of me, but it was for her own good. I can't have her here when I follow through with my plan. She would get hurt. But I should have known Lia would find a way back.

"What are you doing here?" Nash asked.

"Enjoying myself. What about you?" She must have been wearing heels because she was three inches taller. "You want to dance."

"You shouldn't be here."

Lia pouted. "You don't have to be mean, you know. Just one dance. I so enjoyed the one we shared at Lucifer's party." She touched his hand. "Please." Her eyes twinkled. Her features made her an exotic beauty.

Nash gripped her hand more tightly. "Alright." His voice came out in a whisper, but Lia was close enough to hear.

She followed him out onto the dance floor, and he pulled her into his embrace. They swayed. Lia's eyes were on him.

"It's so easy with you," she said. "I wish it was like this every day."

"How did you get back here? Did Adriel help you?"

"Would that make you mad if Adriel helped me?"

"It makes me mad that you didn't listen to me. I shoved you through that portal because you refused to leave."

"Tsk. Tsk." Her hand ran up his arm to his shoulder. "You should know by now, I could never leave you, Nash." Her lips inched towards his. "I just want . . ." she whispered.

Lia's movements were smooth and delicate, and not like her at all!

Nash jerked her back.

"I was going to say *you*, silly." She laughed.

"Ashmedai."

"Oww. I didn't act out that too well, did I? Well, in my defense, I've only met Lia once."

Nash frowned.

"But my," Ashmedai said. "You push a girl through a portal and then you go to kiss her, talk about mixed messaging."

"You were going for the kiss."

"But you wanted it. Be honest, you would have gone for it if you thought I was really her."

"I'm looking for Belphegor."

Ashmedai slapped him on the chest. She still looked like Lia. "Straight to business just like her. You two belong together."

But we couldn't be together. Not if my plan works.

"I'm not telling you that," Ashmedai said. "I came here to see Bell myself. He's been avoiding me for days, and I have something I desperately need to discuss with him."

"I know what Bob is trying to do."

"That makes two of us."

"Really. Do you think gluttony will want to *divide* the power? He's as bad as Pride if not worse."

"You're a real pessimist, aren't you?" Ashmedai put her hands on her hips. "Bob loves me. He wants me to be in power as much as I want him to be."

"How can someone with the power to seduce anyone be so naïve?"

"I think I'm done dancing with you."

"I didn't care to dance. All I want to know is whether Lia is part of Bob's plan."

Ashmedai folded her slim arms, Lia's arms. She smiled. "I'm not going to tell you that, and neither will Bell."

"Belphegor is too lazy to lie."

"Well, good luck. I don't know what you're up to, Nasriel, but if you keep getting in Bob's way, you might lose your head. Whether on Earth or Sheol, that's a one-way ticket to the Pit."

Nash backed away from her before turning to leave the dance floor. He didn't want to turn away from her while she was right next to him. She might plunge a dagger in his back.

After returning his coat to the lounge attendant, Nash jabbed the button to the top floor. Belphegor could be anywhere in the hotel, but Nash guessed he would want to be as far from the other guests as possible.

The elevator doors open. Nash jogged down one end of the hall and peered around the corner. The hallway was empty. Belphegor went everywhere with at least two attendants and a wheelchair. He never walked. He barely sat, but slumped in his chair in a reclining position.

Nash ran to the opposite end and looked down the corridor. Two guards stood on either side of a door at the end of the hall. A corner room, possibly a suite.

Belphegor was in there.

Nash withdrew a dagger. He approached the guards.

"What are you—?"

He elbowed the first guard in the neck. Before the second guard drew his sword, Nash was behind him. Nash slit his throat.

The first guard had caught his breath. Nash kicked him in the gut. The guard doubled over. Nash smashed him in the forehead with the hilt of his sword. The guard fell to the ground.

Nash tried the door. It was unlocked. He stepped inside the suite. Gold trim ran along the crown molding. A painting of people drowsing in the forest was painted on the ceiling. The window was framed in gold curtain. Two loveseats faced each other and a large couch ran along the back. All had red cushions and golden pillows. A white fur was draped across the table in the center. On top was a bowl of fruit and a large flower arrangement.

Across the long couch lie Belphegor. His golden wheelchair sat alongside the couch.

Belphegor was too lazy to Veil himself. His horns jutted out on either side of his head. He had them filed down so they wouldn't get in the way of him laying sideways. His large nose hung over wide lips. His hands and feet were long and his fingers and toes were stringy bits of flesh that seemed to have no bones in them. A tail whipped his face as he snored.

"Belphegor!" Nash yelled, hoping he had no other attendants that Nash might have to put out for a while.

He opened his squinty eyes. Sleep had crusted over them. "Who are you?"

"Someone with questions."

"I don't have time for questions. Time to sleep now."

"This won't take long."

"It's already taken too long." Belphegor slapped a limp hand to his head. The fingers wiggled like jelly.

"One of the Princes has spoken to you about Beelzebub's plan?"

"I don't care about Bob. Let him do what he wants. Let Lucifer do what she wants. I don't care."

"You know the details."

"Details escape me."

Nash walked to the table and pushed it away from the couch along with all the fruit and wine set upon it.

"Oh, now what did you do that for?"

"Tell me one thing," Nash said. "What are Bob's plans for Lia Hebert?"

"The girl? She's nothing. She's nobody. He wants to make her a figurehead."

"A figurehead?"

He couldn't mean—

"Yeah, he says we'll be running things, not that I'm interested in running anything. But she'll have the title."

"What title?"

"Ruler of Hell."

NASH left the Angel District behind him. He locked his glove compartment and removed a key from it. The key came from a ring of keys taken from the demon Surgat.

He parked a couple blocks from Lucifer's skyscraper and walked the rest of the way. He didn't want her to know that he was there. Lucifer had grown suspicious of someone entering her office uninvited. That's why she had installed the lock to get to her floor. *She would have called me out if it was me she suspected*, Nash thought.

Behind the building was a back entrance for employees. Nash put the key into the lock and opened the door. *I must move quickly with my plan. I can't let Bob corrupt Lia like I did to Lucifer.*

Nash curled around the corner to the elevator. The secretary was on the phone. He pressed the button and the elevator doors opened. Key in the lock, he sailed up to Lucifer's floor.

I must make sure things are tied up tight.

The doors opened, and Nash snaked down the hall. He stopped at a door. His eyes darted up and down the hall before he slammed the key in the lock.

Nash stepped inside and closed the door behind him. The only light in the room cast a glow on the one-winged angel stooped over his work.

Nash's hand tightened on his dagger. I could kill him now. That way I wouldn't have to worry about Lucifer finding out.

Nash approached him. I can't do it! Metatron is sneaky. What if he needs to be alive for the Staff to work?

"How does the Staff restore a fallen angel's Grace?" Nash asked.

Metatron looked at his work. "Only God restores Grace, if such a thing *could* be restored."

"I watched it happen."

"You wish to restore your Grace?"

Nash had stood with the Staff poised to his chest and dared himself to plunge it into his own heart.

Nash placed a hand on the staff in front of Metatron. This staff was a fake. A decoy. Nash had the real one.

"You must continue lying to Lucifer," Nash said.

"You promised to get me out before it is done?" Metatron asked.

"If you keep this secret. I'd hate to see you locked in here when it happens. And it will happen. Despite any attempt to foil it. I have others on this, ones you don't know about who *will* follow through as soon as I am captured."

Metatron nodded slowly. "And Michael will be down here when it happens?"

"Yes."

"Then I can sleep at night." Metatron turned in his chair. His eyes were milky white. "I know you're a fallen angel. I can sense it off you. Show me what you were. I need to know if there was ever honor inside you."

Before Nash could back away, Metatron planted the points of two fingers against his head, and Nash's vision went white.

SILVER blood glittered in the sky.

Nasriel plunged his sword, Eternal, into the belly of the angel. Eternal had silver threading crossing the grip. At the pummel was the symbol of the sword—infinity. A set of wings angling down over the hand made up the crossguard. The long, silver blade was barbed on either side in three places: at the base, in the middle, and near the tip.

The sky was bright. The clouds floated far below him. A crystal tower shimmered in the background. The gates of the silver city glowed with light.

A grunt sounded behind him.

"You have to watch your back, Nasriel."

Nasriel spun around.

Lucifer stood behind him. Her long, black hair floated on air. Her eyes were silver. Pure white wings reached to the sky as she hovered before him.

An angel flew from the sky. An arrow between his shoulder blades.

Lucifer held her bow in one hand. The bow limbs were silver with sharp wings jutting out. The tips were like scorpion stingers. *Fatemaker*.

Nasriel grabbed her hand and pulled her toward the crystal tower as their enemies and allies fought in a cacophony of screams and metal.

Nasriel pressed her back to the crystals and crushed his lips against hers. Her lips were warm and held the sweet taste of the fruit of the Golden Gloriosa tree on them.

He pulled away. "We're winning. Michael will no longer rule Heaven under the authority of a false God."

Lucifer latched onto his shoulders. "I will make Michael's little world shatter."

He planted another kiss on her lips. Without her, Nasriel would have never been able to rally so many to fight. The angels looked up to Lucifer, and she could talk her way into anything, even fighting Michael, the Ambassador of Paradise.

Nasriel's eyes darted to the fight.

An angel in shining silver armor rose above the battle.

Michael had arrived.

Nasriel and Lucifer rejoined the battle.

Nasriel darted towards Michael. Anger raged. Nasriel launched himself at Michael, and Eternal met Soulshatter.

"You know not what you do, Nasriel." Michael crossed his sword in front of him.

"I know exactly what I'm doing," Nasriel said. "I am forcing you to reveal God or to admit that you have lied. That there is no God, that you have been running Heaven."

"Lies!" Michael shot forward, Soulshatter pointing at Nasriel.

Nasriel darted to the side, avoiding Michael's blade. He swung at Michael, and Michael dodged.

Light saturated the clouds below them. Colors danced along the clouds, mingling in blue, gray, and white.

"You want to see God. I will show you God." Michael flew at Nash, steel flashing. Nash deflected the blow with Eternal. Michael flew backward, retreating into the sky.

Nasriel looked in the direction he had gone, puzzled. He glanced at Lucifer who fought Uriel, and Nasriel flew after Michael.

Silver blood sprinkled through silver clouds. As they flew the clouds darkened and sparked with lightning.

Heaven . . . He was far from the fight now. Was the tide of the battle turning? Were his followers losing?

Nasriel flew towards Michael. Picking up speed, he drove his sword at Michael. Michael parried the sword thrust with ease, while continuing to fly through the air.

Where is he leading me?

Wind swished below him, the sound of wings.

Nasriel glanced down. Lucifer followed, though her form was distant.

Nasriel darted in the air, ready to bring his blade down on Michael, Michael jerked into the air, avoiding Eternal.

Nasriel sank below the clouds, darting up in a rush beside Michael and striking twice. One strike sliced Michael's arm right above his silver bracer.

Michael continued flying.

He's not fighting me!

Nasriel swung his sword, but Michael only jerked and twisted away from it. He didn't strike.

Michael darted down, pinning his arms to his sides as he dove.

Nasriel followed Michael. He dove into the silver city and zoomed through the streets to a low silver building and disappeared inside.

Nasriel stopped at the building. He walked through the silver archways, his sword gripped tightly in his hands. *Was this a trap?*

He turned the corner. Light emitted from a room and into the hallway. Nash peered into the room and shock ran through his body. He stepped back.

"Nasriel, what have we done?" Lucifer's voice was a whisper behind him.

Michael walked down the sparkling hall, his wings tucked behind him. His sword drawn.

Lucifer's hand shook as she nocked an arrow. The arrow zoomed toward Michael.

With Soulshatter, Michael swiped the arrow, silver body and tip. The arrow clanged against the wall as Michael approached.

Before Lucifer nocked another arrow, Michael closed the space between them. Lucifer launched forward, shoving the sharp edges of Fatemaker into Michael's chest. The steel sparked against Michael's metal chest plate.

She pushed.

Michael ground his feet into the floor.

Nasriel gripped Eternal. He couldn't strike with Lucifer so close.

Lucifer used her bow like a sword, slashing at Michael. Michael dodged, parried, and swung back.

Lucifer deflected his blow with Fatemaker. Michael pushed, and Lucifer staggered back.

Nasriel moved in, swinging Eternal at Michael. Soulshatter met his blade. They struggled.

Lucifer rose, swinging Fatemaker against Michael's back. A long fissure ran down Michael's steel armor.

Michael jerked his arm back, elbowing Lucifer in the face.

Lucifer wiped the silver blood from her lips and rushed at Michael.

Nasriel cut Michael's arm with his sword.

Michael pushed Nasriel away and jabbed the hilt of his sword into Lucifer's stomach. Lucifer bent over, supporting herself against the wall.

Nasriel's eyes latched onto Lucifer.

Michael battered Nasriel's hand with the flat of his sword. Eternal fell from his hand. Michael grabbed the sword, pointing it at Nasriel.

"Without me," Michael said. "They would doubt. God cannot do what man believes, what angels believe. I stand as the only one between tranquility and utter desolation. They can't know the truth."

The secret was too terrible. It was right of Michael to keep it away from the others.

Lucifer looked up at Nasriel. Her eyes were wide and frightened. She had doubt. Fire erupted. She screamed. Her feathers were on fire. Flames burned within her eyes, tarnishing the silver to black.

"Now, you see that what you have done is wrong." Michael sank Eternal into Nasriel's chest. He raised Soulshatter and crashed it down on Nash's blade. The sword broke in two. A piece of Eternal jutted out of Nasriel's chest. Michael kicked Nasriel, sinking the blade into his heart. Nasriel fell.

Nasriel had never felt such fire. The flames burned him deeper than he'd ever known. And he fell through the sky. A shooting star among many. His followers, the Rebel Angels, darted down with him. All burning.

Ash trailed from their bodies as they plummeted. The ground was hard beneath them. Fire cracked below. But nothing could ever be hotter than when his Grace had burned away.

Nasriel stood.

Lucifer held fistfuls of her blackened feathers. "What have we done?" Her hair was ashen. Her eyes black, skin grayed. Black bones hung uselessly from her back. She was beautiful once.

The other angels stood around them.

"What is this place, Nasriel?" Lucifer asked.

"Home." Nasriel looked at his hands. They no longer glowed, but were the same pale gray as Lucifer's skin. He looked over his shoulder. Arched bones rose at his shoulder blades.

The fallen angels around him knelt, begging for God's mercy, renouncing what they had done. Seeing Lucifer and Nasriel leave the battlefield must have weakened their faith. Lucifer's legs wavered. Nasriel would not have her kneel.

He dug his fingers into his wound and pulled the cracked blade from his body. The barbed edges pulled at his insides. Nasriel cringed. The sharp blade cut into his hand.

He breathed a sigh. The blade was out, all he had left of Eternal, not even half the sword.

Gripping the broken blade in his hands, Nash reached behind him. It was awkward, but he managed. He sawed away at his wings.

Lucifer looked at him, wide-eyed.

He continued to saw until the bones fell to the ground. He went to work on the other one. The bones gone, Nash tossed the blade to the ground. "This is what we are now."

Lucifer's face matched Nasriel's resolve. She laughed an ironic laugh. And all went mad.

part three
excision

Twenty-four

I staggered back as the portal disappeared in front of me. Damn it, Nash! I won't listen to you, so you shove me through a damn portal!

No people or cars passed on the dark street. One solitary street light glowed in the distance. Trees lined the streets. A tall, black wall rose on one side, a short chain-linked fence on the other. No sidewalk bordered the street.

A building glowed orange beyond the chain-linked fence, but it wasn't a house. It looked like a school, or maybe a library, but it wasn't anywhere I could go in the middle of the night.

Great! Nash sent me to the middle of nowhere with no phone and no money.

"Caiduc!" My voice echoed into the still air. I turned. The volume of my voice sent a chill down my back. It made me realize how quiet the street was. Silence happens for a reason. I felt as if my voice might rouse a dragon.

Don't be silly, Lia. Dragons don't exist. Or do they?

I walked along the road with my hands in my pockets. *Nash could have at least sent me someplace warmer.*

He should have sent me to a resort or something. *Here, Lia, thanks for all the help hunting demons and making angels fall, why don't you take a break at this nice beach front resort?*

At least that would be something.

I hope Adriel finds out about this. He would come and get me in full body armor of course, so there would be no risk of me touching him. That would show Nash that he couldn't get rid of me so easily. Wait! Did Nash know where he had sent me?

I had to tackle the very real possibility that I wouldn't make it back to Sheol anytime soon. Where was I going to sleep? What would I eat?

Forget Michael. I was going to die from lack of survivor skills.

The chill numbed my nose. How late was it? Maybe I could find a store open at these hours. At least, I'd be out of the cold.

My earlobe itched. I hoped I wasn't getting an infection. I stuck Caiduc's earring through my lobe without any disinfectant. My nose ring was done by a professional, and still my nostril and the left cheek was red and swollen for a week.

I touched the beaded earring that dangled from my ear.

"What are you doing out here?"

Relief washed over me.

Caiduc stood in the street behind me.

"How did you know where to find me?" I asked.

Caiduc approached. "I can always find you when I'm looking for you, but when you touch the earring, it summons me."

"Well, that might come in handy."

"What is this place?" Caiduc asked.

"Somewhere on Earth." I shrugged. "Nash pushed me through a portal so I don't know."

"Why did he push you?"

"He doesn't like me very much."

"I thought you were friends."

"Friends don't push friends through portals." *They don't lie to them either.* "Can you take me back to Sheol?"

Caiduc grabbed my arm.

I blinked against the light.

Around me swirls of green and blue came into focus. Children laughed and swerved between trees. Women powerwalked along the curved trail. Earbuds plugged their ears. People stood in line at a metal truck. A man handed a snowball to a waiting customer from the window of the truck. Birds chirped. Ducks swam on the water.

What happened? Caiduc had to know I meant for him to bring me back to Nash's. But I wasn't in Sheol.

"Miss, are you okay?" A man stood in front of me. His eyes narrowed. "Rachel," he whispered as if he couldn't quite believe it.

His hair and eyes were dark. I recognized him from my memories, my dreams, and the time I saw him from the window as I stood outside my house. *Dad.*

My birth father, Robert Palermo, stared at me like I was the second coming of Christ.

"How did you know?" I blurted out.

"How . . ." he paused. "You . . . you look just like her. Your mother. Rachel, but how . . . where have you been? How did you find me?"

"Why did you leave?" My face tensed and tears were in my eyes.

People stared.

"Let's sit down," Robert said. "We can talk."

"No," I said. "Tell me. I want to hear it from you."

"It was your mother. She took you away from me. I looked for you. But your mother . . . this is going to sound strange, but she saw things, Rachel. Things that weren't there."

"What things?"

Robert looked down. "When I met your mom, she majored in theology, studying religions. But she became interested in demonology."

My mother studied demons! She saw them too.

He gave a short breathy laugh. He swallowed. "She thought she sold your soul to save my life." He shook his head. "I'm just so happy to see you. I shouldn't be telling you this."

"Tell me." The hot sun was at my back.

Robert pressed his lips together. "She did save my life that day. The doctors said because she put pressure on the wound. She didn't say anything until years later when you were born. She was depressed, overprotective. But when you got older, she would read to you from these, books about demons and Hell. I put a stop to it. But your mother, she . . . she couldn't let it go. She was convinced of what she had done to you. Said that I couldn't save you. I reported her, and she ran."

"You should have believed her," I said under my breath.

"What?"

"I said you should have believed her."

"Rachel, no. What happened to you? Where did you get those cuts? Where's Lydia?"

She's dead. But I couldn't tell him that. I felt suffocated.

"Rachel, you have to come with me, okay?" he said. "I'll get you help."

I shook my head. He didn't believe me.

A girl of six or seven ran up to us. A snowball melted over her hand. The syrup dripped onto the grass. "Who's that, Daddy?"

Robert knelt to the ground and spoke to the little girl.

I turned and ran. He shouted my name into the distance. Not my name. *Rachel.*

I stopped behind an SUV in the parking lot and breathed with my back against the car. "Caiduc," I hissed. "I'll find a way back with or without you. If you don't get me out of here, I'll never forgive you."

The parking lot was empty of people and Jinni.

"You heard me?" I shouted.

The earring. If I touch it, he'll appear.

I grasped the beads.

Caiduc appeared between the cars. His eyes glued to the ground.

"Take me back," I said.

Caiduc shook his head. "No. It's not safe."

"Friends don't push friends through portals, remember?"

"It wasn't a portal." Caiduc scratched his wrist. "I want you to be safe. You don't belong in Hell."

"So, you sent me to my birth father?"

"He's your family."

"I don't know him."

"But he loves you. He will protect you."

"I don't need anyone to protect me. You're acting like Nash. You have to take me back. And you don't have a choice as long as I have this." I pointed to the carring.

Caiduc's eyes looked like those of the animals in a ASPCA commercial.

I hated to do this to him. But I needed to get back to Sheol. And I wasn't ready to have a relationship with my father. I don't know if I'll ever be.

"Take me back to Sheol," I said.

"As you wish."

I came out through the water. I stood in a dim room. Light cast my shadow on the door. I turned.

Light glowed around the room's only occupant: the one-winged angel.

Why hadn't Caiduc brought me back to Nash's? Was this another attempt to get me to listen to him? We needed to set some Jinni Siphon ground rules.

I tried the door. Locked.

I couldn't call for Caiduc, the one-winged angel would hear me. Would he tell Lucifer that I was here? Wait! The earring, it would summon Caiduc. My hand reached for the wooden beads, but stopped.

"Who's there?"

I looked over my shoulder.

The one-winged angel had turned. His milky eyes stabbed me. He sat, looking at me. I waved a hand in front of me. He couldn't see me.

"I know someone's there. Lucifer?" He stared. "You have not come to execute me. I will scream."

I put my hands out in front of me. "No, don't do that. I'm not here to hurt you."

"Who are you?"

"I got here by accident," I said.

He considered my words.

Above his head were drawings. The drawings were detailed and depicted images of a staff. *Endbringer.*

But that must mean . . .

"You're Metatron." I approached him, but stayed one or two feet away. What could he be capable of? He had evaded Michael for thousands of years.

Metatron used to be called Enoch. He was the offspring of a human and an angel. A Nephilim.

"What are you doing here?" I asked.

"The Queen of Hell is protecting me from Michael."

That was too selfless of Lucifer. What was she getting in return? The table came into view. On top of the table was a Staff with images etched into the steel. Another angel-killing staff!

Hadn't one been enough. *Not when Nash stole it*. That must be why Lucifer upped her security recently.

"Why is the door locked? That doesn't seem like protection. It seems like imprisonment."

Metatron put his hand on the staff.

I backed away and withdrew my dagger, but Metatron didn't attack me.

His hand rested on the staff. He frowned. "I must finish my work. Then I'll be allowed to go."

So, he *was* a prisoner. Did Lucifer do that to his wing, to his eyes? "What happened to you?"

His sightless eyes followed my voice. "My wing? Michael sawed it off so I couldn't fly to Heaven."

"So, that's why the angels came to the Angel District. They were looking for you. Why does Michael hate you so much?" I asked.

"Because God loves me. He spared me when all the other Nephilim succumbed to Michael's sword."

"Why you?"

Metatron furrowed his brow. "I am destined for great things."

Or destined to be the greatest bull-shitter on the planet. Metatron probably ran. That's why he survived Michael. And he was still surviving but only as far as he could run.

"But if God wants you alive, why does Michael still hunt you?" I asked.

"Michael has been ruling Heaven while telling the other angels that he has seen God, but he hasn't. I saw God, and His face was so beautiful, it blinded me."

"What did he look like?" I raised an eyebrow.

"His visage was so beautiful it cannot be described."

"So, if God knows what Michael is doing, why doesn't he stop him?" I asked.

"God is not in Heaven. Heaven is an intermediary to prepare us for the bliss of true death which will only come on Judgment Day. Nothing here is real. *There* is the only reality."

"Ramiel, my father, gave me this gift."

Ramiel. The fallen Archangel, he was replaced by Phanuel when he slept with a human woman and had a child. That child was Metatron.

"Your father was an Archangel," I said slowly.

The lock clicked. Someone was coming into the room. *Oh, no! I can't be discovered here.* I touched the earring.

Twenty-Five

CAIDUC gripped my arm. I stood in my bedroom at Nash's house. Caiduc let go of my arm and backed away. He swayed. I rushed forward and grabbed his arm to steady him.

"Are you okay?" I asked.

"Dizzy," he said.

"What happened? I thought you would take me straight to Nash's."

"I am sorry." Caiduc hung his head. "I attempted to suppress my magic. It is overwhelming and makes it difficult to focus. You provide me with immense power. It is like two souls are using my earring at the same time. A thing forbidden to Jinni. They can neither have two earrings, nor two Siphons."

I glanced at the clock and squinted. Two in the morning. That can't be right. Time between Earth and Sheol was a little off but only by minutes not hours.

"Caiduc, where was I?"

"You were in-between." Caiduc lowered his head. "I'm sorry."

"What is in-between?"

"When I move you from one place to another, you are temporarily in-between. Time moves fast in-between. I had to keep you there longer this time. I lost control."

"How much longer?"

"Five minutes."

"That's strange. I didn't feel like I was anywhere else for five whole minutes."

"You wouldn't feel it."

A knock sounded.

Caiduc disappeared.

I opened the door. Adriel stood in the hallway. "I knew you'd find a way back." Adriel walked into the room.

I backed away, afraid to touch him. "So, you know what happened."

"Nash can be rude."

"Yeah, rude is an understatement."

"I'm glad he couldn't keep you away." Adriel edged closer. "I don't know what I would do without you." He reached out to me.

"Adriel, don't!"

He grabbed my arm and pulled me into a kiss. He didn't scream. He didn't burn.

His lips left mine.

"Adriel . . . you didn't . . . I didn't."

"Make me fall?" His voice was a soft whisper in my ear. "But you did."

"You're fallen-proof." I threw my arms around his neck.

"Nash shouldn't have done that to you," Adriel said. "Maybe he needs to go away."

"Someone should push him through a portal."

"That wouldn't work," Adriel said. "He could come right back. Maybe we could do something more permanent."

I released him from my embrace. "Adriel, I wasn't serious."

"Nash is reckless. I don't trust him. We could lock him away somewhere. Perhaps send him to the Eighth Circle. At least he can't portal his way out of the Circles."

"You want to send Nash to the Circles? I thought you two were friends now. You said you would help him. Was that all an act?"

"I told him that to appease him."

"You lied?" *Angels can't lie.* Adriel's own words. "Who are you?" The words shuttered from my lips.

Adriel snickered. His white, feathered wings disappeared. His body morphed into a smaller more feminine form.

She wore a long, red dress and burgundy lipstick. *Ashmedai.* A Prince of Hell.

"I am off my game tonight." She watched as her fingernails lengthened to manicured points.

"Bob sent you to turn me against Nash," I said.

"Hardly, I was just having a little fun. I didn't know who to choose though. Are you more taken by the fallen angel or the angel once fallen? Adriel is a bit taller, but Nash's eyes! There's just something about the eyes of an angel who's had his Grace burned out."

I glared at her.

She was Lucifer and not Lucifer. Did she have the same feelings for Nash? No, that would mean Bob did too, and Bob wanted to kill Nash.

"I came," Ashmedai said, "because we want the same thing. Lucifer shouldn't be Queen of Hell."

I folded my arms. "And let me guess, you want the title?"

"No, no." She tossed her hair. "Can you imagine all that responsibility. I have more important things to do. But some people are born leaders. They have powers no one else has. Powers that can make angels kneel."

I narrowed my eyes.

"Your soul is damned. If Lucifer still rules, you will suffer. Maybe get tossed into the Pit. But if you stand up and take her place, you can change things. You could clean up the Circles. Bring color back to this place. You could make it a second Paradise."

"You want me to be Ruler of Hell?"

"I know it sounds bad on its face, but you would change the perception of Hell. Imagine a different, far better place. You could bring your mother to the Outer Region. You could force the angels to bend too. And maybe open communications between Heaven and Sheol."

And see my parents again.

"That's impossible."

"Difficult, maybe," Ashmedai said, "but far from impossible."

"How?" I challenged.

"Do you know why Lucifer trapped Satan under the frozen lake of the Ninth Circle?"

Because she fears that part of herself. Wrath.

"Because Wrath was the real reason she started the rebellion. Michael's lies angered her. Why should he speak for God when she was the most beloved? Wrath destroyed her."

"Sounds like it was mixed with a little envy too. I bet if she ran things instead of Michael, she wouldn't feel as if she slighted other angels who didn't have the privilege."

"Perhaps, but that isn't how Lucifer sees it."

"I don't see how that helps," I said. "Satan is trapped under the ice. In the Ninth Circle."

"But you could get him out," she said, "with your powers . . . and your Jinn."

How did she know about Caiduc? The earring! Had she seen it? I reached for it, but stopped. My hair covered it.

Maybe she had guessed. She had known that Nash pushed me through a portal. She probably was grasping at straws, wondering how I got back so fast.

"I don't know what you're talking about. And I don't know what makes you think I want to rule Hell."

"I'm just giving you something to think about. Someone must rule after you kill Lucifer. Wrath is the one Lucifer fears most. But your willingness to free him depends on how much you hate her."

Ashmedai walked to the door. "I'll be in touch." She disappeared into the hall.

Queen of Hell. Me? I wanted things to change in Sheol, but not enough that I would risk everything to take over.

My mother. Lucifer had her locked up somewhere. What if she tortured her like she did to the people at her parties? Had that happened to my mother? Had Lucifer watched while demons sawed her limbs off?

Freeing Satan. Becoming Queen of Hell. The one thing I did know is that I didn't want my mother in Lucifer's hands.

I touched the earring.

Caiduc appeared.

"Caiduc, please take me to my mother."

"Lucifer has her locked up under the tower."

"Her skyscraper?"

Caiduc nodded. "I can take you."

WATER splashed onto my face. I stood in a dark room. Dim, ember light glowed from a single lantern that hung over a steel door. On the stone ceiling were wooden beams. Cells lined the stone walls.

I stood in the basement of Lucifer's skyscraper, so different from the cold, sterile rooms above.

I walked along the cobblestones.

"Rachel!" A hand reached out from the bars of a cell.

"Mom!"

Dirt covered Lydia's face as if she hadn't bathed in days. Her arms were thin. She wore a rumpled black dress. Her hair was matted in tangles.

"I'm getting you out of here." The dungeon ended in a bare, brick back wall. I stood back. "Take your hands off the bars."

Lydia stepped back towards the wall of her cell.

I focused. Pain, not anger.

The bars of the cells rattled. *Come on.*

The stone walls around the bars crumpled, sending dust down. With a loud screech, the metal pulled away from the walls. The bars crashed against the opposite cell.

The door to the dungeon opened.

Four demons entered. Chains draped across their muscled chests. Dark hoods covered their heads. Besides the hoods, they only wore ragged pants. Red eyes and white teeth glowed from the darkness.

I rushed forward and grabbed Lydia's hand. I touched the earring.

Caiduc appeared.

"Take us somewhere, Caiduc. Somewhere on Earth."

Before one demon brought his sword down, Caiduc flashed us out of the dungeon.

WE stood in a room with yellow carpet and paneled, wood walls. The low ceiling made me feel like a cricket trapped in a box. Light pierced the thin curtains. A single sofa rested against one wall. A blanket had been thrown over it, and a small coffee table covered in papers sat in front of the sofa.

I picked up one of the pages, written in a language I didn't understand.

"Latin," Lydia said. "They're incantations."

"This is where we lived," I said.

Lydia nodded. "I'm so sorry, Rachel. I didn't mean for any of this to happen to you." Her eyes quivered.

"You did what you thought you had to do to save me," I said. "I don't care why you sold my soul. You would have spent an eternity making up for it."

Lydia's smile could collapse at any moment.

"I don't think this place has any running water. Can you still do magic?" I asked.

Lydia shook her head. "Only the living can do magic, the dead don't have the same spiritual energy."

That's why Lucifer was concerned that killing me would take away my ability to make angels fall.

"I have to go back," I said.

"No." Lydia took my hands. "You don't belong in Hell."

"There are things I need to do. I can't stay. I'm sorry."

Lydia's eyes glistened. "You will be safe." She said it more to comfort herself than me. "You were always protected even before you were born. An angel followed you from the moment you were conceived."

I wanted to get to know Lydia. She was my mother, and I was only starting to feel the love I once had for her.

My memory was still fuzzy as if someone was desperately locking them away from me. "Mom, who was the man who told you to perform the spell on me?"

Lydia frowned. "He called himself the Redeemer."

"What did he look like?" I asked.

"It's been over ten years, but it feels like a thousand. He was tall. Dark hair. He looked sad."

"Show me." I clasped her arms and closed my eyes.

Silver blood wet the room. Sydriel lay headless in a large cage. I turned. My mother cradled my younger self in her arms. She cried, hugging me and rocking back and forth.

"Lydia." A man spoke from the shadows.

I tried to step towards him, but I was tethered to Lydia.

"It's time," he said. "You must make her forget."

Lydia stopped rocking. Tears wet her face. She picked up an old book. A single walnut nestled in a glass cup. She removed the walnut and placed it on my forehead as she cradled me in her arms. Silvery blood coated my mouth like a vampire after having a meal.

Lydia chanted, holding the walnut to my forehead. She said the final word and placed the walnut on the ground in front of her.

"Very good, Lydia." The man stepped from the shadows. He had the eyes of an angel with his Grace burned out.

Nash!

I fell to my knees.

Nash approached Lydia and crushed the walnut beneath his foot.

Lydia kissed my forehead. I fell asleep in her lap.

"Now, it's time for you to go where you belong." Nash removed a dagger from his belt and slashed Lydia's throat.

I screamed so hard, tears burst from my eyes.

Blood sprayed onto the face of the young girl cradled in Lydia's lifeless arms.

Nash picked up the little girl and placed her on the ground beside her dead mother, the mother she would forget. He took Lydia from the ground and opened a portal. Her body draped across his arms. He stepped inside, and the portal zipped out of existence.

Twenty- six

M Y eyes ached not from the tears, not from the sadness, but from the anger that rose like hot lightning burning up my body. It was Nash. He did this to me. He killed Sydriel. He murdered my mother.

He is the Redeemer!

I stood in my bedroom at Nash's house. My hands were tight fists. I screamed and tore open the door.

Marching through the house, I searched every unlocked door. I would find him and confront him about what he had done to me.

I stopped at the library.

"Lia," Adriel said.

"Are you really Adriel?" I asked.

"Umm. . ."

"What's my cat's name?" He'd been watching me for years. Adriel should know the name of my cat, shouldn't he?

"Sim. Lia, where have you been? I searched for you for five days. I went to your house, to Jonah's apartment. I came back to see if I could find any clues to where you had gone."

Five days. I was in the in-between.

"What's going on?" Adriel asked.

"Where's Nash?" I asked through gritted teeth.

"He left an hour ago. What's wrong?"

"He did this to me," I said. "He killed Sydriel."

Adriel narrowed his eyes. "What are you saying?"

"He killed her, Adriel. The angel my mother used to perform the spell on me that was Sydriel. He cut her head off. They forced me to drink her blood."

Adriel paled. "No." His voice was a whisper.

I was crying.

Adriel marched past me.

"Where are you going?" I choked on the tears.

"To find Nasriel."

I followed him, unable to speak through the tears. I left the front door open as I walked across the driveway.

Adriel walked across the street. By the time I made it to the road, he was several feet away.

A car stopped in front of me.

"Hello, sweetheart." Bob stared at me from across the passenger's seat. The passenger's side window was rolled down. "There's somewhere I need to take you."

"I'm not going anywhere with you, Beelzebub."

"I'm only trying to help you." Bob wanted me to become Queen of Hell. He wanted things in Hell to be better, like I did. He wanted to kill Nash, the one who did this to me, the one who killed my mother and my guardian angel.

I opened the door and sank into the seat. The car zoomed ahead. Images flashed and blurred. Nash would pay for what he had done.

Bob stopped at the Pit.

"What are we doing here?" I asked.

A crowd gathered around the Pit. Adramelech among them. Lucifer's head bobbed above the crowd. Screams rang through the air.

Lucifer broke the crowd. She dragged someone by the arm. Lydia! How did she find her so fast? Caiduc—he lost control again and kept me in the in-between place where time moved ten times faster. *Five days.* And they found her.

They found my mother. Time moved so fast. My world spun and shifted as if none of this was real. Lucifer pushed Lydia into the Pit.

"No!" I screamed. I tried to open the car door, but it was locked. I beat on the window. "Let me out!" I turned to Bob.

"There's nothing you can do, sweetheart."

Lucifer smiled at me in the distance.

Bob slammed the gas petal, and the car spun a cloud of dust as we zoomed away.

My hand pressed against my chest. Lucifer found her, my mother. I tried so hard to get her out of here, to protect her.

Images blurred out the window in streaks of gray.

I shook my head as tears forced their way from my eyes. She did this to show me she had the upper hand, that she could hurt me in ways I never imagined. She wanted me in line, to be her tool, her weapon. Weapons don't pull their own triggers.

My eyes shot toward Bob. "Did you know about this? Did she tell you to take me here?"

"I can't do anything," Bob said. "She would toss me in there. You in there. She doesn't care about any of us. I want to change things, Lia, but I need *you* to do that."

I growled and touched Caiduc's earring. "You need Satan out of the Ninth Circle? Consider it done."

*   *   *

THE cold air burned my skin. The pain was excruciating. My fingers and arms turned blue then black. I healed them with my power, but the frigid air continued to freeze them.

I had to keep healing, or I would lose function of my hands. Caiduc walked beside me, unbothered by the cold, his skin unaffected by it. He was mostly tree bark. So, that might explain it. Or maybe it was part of Jinni magic. There was only one way a Jinni could *die*. It had to exhaust all its magic and become a single molecule of air.

The ice was slick beneath my feet. Every step made me feel like I was on rollerblades. The ice was blue. The clouds a mix of grays, blues, and violent violets. Riffs and platforms of ice rose above the frozen lake.

Heads bobbed above the ice, the bodies buried below. The faces were blackened. Noses and ears fallen off.

I cringed. Must keep healing. What would happen if I succumbed to frostbite and lost a limb to the biting winds? Could I heal to grow it back? I dared not gamble with that answer.

"Where is he?" I asked.

Caiduc stepped up beside me. "I do not know."

I pushed my hair over my ears to buffer the wind. My ears ached inside, and blood cooled on my neck. This couldn't be good for my eardrums. I'd rather lose my sight than my hearing. How would I ever be able to play music again?

"It's an icy tundra." My breath puffed in front of me. "I can see clean across. There's nothing here."

Few obstacles blocked the wind that blasted into my bones.

"There." Caiduc pointed a branchy finger.

A cave nestled within a tall rift, which looked like it had once been a glacier. I marched towards it. I wanted to free Satan and get the hell out of the Ninth Circle before my fingers fell off.

I tried to push aside my anger towards Nash. I needed to focus on the pain of what he did rather than my anger at him for doing it. The pain would help me focus my powers. It would keep me alive.

Nash was the reason I was here. He led my mother astray and made her turn me into a monster. He took my memories so he could use me in his corrupt game. *To do what?*

Did Nash want to take over Heaven? I'd been looking at Lucifer the entire time, thinking she was the one who envied Michael's position, but Nash put the idea in her head, just like he did my mother.

Nash is greedy for power. He controlled which angels we went after. My hands balled into fists. He made me attack angels who never followed Raphael.

How could I have been so stupid?

Bob had warned me not to trust Nash. I should have seen the signs.

My fingers turned black. *Oh no!*

I tried to focus on the pain, but hatred filled me like water in a plugged sink, left abandoned to overflow.

There wasn't time. I ran to the cave, holding my hands to my body, trying in vain to warm them. I couldn't feel them anymore. But I was hot. I had a terrible urge to rip off my clothes.

Caiduc followed. His hooves sounded close behind me. We were in the cave. The wind no longer rushed in my ears.

The gnashing of teeth echoed off the walls of the cave. A large icy wall separated the cave entrance from the inside. I walked around the wall and stopped.

A pile of frost-bitten body parts littered one side of the cave. Shaking, my eyes drifted to the center.

A demon, lower half frozen in the ice, tossed the half-chewed body of a man onto the pile. The demon's lips, chin, and jaw were bloodied. His head reached the top of the cave. His muscled arms stretched out. He grabbed another screaming man and pulled him in half, entrails dangling from the man's body.

The demon's teeth came down on the man's neck, severing his head.

Satan.

The top of Satan's head was bald. Long, stringy hair grew from the sides. Two massive horns sprouted from his forehead. Blood seeped from around the horns, and the skin was enflamed.

Caiduc hid behind me.

Satan's fingers stained red with blood. The rest of his flesh was gray.

"Satan!" My voice quivered.

Satan stopped chewing. His solid black eyes darted to me, and I felt as if his darkness spilled into me. My skin prickled. I wanted nothing more than to leave the cave.

He tossed the torso he held, and it slammed against the cave wall. Satan growled low and deep.

I tried to put my hands out in front of me, but I couldn't spread my fingers. My hands were dead lumps at the ends of my arms. "Beelzebub sent me to get you out of here."

"Lucifer's lackey." Satan's voice echoed like two voices speaking at once.

"He wants to defeat Lucifer," I said.

"Lucifer." He growled. "She did this to me." With one long nail, he skewered the body of a man. "Beelzebub sent *a girl* to free me from her prison?"

"I'm important to Beelzebub's plan, so you can't kill me. Besides I can't set you free if I'm dead."

Satan laughed. "Not even I could break this ice." The second voice caught up in a harsh whisper. Every sentence was punctuated with a distant scream like Satan had swallowed a woman alive and her cries still echoed from his belly.

"You don't look so good, little girl," he said. "Why don't you come closer so you'll die here, and I'll have something fresh to feast on."

He might kill me, but if I died, I could still rule Hell. I'd be immortal. *Rule Hell?* No, I didn't want that, and I didn't want to be dead either. But I wanted Lucifer dead, enough to risk my own life.

I hated Lucifer. She used me. She was the reason I'd never get to know Lydia. She held my soul in her hands.

The diamonds dimmed. They were translucent. I couldn't grasp them.

"What's wrong?" Caiduc whispered behind me.

"I pushed the anger away," I said.

"Search beneath the anger," Caiduc said. "The hurt is there that fueled wrath."

I focused, thinking about the pain. Sydriel, my protector, dead in a cage, headless. Lydia pouring silver blood into my mouth, choking me. Nash, heartless, watching his plan unfold. Lucifer pushing Lydia into the Pit. Michael throwing Raphael down onto our car, killing Mom and Dad.

I pulled and pushed. I could feel my fingers again. The worse pins and needles ever. I ignored, pushing forward, pulling at the power. The ice cracked.

Satan looked up. Eyes wide. A cruel smile on his lips.

The ice shattered. Pieces lodged into the walls of the cave.

Satan pulled his long, muscled legs from the ice. The cave walls had lengthy, silvery fissures in them where the ice embedded. Satan stood, bursting through the ice.

Bits of the wall showered down like hail.

I knelt and put my arms over my head, shielding myself from the chunks of ice. Pushing them with my powers.

Satan was free.

He turned on his heels and ran across the icy plain. His feet thunderous. His aim Lucifer. He would pull her apart, and her entrails would dangle out.

Twenty-Seven

IGHT blasted through the sky of Sheol. Caiduc walked beside me.

"The scars are bigger," I said.

"More have come." Caiduc scratched his wrists. His eyes quivered. "Michael has come for you."

"You have to take me there."

"Not wise."

"Michael won't stop until I do something. He'll come after me until I die. I must face him. Better to do it now with an army of demons at my back than when I'm alone." *But I can't trust the demons at my back.*

"I am scared," Caiduc said.

"You, scared? Why? You can't be harmed."

Caiduc scratched his wrist. "The penalty for allowing a Siphon to die is be Voided."

"Voided?"

"To have my power vacuumed out of me until I am nothing."

"Your own kind would do that to you?"

"It is the rule. But I do not want you to die. Not because you are my Siphon, but because you are my friend."

"Well, I won't die. Promise. But you have to take me. If I walk, I'll never make it in time."

Caiduc nodded. He reached out a branchy arm.

I came up through the water. My world flashed and burned. Bodies moved around me. I withdrew my sword in time to meet the blade of an angel. I screamed and pushed, throwing my weight into my thrust.

"I can help." Caiduc's voice came from behind. "Teleportation in battle can be advantageous."

"What about the in-between?" I asked.

"That is concerning."

"You have to let go," I said. "You can't be afraid. Let the power flow through you, and don't fight it."

Caiduc touched my shoulder and zapped me behind the angel. I touched the feathers of his back, and he burst into flames.

Heat radiated off the bodies surrounding me. The metallic taste of blood was on my tongue. Only rock concerts were packed as tightly as this.

An angel struck at me. Caiduc teleported me before the blow landed. I slashed the angel across the back and grabbed a fistful of white feathers. The feathers blackened and ash rose in the air.

I sidestepped another strike. I found a rhythm: strike, doubt, zap, grab. I lost count of how many angels I burned.

* * *

NASH'S eyes locked on Michael. Despite the heaviness in his legs, he ran. Michael wouldn't win. No false gods could sway Nash this time. And he had Endbringer.

Michael turned as if he were anchored to Nash. "Nasriel," he hissed. He had a sword in his hand, not Soulshatter, but a long sword with barbed edges. *Eternal.*

The blade was perfect, unbroken.

My sword! How dare he take ownership of my weapon!

With a roar, Nash rushed forward, pointing Endbringer in front of him. Michael swung Eternal, blocking the Staff.

Nash swiped with the opposite end.

Michael jumped back. "You can't win, Nasriel. Your strength has been draining since you fell. You failed to defeat me as a full angel. What makes you think you can defeat me as a fallen one?"

Nash jabbed. Michael blocked.

Eternal danced with Endbringer.

Ash erupted into the sky. Flames sprang from the crowd.

Lia!

She had made it back. Nash should have known she would. He gritted his teeth. *This is bad timing.* But Adramelech fulfilled her part of the plan. Fallen angels and demons from the Circles would march upon the Outer Region. Nash couldn't wait now. It would ruin everything.

Michael looked across the battlefield to the burning spotlight. He pushed off the ground and darted towards the flames and smoke.

Shit! Nash raced towards where Michael flew. The battle was thick, but Nash would kill both angel and demon to get to Lia.

*   *   *

I used my power to strengthen my wary shoulders and liven my tired feet.

An angel launched from the sky and landed in front of me. *Michael!* This is it.

I twisted my blade in my hand.

Caiduc reached for my shoulder, and I was behind Michael.

Michael spun, swinging his blade in front of him.

Caiduc jolted me back.

He swung, and Caiduc teleported me back with each thrust.

The sword Michael wielded was massive with barbed edges. The blade was not the one he usually carried.

Caiduc saved me from another blow.

Michael's eyes locked on my earring. *He knows!*

I pressed forward and swung my sword.

Michael sidestepped me and moved forward. He grabbed the earring and yanked. The beads broke free. The hook ripped my earlobe. I held back the sting with one hand.

Michael tossed Caiduc's earring to the ground. He marched towards me.

Caiduc darted me to the left.

"Caiduc, don't," I said. "I don't have the earring in."

"I have power saved." Caiduc moved me as Michael brought his sword down where I stood.

We danced on the battlefield. I blinked in and out of existence, and avoided Michael easily with Caiduc's help. *Was Michael getting winded?*

I cut his bicep. Silver blood oozed out. As Caiduc teleported me, I made cuts on the exposed areas of his body where his armor was jointed or didn't touch.

Caiduc had lost a large section of his chest fur.

"Caiduc, you can't do this anymore," I said.

"I must," Caiduc said.

"You can't. I want you to go."

Caiduc shook his head.

"Now!" I didn't want Caiduc using up all his energy to save me. I had my powers. I could defeat Michael on my own.

"If that is what you wish. Be careful, my friend." With a frown and a glisten to his eyes, Caiduc blinked out of existence.

It was me and Michael now.

He glared at me and was fast to close the distance between us.

I met his blade. "I know what you did."

Michael threw my blade off his, and I staggered back.

"You lied to the others about Raphael," I said. "He didn't want to start a war with Heaven to keep humans out. He wanted to call *you* out on playing god."

Michael laughed. "Is that what you think, human?"

"You don't want your warriors to know the truth because you want them to side with you. But the truth is Raphael has always loved humans."

"Raphael's love was misplaced." Michael kicked, and the blow landed on my chest.

I fell back and hit the ground, knocking the air from my lungs. I had to summon the pain. I reached for the diamonds, but they slipped from my fingers.

Michael stood over me.

I had to reach. I couldn't breathe.

The sword hovered above me. Michael's arm drove down. Hot metal invaded my chest. I was drowning in the warm blood that invaded my lungs. I could hold on no longer.

I gasped for air.

The sky was gray above me. The clouds moved. *Wind. I'm not in Sheol.* I lay on soft ground. Leafless trees stood around me. The grass was brown and dead.

I rolled onto my stomach and stood. My legs wobbled. Touching my chest, I discovered no wound. I must have healed myself.

The dry blades of grass crackled under my feet. The smell of rotting fruit wafted in the air. *Where am I?*

I walked and found a river. The water was brackish and splashed out on the banks as it funneled down. I followed the river.

What happened? Did Caiduc come back to teleport me one last time? I reached for my earring, but it was gone. Michael ripped it out.

Caiduc. Would he be able to bring me back from this place? Did it cost him all his energy to bring me here?

Dead leaves lined the banks of the river. The grass grew in patches of yellow and brown. No noise except the rushing of the river and cracking of twigs as I stepped. How odd? Not even Sheol was this quiet.

I dreaded the noiselessness.

My legs ached. Nothing changed.

I sat on a flat stone near the river. Water sprayed onto my arms and face. *How long was I walking? Thirty minutes? An hour? Three hours?*

My sense of time was off in this place. I touched the ground, soft near the rock where I sat. I settled down on the ground, the rock blocking my face from the water. My eyelids were so heavy. I drifted as soon as my body touched the ground. Why hadn't I rested earlier? Such bliss! I sank lower and deeper into the ground. Every muscle in my body earned its ease.

RAPHAEL walked among the dead trees. He wore tarnished armor and carried his staff. His blue eyes quivered as he looked around. All was dead and dying. This was not how it was supposed to be.

I was seeing a memory. I stood anchored to the spot, unseen, but all-seeing.

Raphael's wings were tucked back. Dead grass crackled behind him. Raphael spun.

Michael stood with his sword at his side.

"Arcadia. What have you done?" Raphael asked.

"What needed to be done." Michael stepped forward.

"You have played god for too long, Michael. You must be stopped." Raphael swung his staff.

Michael parried the blow with his sword. He bore down on Raphael.

Raphael put his weight behind the staff.

They struggled and broke contact.

Raphael rushed at Michael, staff pointed at his middle.

Michael sidestepped, causing Raphael to run past him. Michael slashed him in the back. Raphael's back arched violently. Silver blood sprayed from the long cut that ran from his shoulder blades down his backbone. The blow had cut the bindings of his chest plate and the metal thumped to the ground.

"You never were the best fighter," Michael said. "You love humans so much it has blinded you to their imperfections."

"God made us to love humans and to take care of them in Paradise. This is no Paradise!" Raphael swiped his staff at Michael's legs.

Michael stepped back, hitting a bare tree. "Those with sin cannot pass through the gates of Heaven. I am doing as God commanded. Humans cannot be without sin." He lunged at Raphael, kicking him in the chest.

Raphael fell back. The impact knocked the staff from his hand.

Michael, sword raised, stood above him. He ran the blade across Raphael's neck. Blood sputtered from Raphael's mouth. His head lulled away from his body. The spinal cord not fully severed, but damaged.

Arcadia! This was Arcadia. It was supposed to be beautiful with lush full trees, sparkling water, and fruits always ripe. Arcadia, the sector of Heaven meant for humans, was dead.

Raphael's body twitched. He was still alive.

But I couldn't be seeing Raphael's memories. He wasn't here. He was in the Angel District, chained to a wall in the sewers.

I looked around.

A woman leaned from behind a tree. Her hair and eyes were black. She wore a long, red skirt. The ends were tattered and caked in dirt. Her chest was bare except for a long, black snake that draped across her shoulders and over her breasts.

I jolted from my sleep. The woman from the memory stood over me. The black snake curled above me.

"You!" I said.

She backed away from me. The snake hissed.

I stood, holding my hands out. "No, it's okay. I'm sorry. I just got here. I don't know what's going on. I'm trying to find some answers."

"You don't remember." The woman cocked her head as she approached me.

"What would I remember?" I asked.

"Your choice."

My eyes darted. *My choice.* I died. That's why I was in Arcadia. Lucifer's contracts. They weren't enforceable. I still got to choose. The contracts were only meant to make people think they belonged in Hell. That way they would end up there because they thought they sold their souls. The deals fueled doubt. Tom was right. Doubt was the greatest of sins.

The Queen of Lies. The contracts were all lies.

And I was dead.

"My name is Lily," the woman said.

"Where is everyone?" I would be damned if the next person I saw wasn't Mom or Dad. I might be dead, but I was with them now. I had to see them.

"Humans are forever in Purgatory," she said.

I stared. *Arcadia wasn't just dead. It was empty.*

"But people are tortured in Purgatory to purge them of sin so they can end up here."

Lily shook her head. "Humans can never be purged of sin. God is angry and imperfect. He doomed us with his imperfections and blamed it on us."

In his image. Humans are imperfect because God is imperfect?

"Then, why are you here? Why am I here?" I asked.

"I hid." Lily petted the serpent's head. "I used to live here. When Michael banished the others, I ran and hid in the Steel mines. He could not find me. Others come, but they are taken away."

"What happened to the garden? Why is it dead?"

"Not enough spiritual energy flows in this place."

My parents. They were suffering in Purgatory because of Michael. As long as Michael lived, he would never allow them into Paradise.

Caiduc would be punished because of me. Because I died.

Could my powers bring back the dead? I reached. The diamonds were gone.

"I need to get back," I said. "I have to stop Michael."

"To stop him?"

"I have power," I said. "I can make him fall. But not like this."

"There's a tree," Lily said. "If you go to it and eat of it, you can come back. But you must be careful. The tree is guarded."

"By what?"

"Cherubim. If they find you, they will bring you to Purgatory. There will be no hope."

"Where is this tree?"

"Follow me." Lily led me to a hill overlooking Arcadia. "There." She pointed.

In the distance stood a tree with rich, sage-colored leaves and small fruits. Surrounding the tree, angels hovered. Their features were difficult to make out from a distance.

"You must go," Lily said. "You must eat from the tree."

I ran through the trees, breaking blades of grass, dried leaves, and twigs under my feet. The wind rushed past my face. I leaned against a bare tree to catch my breath. I made it.

The tree with the sage leaves was on the hill in front of me, but Cherubim hovered around the tree. The Cherubim had four sets of silver wings. The feathers looked more like blades. They held long, silver swords. Their bodies were naked, white, and veiny. Each had four faces: one human, the other an eagle, a bull, and the fourth a lion.

How am I supposed to get past something with four faces?

I needed a weapon. I reached for my sword. It was gone. I must have dropped it on the battlefield before I got here. I withdrew something from my pocket. Bob's MP3 player.

Turning the volume up, I picked a song and threw the MP3 player as far as I could. *Enter Sandman* blared from across the hill. The Cherubim turned towards the music.

I rushed for the tree. The leaves were crisp and green, but the fruits of the tree had rotted. I reached for the fruit.

My body lifted from the ground. Something between a shriek, a squeal, and a roar echoed above me. The Cherub had me in its clutches.

I touched its exposed chest. My power didn't work. I couldn't make angels fall. A dagger gleamed at his waist.

The music still rang out.

I grabbed the dagger and sunk it into the Cherub's side. It howled and dropped me. I landed on the ground with a thump. Adrenaline pumping, I stood and ran for the tree, drums and guitar pings urging me on.

I reached among the leaves and grabbed the fruit. It was mush in my hand. The sour juices ran between my fingers. Worms ate through the flesh.

"Not the fruit!"

I turned.

Lily shouted from the tree line. "Not the fruit. Eat the leaves."

A Cherub zoomed towards her. Lily ran. Another Cherub stabbed me with its eight eyes.

The leaves? Who eats the leaves of a tree? Tea leaves! Void Mortem! The real thing, only found in Arcadia.

I let the fruit plop to the ground. I crushed the leaves into my mouth, taking large fistfuls and chewing. The bitter taste coated my tongue. Steel flashed.

MY legs shook. I stood in a white room, bare except for two columns rising above a set of white, marble stairs, and leading to a wide, silver chair.

"You've grown up so much!"

I turned.

An angel stood before me. Her hair was as silver as her eyes. She wore a long, white dress.

"Sydriel?"

She nodded.

"I thought you were dead."

Sydriel smiled. "The spell kept me alive. My energy gave you the power to defeat angels. I have lived in you. I've been with you always."

The thought was so beautiful. I had been loved always. Even before Mom and Dad found me, I was protected by someone who loved me unconditionally.

I burst into tears and clung to Sydriel's long dress. "I'm sorry for what I did." *For killing angels, for turning to darkness.*

Sydriel's hand was on my head. "You still have the blood magic. Use it to do what is right."

"I don't know what is right anymore."

"You will find it. It's time to let go."

"But what will happen to you?"

Her face glowed. "I will go to my God."

"To Heaven?"

She shook her head. "Beyond Heaven."

I knelt before the Throne of God. My locket and Dad's cross fell against my chest. I screamed as I pulled Sydriel's spirit away from me. Light flooded my eyes.

The penny scent of blood stung my nostrils. The heat of battle waged around me. I picked up my sword.

Michael turned. "What?" His voice carried to me.

I pulled from within me and pushed.

Michael fell to the ground. His sword clattering beside him. He reached for the sword. I focused and pushed it away.

Michael had to be stopped.

He stood. "God is too imperfect to see that Lucifer wasn't His rock, I was."

I marched forward. I tossed my sword to the ground and picked up Michael's.

I have to make it right, all of it. Heaven and Hell.

Michael hovered in the air, ready to dart away, to grab my sword, to fight, to be God's General.

I held out my hand and bolted Michael to the floor. He tried to fly, but he was locked in place. I reached for a fistful of diamonds and threw all my power into pinning him to the ground.

Michael grunted as I forced him to his knees.

God's most perfect angel. He wasn't evil or wrong. He did as he believed God wanted.

The sword was heavy, but I sent power into my arms and lifted the blade. "Now, you will see God!" I swung, cutting into Michael's neck, past skin, muscle, and bone. Michael's head fell from his body.

Twenty- eight

MY shoulders heaved. I dropped the sword and picked up my lighter one. Caiduc's earring lay on the ground. I hoped he was okay.

I pocketed the earring. I would continue to wear it, but I didn't want anyone else tearing it away from me again. Besides, this was no time to pierce my other ear.

Michael's headless body slumped to the ground. *Surreal.* I had killed Michael, Archangel, Ambassador of Heaven, and Commander of God's army. I felt neither regret nor victory. I did what needed to be done. Michael had his mission, and I had mine.

Demons still fought angels, but their numbers dwindled, and the battlefield became sparse.

Three slow claps echoed behind me.

I turned.

Lucifer wore black, steel armor. "Well done." A black bow peeked from above her shoulders, along with a silver staff. An angel killing staff?

"I didn't do that for you." I held my sword in front of me. *This to kill the Queen of Hell.* And someone needed to take her place. I stepped forward.

The ground shuttered behind me. I glanced over my shoulder.

Adriel!

He approached us. "Lia has done what you asked of her, Lucifer."

He spoke with the Devil!

Lucifer smiled. "Adriel, it's been a long time. I expected to see you a little less . . . glowy."

"Are you going to release her soul?" he asked.

"That wasn't our deal," Lucifer said.

"Then, I want to trade mine for hers."

"Adriel, she can't—"

"Done," Lucifer said. "But you'll need to let go of that Grace you just got back."

"Adriel," I whispered. *She can't enforce her contracts. They're lies.*

"I can't live an eternity without touching you again." He pulled me into a kiss. His lips warmed mine. Jolts of joy rang through my body.

When Adriel broke the kiss, confused, he looked at me. His feathers hadn't burst into flames. His Grace did not burn from his eyes.

"I let go of Sydriel," I said. "The spell, it bonded her soul to mine. She's alive, Adriel."

"So, you are of no more use to me." Lucifer drew the long, black bow from her back. She nocked an arrow. "Why don't you run? Give me a good target to aim for."

A shadow loomed above.

I jumped out of the way. A large, gray slug-like tentacle landed between us. The appendage must have been fifty feet high. An echoed screech sounded in the air.

Above the army of demons and angels, a tentacled creature rose. Its body looked like seven snakes conjoined in the middle with seven separate tails. The length of its body was spiked. Its heads each held glistening, sharp teeth. Its eyes were deep impressions. On the sides of each head were two long spikes. *Leviathan!*

The tail moved away.

Lucifer had fallen. Her bow rested several feet away from her. She grabbed the short sword from her side and rushed at me. I met her blade.

Adriel attacked with the Twinblade. Lucifer spun out the way. She fought both of us and pushed us further back into the battle.

I hoped I wouldn't trip over any bodies. Injuries ranged from stabs to missing limbs. It would be a day or at least a few hours before either angel or demon got up again.

I glanced towards the Pit.

Muscled demons grabbed angel bodies and tossed them in.

I ducked as Lucifer's sword came for my head.

Demons fought demons. Cambions jumped onto their assailants and sunk their teeth into their flesh. Furies screeched and clawed. Bob's demons, the ones he had saved just for this occasion: to defeat Lucifer.

*   *   *

NASH ran. He slowed to a jog as Michael's lifeless body came into view. Someone had cut off his head. Eternal rested on the ground in front of the body.

My sword! Nash picked it up and looked over the blade. It was perfect as if it had never been broken.

His sword in his hand and Endbringer on his back, Nash scanned the field for Lia. Leviathan screeched in the distance, their tentacles long enough to crash down on the field. Ashmedai and Bob fought demons and angels. One of Belphegor's attendants wheeled him at the edge of the battlefield. Mammon stood next to him. Lucifer had sunk a few arrows into their enemies earlier in the battle.

They were all here except one. *Perfect timing, Bob.*

*   *   *

I swung at Lucifer. She parried, meeting my blade with her armguard, and matching the Twinblade with her sword.

Time to use my powers. I can do this. I can become Queen of Hell. I reached inside.

"Move aside, sweetheart." Bob carried a shotgun. He blasted a bullet into Lucifer's chest.

Lucifer's armor splintered, shards falling to the ground. Round wounds speckled her stomach. She stumbled back. "Beelzebub!"

Bob kicked her down. "No offense, Lucy, my dear, but you're one bad bitch!" He shot her in the face.

"Chain her up!" Bob demanded.

"Why not toss her into the Pit?" I asked.

"It doesn't work that way, sweetheart." He turned to me. A hand gripped his neck.

Lucifer rose. Chunks of her face fell away. Her jaw dangled to one side. With her other hand, she straightened the hanging jowls. The flesh fused back together.

"Did you think it would be that easy, Beelzebub? Did you think when we separated that I endowed you with equal power?" She tossed him.

Bob rolled along the ground, stopping at a pile of three bodies and a torso.

"Angel Killer." Her voice was layered. One deeper voice spoke underneath. She gestured for me to come to her. Chunks were still missing from her face, but they filled in quickly from the inside out.

I held my sword in front of me.

Lucifer jumped and landed before me and Adriel. "You want to play too, Seraph?" She lunged her blade at Adriel.

Adriel sidestepped her.

I swung my sword, cutting into Lucifer's arm. The cut healed.

She barreled into Adriel, pushing him back across the field. She turned to me. Our blades met. I tried to reach for my power but had to focus on deflecting her blows.

Adriel ran forward.

Lucifer turned and cleaved him in the chest.

Adriel bled.

I sank my blade into Lucifer's back and pulled it out. Lucifer faced me. She grinned. She swung at me.

I dodged, only a whisper of air separating me from her blade.

A growl sounded from across the battlefield. I knew that growl.

Lucifer paled.

The ground shook. Satan trampled on angels and demons on his way to Lucifer. She may not have given gluttony as much power as pride. But wrath was the biggest part of her. It consumed her.

Satan grabbed Lucifer and slammed her to the ground. She scrambled to her feet, coughing from the impact.

She darted away from Satan, but he pursued her, causing the ground to quake with each step.

* * *

NASH turned, searching for Lia. *I must get her out of here before this is done.* More came into battle. Fallen angels with blacken bones hanging from their backs. Adramelech had pulled through. The Chancellor of Hell had one thing left to do.

When he met with her as the Redeemer, he convinced her to demonize her soul to become Chancellor. "If I must be down here," she had said, "I will do everything in my power to bring this place to its knees."

Getting rid of the first Chancellor was quite a job. He convinced Lucifer to toss him into the Pit. "Demons are leaving the Circles on his watch." It was true, but he concealed Bob's treachery. He needed Bob to gather the Princes.

"Nasriel, so nice to see you again." Azazel grinned.

He brought the Furies to this battle as Bob instructed.

"So sorry I stabbed you last time." Azazel moved towards Nash. "You know, I think we could have been good friends. If you weren't so busy starting rebellions, and I wasn't so busy convincing angels to mate with humans."

Azazel's black feathers were molting away. Nash held Eternal in front of him.

"Oh, that's a shame," Azazel said. "I thought we could make amends." He came at Nash with his black sword.

Steel clashed against steel. Feet danced. Arm bracers blocked.

They struggled, locked together.

"You could be on the right side, Azazel."

"I'm not interested in being on the right side. I'm interested in being on the winning one." He fought under the weight of Eternal.

Nash glanced across the field. Adramelech liberated the demons and the dead from the Circles. Horned beasts with Arcadian Steel laced whips, Hades, Cerberus, Geryon, they all came in hordes to fight the remaining angels and the Princes of Hell.

Leviathan screamed above them. They brought one head down to Nash, snapping at him with sharp, wet teeth. Nash leapt away.

Azazel laughed. "I think they like you."

One of Leviathan's tails came down beside them. The tails swept the ground. Nash ran.

"Where are you going?" Azazel asked.

"Leviathan!" Nash yelled through cupped hands. "How does it feel to be Beelzebub's lackey? How does it feel that he was picked by Lucifer over you?"

All of Leviathan's heads were pinned on Nash.

"What are you doing?" Azazel asked.

"Do you think he'll keep his end of the deal?" Nash asked. "To let you rule beside him? You can't even fit in the conference room."

The heads snapped towards Nash.

Nash ran. "Come on. You wanted what Michael had. Now you want what Lucifer has, but you can't have that with Bob around, can you?"

Leviathan moved close to Nash.

Nash neared the Pit. Leviathan brought a tentacle down. Its shadow hovered over Nash. Nash darted away as it crashed down.

"You can't do it with him because you're weak. Even I outsmarted you." Nash gripped Eternal and leapt.

His sword cut into Leviathan's tentacle. Leviathan screamed. Nash used his weight to cut downward. Eternal managed to cut one fourth of the way through. The tentacle dangled dangerously over the Pit.

Nash spotted Lia and Adriel. "Adriel!" he called. "I need you."

Adriel's eyes stabbed Nash. Lia's lips pressed together in a grimace. She said something to Adriel and pulled on his arm.

She touched his arm!

Yet, Adriel didn't fall. He cradled her face in his hands, and Nash had to look away.

Nash hacked into Leviathan, slicing into the middle of the tentacle. Adriel hovered on the opposite side of the tentacle. He brought the Twinblade down into the flesh, hacking away with Nash.

The tentacle slid in a wet, bloody trail into the Pit.

Leviathan screeched.

Adriel flew up and battled one of its heads.

Chandra and Kiran rushed up to meet them. And behind, Adrianna wheeled Belphegor to the edge of the Pit.

Nash scanned. Lia was gone.

*   *   *

ADRIEL helped Nash with Leviathan. I told him let Leviathan kill Nash. I don't know if I meant that. At the time, I did. Maybe I still do.

Adramelech entered the battle with an army of demons from the Circles. She carried something that glowed: her Chains! And the demons who fought with her, some of them carried weapons of Arcadian Steel, Angel weapons, the weapons I had stolen.

How did they get them?

"You killed the daughter of my blood." A demon with black eyes and bleeding gums stood five feet from me. *Belial*, the demon who fed my mother his blood.

I held up my sword and stepped towards him. "I didn't kill her. Lucifer did."

Belial frowned. "But you are the reason Lydia is dead." Belial carried a rapier.

I reached for my power.

Belial flew back. He righted himself again. "You drank demon's blood."

"Angel's blood." I shot him across the field.

Nash and Adriel had cut off one tentacle and one head from Leviathan. They worked on a second as Leviathan's screech filled the air. *I'm sure those tentacles can grow back. They better work fast.*

Belial threw his sword against me. I pushed. Belial staggered back.

He sliced. I healed.

Power zapped through me and out.

Leviathan lost more limbs.

Three demons joined Nash and Adriel. One had the hard body of a scorpion and stinger to match. *Chandra.* The second had a long, curvy snake-like body. *Adrianna.* The third had fire glowing in the cracks of its skin and through its eyes, nostrils, and mouth with long branchy horns growing from its head. *Kiran.*

Power flooded me. It broke behind my eyes. Droplets fell on my skin. Rain in Sheol. And I had brought it.

I pushed. Belial skidded across the dirt.

Give up, demon. You're no match for me.

I jumped, using my power to push me towards Belial. I planted my feet on either side of him. My sword left a pattern of cuts on his chest. As I plunged home, Belial grabbed the blade in his bare hands and pushed me away.

I stumbled back.

Belial was on top of me. He bit into his wrist and forced it against my mouth.

His arm muffled my scream.

"I need someone to replace Lydia. She was beloved." Belial's arm smothered my mouth and nose.

I can't drink the blood.

But I couldn't breathe!

I tasted bitterness at the back of my throat. My eyes popped open.

A demon rushed forward. His eyes were black dots in a forest of shaggy fur. Above his eyes, horns curved backward against his head, covered in thick, coarse hair. Fur covered his masculine body. He was twice the height of an average man.

His long hand swept Belial from on top of me. He charged after Belial as he rolled to a stop.

I blinked. I reached for my power. The diamonds weren't bright. They weren't dim. They weren't there.

The demon faded, morphed into a man of average height with messy brown hair and a long, thin sword at his side. *Tom!*

Tom sank his blade into Belial's chest and sliced him to the chin.

Twenty-nine

L EVIATHAN lost another head to the Pit. Envy's brackish blood coated Nash's arms. Adriel flew above him, cutting into the neck of the third head.

Adrianna wheeled Belphegor to the Pit and tossed him in along with his golden wheelchair.

One down. Six to go.

Another tentacle slipped into the Pit.

"My, my, my."

Nash turned.

Lust walked alongside Greed and Gluttony.

Bob's face twisted into a cruel smile. He held a shotgun in his hands. "Oh, Nash, you couldn't leave well enough alone, could you?" He fired.

Nash dropped to the ground. He gripped Eternal, pushing himself up.

Bob fired another shot, but Nash slid towards Mammon. Mammon held a thin, short dagger. He wasn't a fighter. Nash got around him and cut his throat from behind. Mammon slumped to the ground like a worn doll.

Ashmedai lunged forward with a machete. Nash met her blade with his own. "Elegant weapon for a lady love."

"Lust isn't love, dearie." She twisted away from Nash.

I underestimated her.

Ashmedai swung at Nash. He sidestepped her, kicking Mammon into the Pit.

"You'll pay for that," she said through gritted teeth.

Nash jabbed with Eternal.

Ashmedai jumped, missing the blade by an inch. She lunged. The machete cut into Nash's arm. Black blood spilled over his elbow and forearm, mingling with Leviathan's.

"Oh, did I get you?" Ashmedai ran at Nash.

Bob reloaded his shells. His gun was aimed at Nash. He fired.

Nash pulled Ashmedai in close, her machete sank into his side, but her body shielded him from Bob's shot. Tiny, silver shards embedded into Ashmedai's back.

Nash pushed her body from his.

Ashmedai fell into the Pit. Her lovely eyes stared up into the skies of Sheol.

"No!" Bob shouted. He fired.

Nash stumbled to avoid the shot, nearly falling into the Pit himself.

Bob loaded the gun, popping in two shells and closed the break with a loud click. He shot. Twice.

Nash deflected the bullets with Eternal. Sparks showered him. "You played right into my hands, Bob."

Adriel had cut off another of Leviathan's heads. Kiran, Chandra, and Adrianna sliced at the tentacles.

Bob reloaded.

"Wait!" Lia's voice rang out.

*   *   *

I looked to Bob and Nash. They were trying to kill each other, but didn't they both want the same thing? To stop Lucifer.

"Lia," Nash said, "don't trust him."

Yeah, like I can trust you.

"He's using you." Nash held his hand to his side. Blood oozed over his fingers. He was hurt. "He wants to make you Ruler of Hell, so he can control you."

Says the control freak.

"He sent that Jinn," Nash said, his voice growing weak. "He wanted you to see your mother. He wanted you to hate Lucifer, so you would want to kill her, to take over Hell. He needed someone to do it. Someone to replace her."

Caiduc! "Is that true, Bob?" That's why Caiduc knew so much. He knew my father was alive. He knew my mother was in the Seventh Circle. He knew where Lucifer was keeping her. I didn't question it. I thought the knowledge was a part of the Jinn's powers.

"It's true, sweetheart. I had to do something to convince you Lucifer doesn't belong on the throne."

Caiduc. My friend.

I touched the earring in my pocket. Caiduc appeared. He scratched his wrist. "I am sorry. Friends don't lie to friends."

"You see," Nash said through heavy breaths. "He's been trying to trick you, Lia."

"That doesn't make up for what you did to me," I said. "You turned me into a monster. Made my mom think she had to kill an angel to save me. Nearly drowned me in that angel's blood. I trust you a whole lot less."

Nash's face paled.

"Bob, do what you have to do."

Bob smiled. He clicked the gun shut and approached Nash.

I rushed forward, raising my sword, and sank the blade through Bob's back.

"Sweetheart." He chuckled. He looked back at me. Blood dripped from his lips and stained his teeth as he smiled.

I kicked Bob off my blade and into the Pit.

I hated Nash for what he had done, but I didn't want anyone challenging me as Ruler of Hell. I may have lost my powers, but I was immortal now, and I was ready to take this place.

The large head plopped to the ground. I helped Nash push it into the Pit. Nash's hand still held his side. *If I had my powers, I could heal him. No, let him suffer!*

Leviathan had one remaining head. It lunged, trying to bite at Adriel and fell into the Pit along with the rest of its maimed body.

* * *

LUCIFER tried to outrun Satan, but he was at her heels. She couldn't keep power away from him. He was too big a part of her. That's why she trapped him under the ice of the Ninth Circle.

He was the only one who could pull her apart and consume her. She had turned the corner and headed back for the Pit. She'd have to rely on her army to help her defeat Satan and put him back where he belonged.

She put distance between herself and Satan.

An angel landed in her path. *Gabriel!* He pulled a silver sword from his side.

Lucifer reached behind her back and drew the staff.

Gabriel paled as much as an angel could pale.

Lucifer lunged forward. Gabriel dodged. He swung his sword at Lucifer. It met the staff. Lucifer heaved and threw Gabriel back. She charged.

Gabriel fell to the ground.

Lucifer pointed the tip of the staff at Gabriel's middle.

"Kill me!" Gabriel said. "I will go to God."

"You will turn to dust," Lucifer said. "You will be nothing!" She plunged the sword into Gabriel's body.

It sank into his stomach.

Nothing happened.

The staff pinned Gabriel to the ground, but he was still alive. "It doesn't work," Lucifer whispered.

Her hands balled into fists. I will kill that one-winged half-breed!

She looked across the battlefield, Satan tore through the armies. Beyond him, on the edge of the battlefield, a demon escorted a cloaked figure. A hump rose beneath the cloak. A wing. *Metatron!*

Lucifer wanted to tear off that remaining wing, but Satan's feet thundered towards her. She left Gabriel pinned to the ground.

Lucifer leapt across bodies and weaved between warriors. Over a hundred angels and demons still fought near the Pit. Satan swiped them from his path.

Nash stood at the Pit. *Nash.* Her rock. She'd take his guilty loyalty.

She was before him when Satan lifted her body into the air. "Nasriel!" Her skin stretched. Satan would split her in two.

Nash stood with his group, the hunters, and Lia, the stupid girl who was of no more use to Lucifer.

Nash leapt forward and sank his sword into Satan's belly.

Was that Eternal?

Satan growled and dropped Lucifer. She hit the ground and scrambled from beneath his shadow.

She backed away, pulled her bow, and nocked an arrow. The others all attacked Satan, including the former fallen angel, Adriel, Nash's brother, the one who refused to side with them in the rebellion. Well, goody, he got to keep his wings. Then lose them and get them back again.

When she had a clear shot, Lucifer loosed the arrow. It shot through Satan's temple. He growled, but did not go down.

Straight through his damned head, and he's still standing!

Lucifer nocked another arrow.

Satan's hand came down on the hairy beast and scorpion demon, but Nash was still going strong despite the bloody wound at his side. Even little Lia sliced at the creature's legs.

Lucifer planted her next arrow in Satan's thigh. Adriel flew above Satan's head, and Lucifer didn't want to injure someone who attacked the bane of her existence.

Where was Leviathan? Did that traitor Bob run and hide? This time, she would bury him under the ice with Satan too.

*   *   *

I sliced at Satan's muscled legs. The cuts were shallow though I wielded an Arcadian Steel sword. Satan growled and swung his arms. He kicked.

His leg hit me. The air rushed around me. I landed hard on the ground. The breath knocked out of me.

Nash moved quickly, avoiding Satan's hands and feet. Adriel darted in the air above Satan's head, getting a clean jab when he could.

Satan had lost an eye and had an arrow through his head. He still stomped around like a kid attacking an anthill.

And Lucifer fought with us. She didn't suspect Nash. She was a good shot too. Another arrow went through Satan's remaining eye. But the other was reforming.

Geryon cawed as he flew, plucking angels from the sky.

Cerberus was alive and well, his jowls bloodied.

I stood, rushing back to Satan.

Satan reached for his attackers. Chandra battered his knees with her steel knuckles. Adrianna dug her daggers into his back. Kiran left a pattern of cuts on his chest. Tom sliced his legs, taking over my role.

Satan kicked.

Chandra and Tom fell to the ground.

Satan stooped, scooping Tom into his hand. Satan's left eye was fully formed now. He glared at Tom, took either end of his body, and pulled.

Tom's entrails dangled.

I sprinted.

Nash screamed, digging his sword into Satan's body and climbing up, trying desperately to reach Tom.

Satan tossed the two halves of Tom's body into the Pit.

I fell to my knees.

Kiran collapsed at the Pit's edge.

Nash growled. He sank his blade into Satan's chest, grabbing a fistful of flesh, anchoring himself to the spot as he stabbed again and again. His blade left a gaping hole. Nash reached in and pulled.

He fell back, holding a bloody lump in his hand.

Satan kneeled and collapsed to the ground.

Nash stood. He dropped the lump to the ground. It still beat.

Lucifer dropped her bow and rushed into Nash's arms. Her lips locked on his.

I expected Nash to back away, but he didn't. He enveloped her in his arms and sunk deeper into the kiss.

What?

Nash. He tricked me again.

Adrianna grabbed Satan's heart. Adriel and Chandra dragged his body. Together, they pitched both over the edge of the Pit.

Lucifer pulled away from Nash. "What are you doing?" she screamed. She turned from Nash. She looked like she was ready to toss Chandra, Adrianna, and Adriel into the Pit.

Why didn't she want Satan in the Pit if she was so scared of him? Wasn't the Pit a more permanent solution than the Circles?

"Lucifer." Nash held Endbringer. "Let's see if this will restore your Grace!" He sank the Staff into Lucifer's chest. He didn't wait to see what the weapon would do to the Queen of Hell. He pushed Lucifer and the Staff into the Pit.

 Thirty

WIND whipped through Sheol. It gathered at the Pit as if it wanted to push everything inside. I knelt and picked up a sharp tooth, Leviathan's.

Nash turned to me. "I'm sorry, Lia."

The wind rushed in my ears. "Nash, what did you do?"

"I had to do this. I had to fix what I did."

"The rebellion."

"I saw him. Michael showed me God. He was weak and imperfect. Not fit to lead us. His creation was imperfect, none belonged in Heaven. But that was wrong. I was wrong for believing him. I don't think now, that who he showed me was God."

I shook my head.

"I don't know if there is a God." The wind tore at Nash's clothes. "What Lucifer created was too terrible. I did love her once. But what I did to her soul created a monster. And I had to stop her. I know what I did to you was cruel. Unforgivable. But I needed something big to distract Lucifer, to gather an army, and to bring Michael to Sheol."

I looked down at Leviathan's tooth, the only part of Lucifer left.

"You have to throw it into the Pit," Nash said. "End this, Lia."

I died and found out Mom and Dad were being kept from Paradise. They were suffering an eternity in Purgatory like the people in the Circles. That's what Nash tried to fix so no one else would suffer. His methods were wrong, but how far would I have gone to stop the injustices in Heaven. I was willing to become Queen of Hell just to stop Lucifer myself.

"Nash, what did you do?" I clung to his shirt.

"Hell cannot be without its creator. Sheol was built around Lucifer, and now, it will follow her."

My eyes quivered. "What does that mean?" My hand clenched the tooth.

"It's up to you now." He looked down at the last remnant, the final piece of the puzzle.

If I throw it into the Pit, I won't become Queen of Hell. There would be no Hell. It would fix Nash's mistake, the thing that haunted him in his dreams, the reason he couldn't sleep. He had lied to me, but could I trust that he tried to do the right thing?

I walked to the Pit and with tears in my eyes, I tossed the tooth into the abyss. The winds twisted around me.

Nash turned me in his embrace. "You have what I didn't have: Faith."

He spoke without looking away from me. "Adriel, she's all yours now. There's just one thing I need to do first." He pressed his lips to mine. My hands were in fists against his back. He looked at Adriel. "Sorry, but not sorry."

I hated him and loved him. And I wanted only one of those to be true. But most of all I wanted to understand what he had done and why he had done it. But I couldn't comprehend eternity the way Nash did.

I might never understand his sacrifices and what he forced others to sacrifice to fix what should have never been.

"Nash, I can carry you too," Adriel said.

Nash glanced at Chandra, Kiran, and Adrianna. He slapped Adriel's shoulder. "No, you can't. Not all of us."

"I'm not going anywhere," I said. "Nash, you can't do this."

"I already have. Adriel, fly her out of here, for God's sake. You're her guardian angel."

Adriel took me in his arms.

"No," I whispered, but my voice was lost on the winds.

Adriel flew, fighting against the gales. Nash was a dot in the distance. We headed for the scars in the sky of Sheol, but the pull increased.

The winds ripped Adriel's feathers from his wings. He couldn't fight the growing gravity. The Pit was pulling us in, pulling towards Lucifer.

A horn sounded. Gabriel's horn. The shrill sound bit into my eardrums. I screamed. The horn blared again.

Adriel looked down. He said something, but I couldn't hear it. Blood dripped hot from my ears.

No. Was Caiduc still down there? He had worked for Bob, but I couldn't let him die. He was my friend. Despite Bob's orders, he had saved me. I reached into my pocket. I fumbled for the earring, but my hands shook. I grabbed the metal hook. The wind tore the earring from my fingers. I hadn't touched the beads.

Tears erupted from my eyes as the wind bit at my face.

Adriel struggled to fly, but he tossed on the wind, getting sucked in.

Below, Sheol pulled into the Pit as if it was a vacuum. Hell caved in on itself.

Branchy arms touched my shoulders. I came up through the water.

epilogue

HE police found me, wandering the streets of Mid-City. My stomach clenched, and my eyelids drooped. Tears left clean trails through the ash on my face.

I got into the back of the police cruiser without saying a word. The officers tried talking to me, but I couldn't hear what they said.

They brought me to the hospital. After scans, tests, and examinations, a doctor came in and asked me questions about what happened to me. He wrote his questions on a handheld white board in black marker.

I didn't know how to answer them.

How long have you been deaf?

"Only today."

Uncle Jonah rushed into the room. He hugged me. He leaned down, saying something to me. The doctor tapped his shoulder. He talked with Jonah, I heard none of it.

Jonah shook his head.

He brought me to his apartment. I was eighteen. Family services couldn't put me in foster care.

Jonah put his arm across my shoulders as he guided me to the living room.

I stopped.

A painting hung on the wall above the sofa. The angel was bearing down on the Devil. Both were surrounded by flames. My eyes darted to Jonah's.

"That's Dad's painting."

Jonah nodded.

It was supposed to go to a gallery in the city. I saw the painting right before I saw the real thing. "Take it down," I said.

Jonah's hand squeezed my shoulder.

"Take it down!" I screamed.

Jonah sat me down on the couch and covered me with a blanket. I was shaking, but not from the cold. He sat beside me, talking, mouthing words slowly.

"Where. Were. You?"

I shook my head.

Jonah left the room and returned with a few sheets of loose paper and a pen. He turned the paper over and wrote on the back. *What happened to you?*

"Did the doctors say when my hearing will come back?"

Jonah tapped the paper with the pen. *What happened to you?*

"What did they say?"

Jonah jabbed the paper.

"Tell me when I'll get my hearing back!"

Jonah sighed. He crumpled the first sheet and threw it on the ground. He wrote on the second sheet and held it up for me to see. *The doctor said it might have been an untreated ear infection. They said it may be permanent.*

I shook my head.

Jonah nodded. "What. Happened. To. You?"

I'm deaf.

Silence mingled with dry heaves and evenly spaced foghorn sounds. But the sounds were only in my head.

I slapped the papers out of his hands. They scattered onto the floor.

I couldn't hear. All my music was gone. I locked myself in the bathroom and fell asleep in the tub.

Jonah left for work the next morning. I sat in the apartment, screaming Caiduc's name. Had he used all his energy to save me?

I spent my days watching the streets. I looked out for angels, demons, anything that could connect me back to Caiduc or Adriel or Nash. But the gravity of the Pit was so strong, Adriel and Nash couldn't have possibly made it out.

Jonah and I sat at the dinner table. He came home from work early to spend time with me. Jonah looked at me. He stopped mid-chew and swallowed.

He reached for me and grabbed the cross of Dad's necklace. "Where. Did. You. Get. This?"

I snatched the cross from his hands and tucked it into my shirt.

Jonah planted his hands on the table and pushed himself up. He gathered a few sheets of paper from the floor. He wrote: Someone stole that necklace from Micah's grave. The police said someone dug at the dirt with their bare hands. Was that you, Lia?

I narrowed my eyes and shook my head.

Jonah shoved the pages aside and took his plate into the kitchen. He scraped what was left of his fried rice and sesame chicken into the garbage.

Jonah started coming home late. He skipped work a few times and wore the same stained shirt for three days. He became jittery and unfocused. Other times, his eyes were wide and bloodshot.

I discovered a spoon and needles in his room along with several bottles of prescription meds. I wanted to confront him about it, but it was difficult to have a conversation because I couldn't hear what he was saying. I had to say something though.

On nights when Jonah didn't come home, I rocked on the sofa and played the songs I knew in my head. It wasn't the same, but it was something. The silence unnerved me.

The apartment shook as Jonah slammed the front door. He didn't stop to talk to me. He probably thought it was pointless.

His back was to me as he walked into the hallway to his room. My breath caught.

On his back was a skinny, gray-skinned demon. It whispered in his ear as it held itself up by his shoulder.

That night, I crept into Jonah's room. The light from the hall glowed a line through the demon, right over one of its red eyes. A cruel smile was on its lips. The demon wanted me to see it.

It whispered things to Jonah. It wanted him to do things, things that were destroying his life.

I stepped into the room, kitchen knife in hand.

The demon scurried from the bed and across the floor. It darted into the hallway.

I threw myself on top of it and stabbed it with the knife. Where would it go once I killed it? Not Sheol. Hell no longer existed. The few demons who survived the Pit remained on Earth, and I would find them.

I sank the knife into the creature again and again. So much blood spilled on the floor, so much blood for such a small demon.

I didn't see Jonah after that. Where had he gone? Had another demon latched onto him?

The demon I killed days ago was still there. *Its body stinks.* I would have buried it, only Jonah doesn't have a backyard.

When I see the demons, I kill them. My hands are dyed with black blood like ink stains. I can no longer hear their screams. When I'm killing them, my thoughts are as silent as their shrieks.

The world is a broken guitar, and its music is silence.

I couldn't hear the sirens, but I could see their lights flashing blue and red. They took me away in handcuffs and locked me in a padded room, but I'm not crazy.

Have you been living under a bridge?

No, I've been living in Sheol. I've been through Hell. But Hell doesn't exist anymore. You're welcome.

Mad World plays in my head.

I can't live forever like this, without my hearing. And I will live forever. I ate Void Mortem in Arcadia. I sacrificed an eternity with my parents to kill Michael. I still had some leaves crushed into the pockets of my jeans.

I will get some money and buy a ticket to Fengdu, China. I'll visit a little tea house and offer the real Void Mortem to its owner in exchange for healing teas. I'll get my hearing back. And the next thing I will do is find a way to check up on things in Heaven. The angels better have let Mom and Dad in, or they will have to deal with me.

Please enjoy this extended excerpt of
The Elementals Trilogy

THE ELEMENTALS

L. M. PERALTA

Now available in Kindle and paperback

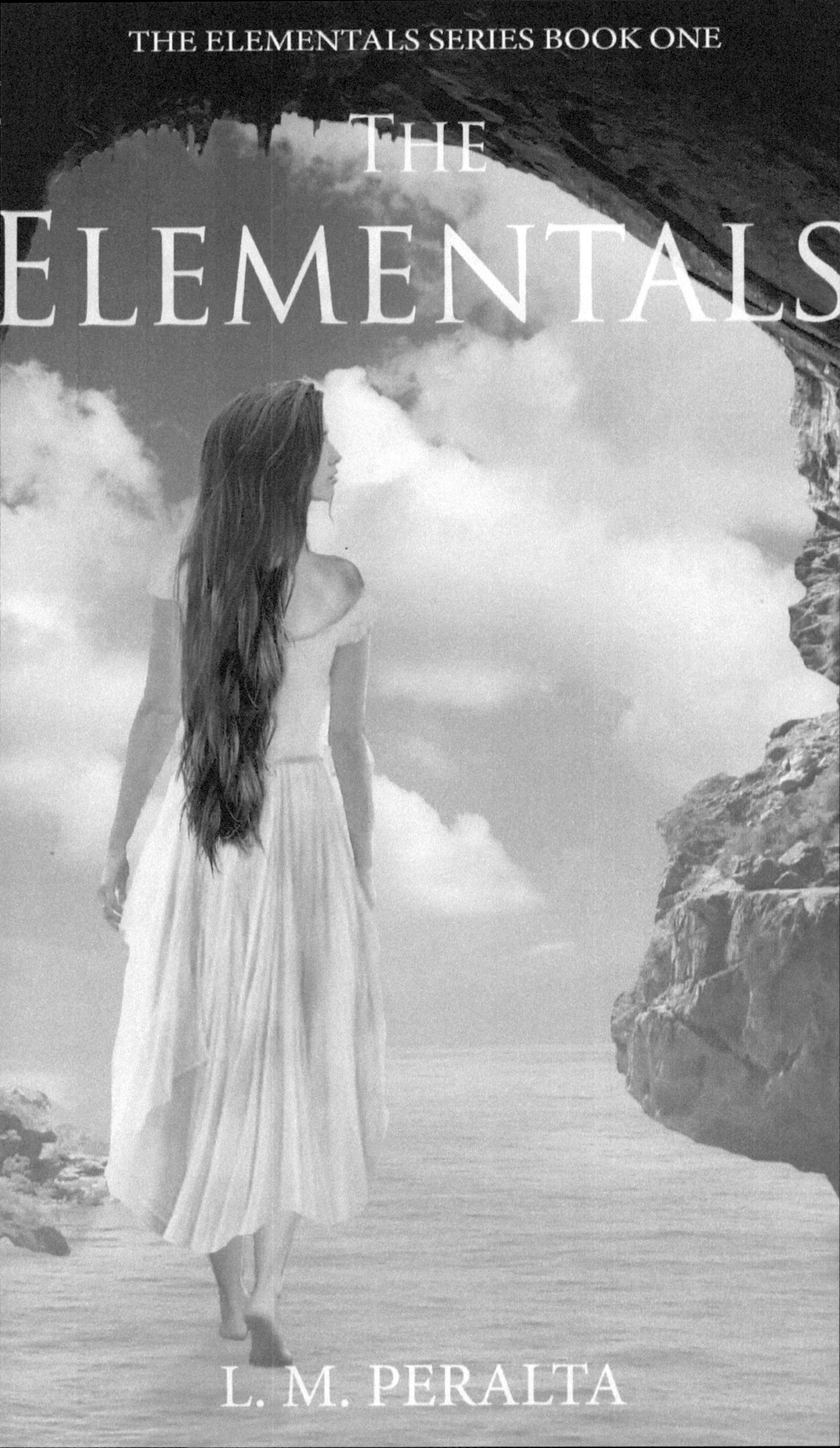
THE ELEMENTALS SERIES BOOK ONE
THE ELEMENTALS
L. M. PERALTA

PROLOGUE

THE city that housed fire was black, and the illumination of the fire's surging brilliance did not extinguish the depth of the shadows. Darkness, alive and threatening, swept across the valley and the worn stone walls of the fortress at its center. Its dark fingertips crept along the cliff and jagged rock of the mountain with its shadow towering over the city.

At the city's core, the citadel huddled among the crumbling buildings. Inside the citadel was a castle made of stone from the surrounding structures. The power of the citizens kept the torches ablaze in the dim-lit streets. The mountains rose on the city's northern and southern borders, and the cliff rested to the east. Stones, fallen from the city walls, bruised the ground. The snow buried the wounds.

Stone houses clustered across the valley. Heavy blankets draped over the shutterless windows to keep out the cold. The doors needed to be replaced after every storm. The roofs wept frozen tears.

Soldiers marched through the mountain pass. Two of them dragged the body of a man. The arms of the men hung at their sides as they labored toward the dark city. The sentry sent a burst of flames into the air. The guards below opened the gate, allowing the soldiers to pass through the walls of the citadel.

The tired feet of the soldiers met the stone steps of the castle as servants opened the heavy wooden door from the inside. The soldiers walked into the ante room and through the doorway to the central chamber.

Within the central chamber was a wide expanse of cracked stone floor, and at the end of the broken stone mass, their leader, Hephaestus, sat on a stone throne. He stared at the men as they entered. He watched as the two soldiers dragged their prisoner.

The long body of the man on the throne hunched forward so that his pale face jutted out while the rest of his body lay hidden in the black folds of his clothes which blended into the dark stone. His long red cloak draped down like a trail of blood. His arms spread to the arms of the throne, and his hands clutched them. His golden-brown eyes fastened on the body of the man being dragged as the soldiers came closer.

Perditus stood at the side of the throne. His pale face and black hair matched that of his leader, but his eyes were gray, like storm clouds or the smoke of a rising fire. He wasn't yet fifteen years old. He would be in a matter of days, but the hours were heavy in this place, and time crept by slowly.

Perditus clenched his hands into fists. His head tilted to the floor, but his eyes strained upwards. He, too, focused on the man the soldiers held between them.

Sores and open wounds, thinly frosted over, covered the man's body. The assault had been the outcome of the dragging. Perditus wondered if they had dragged him all the way from his home despite the cries of those around him who dared not suffer the consequences of fighting back.

Perditus knew what the man was and knew why he had been brought to Omega Ray—so that Hephaestus could play with him as a cat does with a mouse.

Soldiers stepped to the side to avoid the direct gaze of the man on the throne. The two soldiers who held the prisoner remained in the center. One of them averted his eyes, but the other stared straight into the eyes of his leader.

He stood holding one arm of the prisoner. He was shorter in stature than the other soldiers, but his body was broad. He bore the partial weight of the other man with ease. He could have effortlessly held the man slung across his shoulders, but he wanted to drag him from the top of the mountain, across the snow, through the uneven ground of the city, and the stone of the fortress floor.

In contrast to the pale face of his leader, this man's skin was a reddish-brown. Right at the base of his jaw-bone, near the ear, he had a deep red birthmark.

The pale-faced leader turned to the red-faced soldier.

"This is not what I asked you to do," Hephaestus said.

The red-faced man did not avert his eyes.

"I understand that, Sir. But our given task proved once again impossible," he said. "Instead, we have brought this man. We found him near Lumina on Dustpath Road. He's a Water Elemental."

An offering, thought Perditus, so as to divert Hephaestus from thoughts of punishment.

Slowly Hephaestus's shoulders relaxed, and his body curled back against the throne.

"Is that so? I thought we would have gotten them all by now. Is he alive?"

"Yes." The red-faced man kicked the man he had been dragging, causing him to issue forth a loud grunt of pain.

Hephaestus placed his hands firmly on the arms of the throne and used them to prop himself up. He stood in front of the man.

"What's your name?"

"Elias," the man said.

Hephaestus stiffened.

"You know him, my lord," the soldier asked.

"No." Hephaestus's eyes turned back to the prisoner. "Lift up your head."

Elias did so. Bruises colored the skin around his eyes and along his jaw. His eyes were so swollen, Perditus doubted he could see what was in front of him. But he had seen worse off men find their way through the smoke.

The soldiers held Elias, and he could not wipe the dried blood from his lips. His finger moved ever so slightly. He begged, "Please, let me leave. I don't know what this man is talking about. I'm not an Elemental." Tears leaked from the slits surrounded by tortured flesh. "I'm just a man. A poor one. But I have a family, a wife and a son. I have to go back to them."

His eyes moved Perditus more than his words. He imagined that the man was found out when he took a drink from his hands absent any lake or stream. But Perditus had no desire to help the man. His sorrow was too sweet and poetic, and Perditus wanted to see what would happen.

"Fero, hold out his hand," Hephaestus demanded.

The red-faced man let the prisoner's arm slump to the ground before roughly grasping his wrist in both hands and stretching his arm out to present his palm to his leader.

Hephaestus's eyes focused on the hand of the prisoner, and the flesh caught fire.

Elias screamed and tried to pull his hand away, but Fero held it tight. With his hand ablaze, Elias closed his eyes and a mass of water, enough to fill three canteens, hung in the air and splashed down onto his hand, dousing the flames. The skin of his hand was pink, and some of it had burned away, leaving his palm raw and bloodied. The sweat on his brow mixed with the tears running down his face.

"Please, stop," he whimpered. His voice was pathetic and desperate. He was a man with everything to lose.

"Stand him up!" Hephaestus demanded.

Fero and Dirge lifted the Water Elemental to his feet.

Elias stood unsteadily. He tried to touch his hand, thinking that might sooth it, but he flinched as his fingertips touched the burnt skin.

Hephaestus circled him slowly, eyeing him like a vulture considering its next meal. He stopped in front of him.

"Make Water dance for me," he ordered.

"What?" Elias asked, confused by this request. He had been dragged all this way to be a source of entertainment.? It was a cruel joke to be sure.

Hephaestus closed his eyes, and the prisoner's arm began to tingle with heat.

"Wait! Stop! Please!" Elias screamed like a man whose body was over the fire.

"You know the consequences," Hephaestus said, his voice even and calm. "Now, make Water dance for me."

Elias closed his eyes and concentrated. Slowly, a string of water began to twirl in the air in the wide space between the prisoner and the pale-faced man. It was the narrowest stream, without a bank, its source unseen. It spun into an orb and continued to twist in the air. The tiny strings of water twined around each other as Elias focused.

He was an artist in that moment, painting a picture like only he could. He had the eyes of the entire room on the moving water. It was so exceptional and so stunning.

Only Fero was immune to its charms.

It was a perfect watery chrysalis. Elias moved his hands as if molding it, but his flesh never touched it.

Perditus didn't know what he was thinking, but the prisoner had a smile on his face and tears in his eyes. They weren't the tears of a man fighting for his life, but a deeper sorrow that had happiness at its core.

Hephaestus gazed at the display like he had found some rare and beautiful animal.

He reached out to touch the watery orb with a trembling hand.

"Sir!" Fero warned.

"Quiet!" Hephaestus hissed.

His hand inched closer, the water hitting the light of the torches and reflecting it onto his palm. A breath away from the watery orb, his fingers grazed the cool water. But he flinched away as if afraid to touch it.

Perditus thought he heard a tiny gasp of awe escape his lips.

The Water Elemental opened his eyes wider than before despite the swollen flesh surrounding them, and a powerful jet of water from the core of the orb shot toward Hephaestus with profound speed. Hephaestus turned it to steam before impact.

Elias only meant to distract, not to harm. He knew he couldn't hurt this man. He turned to run, but Fero's auburn hand grabbed his shoulder and yanked him back.

Elias was on his knees again, struggling beneath the weight of Fero's hand.

Elias screamed. Smoke issued from his mouth. His insides burned, cooking his organs, filling the room with a rank, meaty scent.

Fero's eyes widened. A look of despair lighted upon his face. "No," he shouted. "We need him!"

But it was too late. Elias slumped to the ground. Smoke trailed from his lips like a serpent.

Fero, looking at his leader desperately, still held the man's limp arm.

"What do you mean we need him?" Hephaestus asked.

Fero continued to look at the dead man with a gaze that made Perditus think that he could stare at the corpse forever.

Hephaestus made a wide circle around the body as if death was a disease he could catch. He sat back upon his throne. "Why would I need him?"

Fero's eyes were anchored to the body, but he responded to his leader's question. "The sphere sanctums . . . we have yet to see a Protector." At this, Fero looked up into the eyes of Hephaestus.

The light glanced off his golden eyes, making fire dance in his irises.

"Fear in my men?" Hephaestus leaned forward in his seat, like a python striking out at its prey.

Fero did not flinch. "Not fear, sir, but a barrier that we cannot break, not without a balance of the elements. The doors to the sanctums remain closed to us. A strange haze floats over them."

"Then tear them down."

"We can't. My men have tried everything. I exhausted my element trying to burn the doors down. Something is keeping us out."

"What?"

"Above the sanctum doors are the symbols for the elements, all of the elements."

Silence hung in the air.

"Go," Hephaestus demanded of the other soldiers.

They left, taking with them the body of Elias.

Only Fero and Perditus remained with their leader.

After the other soldiers had gone, Hephaestus didn't speak for a long time. Time had never crept slower in Omega Ray.

When he opened his mouth to speak it was like the flames had grown in his eyes. "So, you are telling me I need a Water Elemental?"

"That's what I'm saying, sir."

"That man's family?"

Fero shook his head.

Hephaestus put his head in his hands.

After years of taking Water Elementals to their graves, he needed one. The thought made Perditus smirk.

Fero interrupted the silence. Perditus wondered if silence was one of the few things too heavy for him to bare.

"The boy," Fero said, "he was taken to Element."

Perditus's fists tightened when Fero changed the subject. What right did he have to meddle in his joy?

Hephaestus drew his back away from his seat. "Are you sure it's him? It's been years since he ran away."

"Yes, sir. He is the reflection of his father. Should I bring him back?"

Perditus cringed.

"No," Hephaestus said.

At this, Perditus grinned. His down-turned face hid the smile.

"He could be useful in Element," Hephaestus said, "He is a brat, but he was always strong in his element. I'll have my men keep in touch with him. He can be my eyes in that place."

"You want me to arrange for that?"

"Yes, and soon. I don't want him getting too comfortable, thinking he has escaped me. There's nothing worse in a man than the thought of ease. It halts progress and self-improvement."

Perditus wondered if Hephaestus had ever suffered a moment of ease in his life. Maybe when he was a baby in his mother's arms, but Perditus could never imagine him as an innocent or vulnerable child.

He assumed that his cold, pale skin was hard as marble all his life and that the fire had always lived inside him, keeping his rage alive.

Hephaestus wasn't a person, but a monument. Something that could not be reasoned with and had no reason to be soothed.

"What about the sanctums? What do you need us to do?" Fero stood with his hands behind his back.

Perditus lifted his head, but neither Fero nor Hephaestus paid him a glance. He was like a shadow, warranting no consideration.

"Tell the men to search Mirmina for Water Elementals. I must have left at least one alive."

Fero looked at him without expression. He hadn't delivered that man all the way from Dustpath to serve as his leader's plaything. He sought him out. It wasn't Fero's cruelty alone that made him drag Elias to Omega Ray. Fero was angry that Elias had made himself so difficult to find. Fero didn't know that Hephaestus would dismantle his cargo without granting him a mere moment to explain its purpose. Fero had journeyed for years to decipher the secrets of the Sphere Sanctums. How many of those years were dedicated to finding that Water Elemental?

Perditus knew Fero would calm his rage on someone else. He wouldn't challenge Hephaestus. He couldn't blame him for his rash act.

Hephaestus twined his fingers together.

Perditus lowered his head. He watched Hephaestus's shadow upon the floor, and from that shadow came words.

"One day, I will get the spheres, and I will out balance everything."

1

THE FOUNTAIN

SARA curled her legs up so her feet could stay warm beneath the small blanket. Her bed creaked as she turned. Her eyes searched the room. The other girls rested in their beds. Some of them tossed and turned in an effort to get warm. Sara waited and listened to the rain outside. Drops hit her window in a steady rhythm.

The rain reminded her of fear, smoke, tears, and that singular night. She tried to overcome the rain's hypnotic power, but her eyes were drooping, and her mind was pulling her away.

The room filled with smoke, and the water in Sara's eyes blurred her vision. Her mother lifted her up. Glass shattered as her father smashed the back window with his elbow. Her mother helped her out the window, just large enough for four-year-old Sara to fit through. She told Sara to run. Crying and shaking, Sara ran from the house. She hid in the overgrowth near the forest and watched as the smoke became heavier and the fire surrounded the little cottage. Rain began to fall.

Thunder woke Sara. She sat up and pulled her blanket to her chin. Lightning flashed, brightening the room. Her eyes searched the space to find the other girls asleep. The thunder had not awoken them, and their tossing had ceased.

Sara tried to get out of bed as quietly as she could, but the bed squealed as she stepped down. She poked her head under the bed and retrieved a kettle full of water. She sat down on the floor and pulled the kettle toward her. Her eyes focused on the water.

"Please, please, please," she whispered.

Lightning flashed again, and for a moment, her face was reflected in the water. She never saw herself properly before. The orphanage had no mirrors. She wondered if she had grown to look like her mother. She was fourteen, yet shorter than other girls her age. Her mother was tall and slender, her movements fluid like the power she possessed.

She concentrated on the water.

"Come on, come on."

But the water didn't move. It didn't ripple.

Sara closed her eyes. Her mother's eyes were hazel, and her hair was light brown. Her voice was even and soft. Her father's eyes were green, and his smile made her feel at ease. Sara drew their faces in her mind's eye. She struggled to remember who they were, but being so young, she remembered only warm embraces, gentle words, sometimes harsh words, but more so the gentle ones.

Opening her eyes, she turned her attention back to the water. She glanced toward the window as lightning lit the glass.

Drop. Splash.

Water seeped over the edge of the kettle as ripples drifted from the center.

Sara focused more closely, hoping to send the water spilling again. But as she focused, a drop of water landed into the pot, causing the water to ripple and spill over the edge.

She looked up. Another drop of water dislodged from the ceiling and dropped down into the pot.

Sara sighed. She pushed the kettle back under the bed. She got her blanket and used it to mop up the water that had spilled. It was no use. The water continued to leak from the ceiling. The old pot could catch the drops, she thought. But that would only make the water in the kettle splash, causing more of a mess. Sara would go without dinner if Ms. Fiora discovered she took the kettle from the kitchen.

She crawled back into bed, carrying the wet blanket with her. She spread the blanket over the end of the bed to allow it to dry. Reaching under the mattress, she retrieved a necklace. The necklace had a blue gemstone in the shape of a raindrop hanging from a delicate woven cord. She clenched the gemstone in her fist and, colder than before, she tried to go back to sleep.

BLANKETS rustled against sheets as Sara awoke. The other girls were making their beds. She got up quickly to make her own. Taking the damp blanket from the end of the bed, she placed it over the sheets and smoothed out the dank wrinkles. As she bent over the bed, patting down the blanket, she caught the faint scent of rain.

Years ago, she overheard her father and mother as they talked in their dining room. Peering from behind the paneled wall, Sara watched her parents. Her mother sat at the small, pine dinner table, and her father stood across from her. He rubbed his forehead.

"I should go with you," she said. "I can reason with him."

"No, Sara needs you, and I have to protect both of you. He won't stop until he's killed us all."

Her mother knitted her brow. "I don't understand."

"No one can understand the mind of a madman."

"Sara?"

Sara was leaning over the bed. She turned her head. Miranda raked through her long hair with an old comb. The teeth of the comb were missing in places. "It's time to eat. You're not getting sick, are you?"

"No, I was thinking."

"About what?"

Sara sighed as she smoothed down the hem of her blanket and turned to take her dress out of the small drawer beside her bed.

"My mother. I don't want to forget her face."

"I don't remember my mother's face," Miranda said. "But she had long hair. I used to brush it for her and curl up in it at night. This was her comb." She held it up for Sara to see.

Miranda was twelve years old, but she was tall and thin. She combed her hair all day, and she flinched when any of the older girls offered to braid it for her.

The girls had their chores. The older girls helped in the kitchen and laundered the clothes and sheets, while the younger girls cleaned the floors and washed the dishes.

In addition to scrubbing floors, Sara walked to the market every three days. She used to go alone, but her thoughts brought her to her parents, their powers, and the question of why she lacked their gifts.

She asked Ms. Fiora if Miranda could accompany her on the long walks into town.

The market lay in the center of town. Buildings sprawled around the market square. The school of Element sat on a hill, above the buildings. Its ivy-covered, stone walls stood stark against the pale sky. Element was where Elementals went to train. Elementals could manipulate and call the elements. Sara hoped to be an Elemental and to harness the power her parents had.

To block the sun, woven cloths covered the tops of the stands in the square. Various smells accosted market-goers, but the most prominent was the odor of dust and feathers.

Elementals stood between stands and performed tricks. A huge crowd surrounded the Wind Elementals, who played with the autumn leaves, making them swirl and dance. A Fire Elemental sent rings of flame into the air. He was middle-aged and had a scar going from under his ear, along his jaw, and down his neck. People made wide circles around him, giving him narrowed-eyed glances as they passed.

Sara noticed him before when she went to the market. In that mysterious way that people can feel the eyes of others on them, she felt his eyes bore into her back when she turned away from him. She bit her lip.

"Sara, there he is again," Miranda said, "Do you think he works for Hephaestus?"

"I don't know." Sara peered at him from over her shoulder.

"He sure looks scary enough."

Sara turned away from the Fire Elemental. At one of the stands, the merchant sold paper and charcoal. Sara jingled the money in her dress pocket as she stared at the paper.

She forced her eyes away from the paper merchant and walked to the stand that sold eggs and chickens. The chickens were frantic in their cages, causing loose feathers to fly into the air as they moved. The uproarious clucking of the distraught chickens, fighting in vain to be free of their cages, made this stand the loudest in the market. The merchant smiled as Sara approached. He was a calm man among chaos, with a pleasant smile on his face as the feathers of the chickens rested on his shoulders. Sara tried not to look at the struggling chickens.

"Half a dozen eggs, please." She held out the money. She memorized how many sparklings she needed.

"Aren't you one of the little girls from Ocean's Light? Half a dozen doesn't seem like enough to feed all of you."

"Ms. Fiora likes eggs in the mornings."

Sara's eyes drifted to the paper and charcoal.

"I see you're always staring at that paper," he said with a wink.

"I'm saving up for it."

"I didn't know you were given an allowance?"

Sara looked away.

The merchant handed her the eggs. Sara placed them one by one in the basket and covered them with a woolen cloth. She was careful not to let the eggs break. The girls whispered a story about a girl who used to live in the home. She tripped on the way from the market. The eggs cracked on the cobblestone path. After Ms. Fiora was done with her, the girl ran away from the orphanage and never returned.

On the road back, Sara took one coin from her pocket, knelt down, and slipped the coin into her shoe. Miranda combed her hair and hummed to herself as she skipped along the path.

She stopped and turned around. "Aren't you always the one who says Ms. Fiora will be mad if we're late?" Her hands were on her hips.

"I thought something got into my shoe." Sara stood.

"Just shake it out."

"It's fine now. You're right. Let's go."

When Sara and Miranda returned, Mari, one of the older girls, was crying on the steps in front of the house. Rosaleen, the nurse comforted her. "You'll see your father again. He's waiting among the Aethers in the heavens."

Sara and Miranda bowed their heads and climbed the steps to the door. Sara looked back at Mari before she stepped inside.

Ms. Fiora stood in her office, gazing upon the decorative box that rested upon the mantel. The girls believed Ms. Fiora kept the ashes of her late husband in that box.

Sara handed the money in her pocket to Ms. Fiora. Ms. Fiora stood tall, her shoulders back, and eyes at a constant downward tilt. Her dress was freshly ironed, the white collar pressed firmly down. Sara's skin tingled as Ms. Fiora counted the coins.

"Prices are still up, I see."

While the other girls did their chores, Sara returned to the bedroom. She took the coin from her shoe and opened her drawer. Inside, under an old handkerchief, was another coin. She placed the second coin under the handkerchief and closed the drawer.

Weeks ago, she returned with fewer loaves of bread, telling Ms.

Fiora she didn't have enough money for the extra loaves. The next time Sara went to the market, Ms. Fiora had given her extra sparklings for the bread. Sara could have taken all the extra coins, but decided that would be too risky.

That night, the wind beat against the window above Sara's bed. She thought of Mari who lost her father. She wondered what happened to him, if he died like her parents. She waited with her hands up to her chin clenching the raindrop necklace until she heard the gentle snoring of the other girls and felt confident they were asleep. She slinked down to floor, placed the necklace back under the mattress, and pulled the kettle of water from beneath the bed.

She stared into the water until her eyes hurt and clouds covered the dim light of the moon. Too dark to see, Sara replaced the kettle and climbed back into bed. She retrieved the necklace, and holding it, went to sleep.

HER mother woke her in the dead of the night. Her face was pink. Beads of sweat patterned her forehead. A strange and surprisingly loud sound came from outside, a crackling that roared. The fire surrounded the house on all sides. Her father tried desperately to put out the flames that filled the cottage. He drenched the flames with water flowing from his fingertips, but they would not go out.

"We have to get her out!" her father shouted.

Her mother ran, carrying Sara to the back of the cottage. Her father broke a small window. Her mother ripped the necklace with the teardrop gem from her neck and gave it to Sara.

"Always keep it close, my love."

Her father extinguished the flames outside the window. "Hurry," he said. "I don't know how long I can hold them back." Her mother placed her through the broken window. "Run, baby, and don't look back."

Sara ran. She tripped. She glanced toward the house. She expected her parents to climb through after her, but the flames rose in front of the window.

Sara felt warm tears rushing from her eyes aided by grief and smoke. A laugh resounded in the distance, and the fire rose from the cottage as the tears blurred Sara's vision. She did as her mother said and hid behind a wild shrub not far from her home.

The smoke rose and twisted in the night air. A cold, stiff rain fell, putting out the fire, but it was too late. The smoke smothered Sara's parents before the fire ever reached them.

Strong hands lifted her from among the leaves.

MARI was absent from breakfast the next morning. Sara stared into her bowl as Miranda talked and combed her hair. After breakfast, Sara carted the tray of bowls and dishes to the kitchen.

She rolled up the sleeves of her dress and dipped the first plate into the basin of water. Taking the bar of hard soap, she rubbed it between the palms of her hands. The soap would not lather. Sara stopped and put down the soap.

Faint sobs came from the back of the kitchen.

She dried her hands on the worn old dish rag and walked in the direction of the sobbing. Behind the large pots and sacks of potatoes on the floor was Mari.

Sara knelt down, took the handkerchief from her dress pocket, and gave it to Mari.

Mari looked up. Her sobs quieted. Embarrassment overcame her sadness for a moment. She took the cloth from Sara and wiped the tears off her cheeks.

"Thank you."

Sara got up to return to the dishes.

"Wait. Stay with me for a little while."

Sara knelt beside Mari. "Do you want some breakfast?" Sara asked. "I think there's still some porridge left over."

Mari shook her head. Her hand gripped the worn cloth.

Silence hung in the air for some time.

Sara struggled for words as if the silence would destroy them both had she not found them.

"What happened to your father?"

Mari glared at her.

Sara looked down at her hands.

"My father," Mari started. Her voice was softer than her glare. "My father died." More tears leaked from her eyes. "He was a soldier for the Resistance. Hephaestus's men killed him. I got the letter yesterday."

Sara was aware that Hephaestus was the Fire Elemental everyone in Mirmina feared, but she knew very little of what he had done. Her parents had sheltered her from it.

"The messenger gave me this." Mari held up a silver band for Sara to see. The band was large enough to be worn around the arm. "When he was alive, my father wore this as a symbol of his allegiance to the Resistance and to the protection of Mirmina." She balled up the material and threw the silver band across the room.

"Was your father an Elemental?"

"No." She sobbed. "He was just a man, but Hephaestus killed him like a beast."

Sara fought for something to say. "My parents died too. I was with them when it happened, but I don't remember much. I dream about it sometimes, but I forget the details in the morning."

Tears dripped into Mari's hands.

Sara touched her arm. "I'm sorry. No one can say anything to make you feel right again. I just wanted you to know you aren't alone. Everyone here lost somebody."

Mari stabbed her with her eyes. "My grief is cheap. That's what you're saying."

Sara shook her head. She stood. "I don't know what I'm saying. Please, forgive me."

Sara left the kitchen. She might get into trouble for leaving the dishes unwashed, but she failed to sooth Mari. *What was I thinking telling her her grief was on an assembly line?*

A crash came from the kitchen. Sara ran back inside.

A basket lay on its side. Cracked shells and egg guts littered the floor.

"What happened here?" Ms. Fiora stormed into the room.

Sara looked to Mari. Mari's lips trembled.

"It was me," Sara blurted out. "I broke the eggs."

Ms. Fiora grabbed her arm. "What happened, girl?"

"I slipped, backed into the shelf. The basket fell. I tried to catch it, but…"

"You know what eggs cost." Ms. Fiora pulled Sara out of the kitchen and dragged her to the anteroom where the girls read and played jacks and dice. The girls stopped their activities and looked up at Sara and Ms. Fiora.

Ms. Fiora left the room.

"Sara, what—" Miranda stopped and sank back into the crowd.

Ms. Fiora returned with the switch. "Palms up."

Sara slowly offered her hands.

Ms. Fiora snapped the switch across her palms. The pain stung and left heat. Ms. Fiora continued to strike her hands. Sara's palms burned and itched, but she held her hands out.

Mari ran into the room. Sara thought she would speak up and tell Ms. Fiora that what Sara told her was a lie. Mari was the one who broke the eggs. *Don't say anything*, Sara thought. *Ms. Fiora will finish with me. But if you say anything, she'll snap your palms and give me double for lying.* But Mari bit her tongue. Her eyes never left Sara's reddened palms until the punishment was done.

Ms. Fiora snapped the switch one last, biting time and moved away from Sara.

Sara tried rubbing her raw, itchy palms, but they stung worse. She left the anteroom and sat on her bed. Minutes later, Rosaleen walked into the room. "Let me see." She rubbed a gel on Sara's palms. The itching and burning dissipated.

"There," Rosaleen said. "It's not so bad. I've seen worse. This should heal by morning."

Rosaleen patted Sara's arm. Mari entered the room as Rosaleen left. Her eyes were on the floor.

"You didn't have to do that for me, you know," Mari said.

"Why did you smash the eggs?" Sara asked.

"I was angry," Mari said. "You were right. All the girls here have lost someone. But my father . . . he didn't have to join the Resistance. He should have stayed with me. And now he's dead."

Sara looked at her hands.

"Why did you lie for me?"

Sara bit her lip. She was part of the reason Ms. Fiora was so upset about the eggs. Money was tight. Sara was stealing it. "I felt bad about what I said. You have just as much right as anyone to grieve your father. There shouldn't be a contest for who's in the most pain."

THREE days later, Sara and Miranda made the trip to the market. This time, Sara had put the two coins into her shoe. They slid back and forth as she walked.

"What was your mother like?" Miranda asked as they walked to the market.

Sara walked with her head down. "I don't remember much, but she was beautiful. She cared for me. She had powers like my father. They were Elementals."

"How come you aren't an Elemental?"

"I don't know."

Miranda took the comb out of her pocket. She stopped walking. Sara stopped too and looked back at her. Miranda was looking down at the comb. "This wasn't my mother's. When I was five years old, one of the older girls gave it to me before she left. I don't remember my mother. She left me outside of the chapel in Caleena when I was born."

Miranda cried, and Sara rubbed her arm. She wiped her tears with the backs of her hands.

Sara offered to hold the basket, and Miranda gave it to her.

Once in the market, Miranda's tears had dried. Sara suggested they split up to make fast work of their task and impress Ms. Fiora. She gave the basket to Miranda and told her to get the bread, while she would get the potatoes and beans. She handed Miranda coins for the bread and hurried off to the stand that sold the paper.

She stopped in front of the stand. She looked at her palms. Ms. Fiora's punishment had faded, but Sara remembered the sting. She looked back at the paper and charcoal. She swallowed her fear and approached the stand.

"I want three sheets of paper and a stick of charcoal, please," she told the vendor.

"That'll be three sparklings."

Sara took off her shoe and dumped the two coins into her palm. She retrieved one more from her pocket. As she felt for the coin in her pocket her fingers grazed the smooth surface of the teardrop gem of her mother's necklace.

The vendor grinned.

He looked down at the coins in her hand.

"You live in the orphanage, don't you?"

Sara nodded.

"Those aren't your coins."

Sara pressed her lips together and shook her downturned head.

"You shouldn't steal, not even from a bitter, old woman."

Without taking her coins, the vendor offered her a few sheets of paper and a stick of charcoal.

Sara looked at it tentatively.

"Go on, take it," he said. "When everyone in Mirmina wants one of your drawings, you can sign one for me."

"Thank you, sir."

Sara regrettably folded the sheets twice so that they would fit into her pocket. She hurried to buy the potatoes and beans and met Miranda at the fountain. Sara put the small sack of potatoes and the jar of beans into the basket at Miranda's feet. Miranda seemed to be mesmerized by the dancing of the Wind Elementals, who were making leaves and ribbons twirl in the breeze around them as they danced.

"I wonder what it would be like to be an Elemental."

The Fire Elemental with the scar was watching them from a distance.

"It's time to leave," Sara said.

"Wait, I have an idea." Miranda took off her shoes and got up on the ledge of the fountain.

"What are you doing?"

"Take off your shoes."

Miranda reached down to give Sara a hand. "Come on, it'll be fun."

Sara sighed, but she took off her shoes and took Miranda's hand.

Once they both stood on the fountain's ledge, Miranda began to twirl and dance like the Wind Elementals in the square.

Sara looked down into the clear water of the fountain. Closing her eyes, she remembered the face of her mother. She danced, imagining that she could call Water to swirl around her. She moved her feet along the warm, gritty stone of the fountain's ledge. She felt a cool, light feeling on the underside of her feet.

The marketplace became very quiet.

Sara opened her eyes. The eyes of everyone in the market were on her. Miranda had gotten down from the fountain's ledge, and she too was staring at Sara. Sara's feet no longer touched the grainy stone of the ledge. Beneath her feet, the water glistened in the sun.

2

A New Apprentice

SARA stared at the glistening water beneath her feet. She curled her toes, and they dipped down into the cool liquid. All the years she tried to get water to move and failed left Sara thinking that she did not possess her parents' gift. Now she felt the full power of it.

It was strange. She hadn't concentrated like she had for hours, watching the stagnant water in that crude kettle, yet she stood on the clear surface as it was effortless.

She looked around to see if anyone else noticed her new-found power. The people in the market had stopped their shopping and stood around the fountain to watch Sara's dance. However, they did not watch her in awe and wonder as they had with the Wind Elementals or in fear as with the Fire Elemental. Instead, they stared at her as if she was a rare creature that shouldn't exist.

Tense because of the crowd's unexpected reaction, Sara stepped out of the fountain's cool, gently swirling water. Her feet, once flat against the water's surface, now moved out onto the warm, stone ledge and to the ground below. She stood next to the fountain and gazed at the water, swirling where her feet had left it and the watery footprints stamped on the fountain's edge.

A crowd of people gathered around her. "It can't be," she heard someone say among the whispering and sighs of surprise. The crowd was swelling to an overwhelming size. She hadn't remembered this many people in the market before she danced. Unable to see beyond the crowd, Sara began to panic. Someone grabbed her hand and pulled her through the sea of people. *The Fire Elemental!*

"Wait, what are you doing?" Sara tried to struggle out of his grasp. She remembered when Miranda suggested he might be a follower of Hephaestus. Her struggles were in vain. His grasp was too strong.

"Don't worry," he said, "I'm taking you someplace safe."

"Where?"

"To Element."

In Element, trainers helped young Elementals develop their skills. Sara had heard of it in stories. It was the oldest building in Elementa, older than the library or the marketplace.

"Why are you taking me there right now?" Sara asked.

"You belong there," the scarred Fire Elemental said.

Once they were far from the market, the Fire Elemental slowed his pace and loosened his grip on Sara's hand. Sara wriggled her hand out of his loosened grasp. Once free, she shook the pain from her hand. The skin was bright pink. Sara wondered if the color would ever fade.

They walked through the streets surrounded by towering buildings. The buildings stood fifteen feet high in packed rows, making the dirt streets narrow.

The Fire Elemental's scar was light pink against his dark skin, but had looked white from a distance. The scarred skin was uneven, and purple and blue veins were visible through the thin membrane. *Why had a Fire Elemental allowed himself to burn?*

"How do I know I can trust you?" she asked.

He looked straight ahead. His face was discerning.

"I'm Talon."

"Why did you pull me away from all those people? I'll have to go back soon. I can't leave my friend. We're supposed to go to the market together, and we're supposed to be back by a certain time or we'll be punished."

"You belong in Element."

"Wait." Sara stopped walking, and Talon turned around. "I can't leave."

"Do you want to go back?" His eyes looked stern, but not angry.

Sara looked back toward the orphanage and into the distance

toward Element. Ms. Fiora was not an Elemental nor would she have any interest in helping Sara with her new-found power. *If I went back, would she let me go if I changed my mind?* Trainers worked at the school, other Water Elementals who could help her hone her skills. "No. I . . . I want to go to Element."

Talon looked at her for what seemed like a long time. But before she could read his expression, he turned back and continued on his way. Sara followed.

They walked two miles before meeting the steps of Element. Element was on the hill. Ivy covered the stone walls, and green moss grew between the cracks. On the oak door hung a brass knocker.

The Fire Elemental swung the brass knocker three times. It was an odd knock with uneven pauses in between. The door groaned as a short woman opened it. She had a small frame, and faint wrinkles gathered on her forehead. Her hair frizzed out in wispy curls. A smile brightened her face.

"Talon!" she exclaimed.

She smiled so widely and so quickly, her eyes glazed over. She looked like her mind might be in a haze, but steadily advancing on her face was a look of relief.

"It's like you've come back from the dead. Where have you been?" She smoothed out her hair.

"I don't have time," Talon responded.

"You're not leaving, are you? Please, stay longer this time."

Sara stood, half-hidden behind Talon and his long coat.

"Come in." The words rushed out of the woman's mouth and sounded like an order.

Talon and Sara entered, and the woman closed the door behind them.

"Who is this?" Her eyes pierced Sara. "Not your daughter?" she asked. "Doesn't look at all like you with your dark hair and her light brown. She must look more like her moth—"

"No," Talon said. "She's a new apprentice."

Sara looked at the ground. She knew what it felt like to be watched like a rare animal let loose from its cage. But this woman judged her for entirely different reasons.

"Oh," she said, "I'm sorry. I thought..." The woman stopped mid-sentence and smiled, "I'm Brina. Who are you?"

"Sara."

"It's not every day Talon brings in a new apprentice. In fact, you are only the second."

"Brina," Talon stopped her.

Brina smiled. "Would you like me to take your coat, Talon? You could stay awhile."

"I'm fine. I don't think I'll stay very long."

Brina's smile faded. She turned her attention to Sara. "I'll show you to your room."

"My room," Sara said, "as in singular."

"Of course," Brina said. She gave Talon a look that read: *Where did you find this girl?*

Brina turned to lead them to the room, but Talon grabbed her arm and leaned closer to her. "Give her one of the rooms on the top floor," he said.

"The top floor. We haven't been able to fill it since… Well, you know. She would be all alone up there."

Talon held her in his grasp and looked into her eyes. His stare was not menacing or fierce, but determined. He held that stare until she nodded.

Brina led Sara and Talon through the entrance hall and up the stone stairs. The stone steps felt hard beneath Sara's feet. *My shoes? I must have left them at the fountain.* They reached the top floor, and Brina opened the doorway to the hall. Rows of doors lined either side of the long hallway.

"Where is everyone?" Sara asked.

"At mid-day, the apprentices go outside to train."

"When will I be able to train?" she asked.

"You can start tomorrow. I'll set you up with a trainer. What is your element?" Brina asked, as they walked down the hall. Sara opened her mouth to answer, but Talon pulled Brina aside and whispered something in her ear. Brina's eyes widened. "No." She looked at Sara.

"I thought it best not to say it too loud," Talon said.

"Why?" Sara asked.

Brina gently pushed her along. "This room is unoccupied. It's yours."

She opened a door at the end of the hall. A large bed with white, satin sheets rested in the center, and blue curtains hung on the window in the back of the room. The cream-colored carpet felt soft under Sara's bare feet.

"We'll let you get more comfortable." Brina closed the door

behind Sara.

Sara fell to her knees and ran her fingers through the soft carpet. She imagined that the bed must be twice as soft. She sat down on it. She touched cotton once in the marketplace. A vendor brought it from a village across the sea where he said it grew in a large field. The bed felt like that.

An end table sat on one side of the bed. Sara took the paper and charcoal out of her dress pocket and put them on the table. The charcoal had coated the inside of her pocket with black dust. She tried to smooth the paper out on the table to make the folds less apparent. She placed the charcoal and the paper in the drawer.

Reaching into her pocket, she retrieved her mother's necklace. She looked at the necklace for some time. She had never worn it as her mother had. Tying the woven string around her neck, Sara secured the necklace. She held the raindrop gem between her fingers and looked into its clear blue surface before letting it fall to her chest.

The window caught her eye. Outside, the field stretched to a tall, stone wall. On the field, apprentices practiced their elements. They ranged in ages. A group in the center made leaves dance on the Wind. Others summoned Fire to light torches. Earth Elementals stooped with their hands over the ground, causing saplings to sprout.

But no Water Elementals practiced their element. In the distance, was a lake where Water Elementals could train, but it was abandoned.

She was distracted by a boy who seemed to have greater command over his element than the others. He forced his element into the shape of a hand. The Lightning caused the fingers to look thin and wiry. Every time he clenched his own hand, the lightning hand clenched also.

He was a puppet master, and his puppet was bright and terrible. But it was also beautiful. Sara watched him for a long time.